SIMULACRUM

R. H. Gründ

R. H. Gründ Works

SIMULACRUM

THE FUNERAL

1.

Laura was dead.

Kelsey hardly heard anything else Pete said, such were the tremors in his voice, the tremors in her chest. In the dark of her bedroom, she clutched her throat. Laura. A name she hadn't heard in so long. A name she had refused to remember. A name she had willed away.

In the kitchenette, she cradled the phone in the crook of her neck and scrounged for a glass in the cupboard. Pete had not stopped talking since he woke her up with his call. "She thought about calling you," he said, "about getting back in touch. I told her she should. After she got really sick, I kept telling her. 'Call Kelsey. Call Kelsey.' But she didn't. I know she wanted to. I thought she wanted to. You were like sisters. That's how she always said it. But she never told me what happened. Why you stopped talking. She never mentioned it. Even when it was really bad, she didn't tell me. She wouldn't say."

Kelsey stood on the balcony of her Houston apartment and watched the pre-dawn sun shimmer across the skyline, felt the morning breeze on her face. Traffic flowed below in rivers of red and white lights. An ambulance sped through, siren wailing. Crows scattered overhead.

She sipped her bourbon. Her voice shook. "When did it happen?"

"Just a few hours ago. Listen, Kels, you have to come. I want you to come. She did."

After Pete hung up, she returned inside and re-filled her glass. She left the excess bourbon where it spilt. Pointless to go back to sleep, she thought. Pointless when every thought would be of that head of blonde hair, those eyes of ocean blue. Pointless now that Laura was dead.

The memory of Laura had disappeared slowly over time, consumed by the stress of today, the minutiae of now. How strange that her image came back so forcefully now upon news of her death, so vividly, as if the two women had never parted ways. Kelsey would be checking a patient's teeth, filling a cavity, scraping a retainer, and then suddenly, her hands would lock, her eyes glaze. No matter where she excused herself, whether the sterile-smelling lobby or the sunlit breezeway, memories surged. Studying in their cramped dorm. Drinking in the field. Crashing the old Chevrolet. Watching one of Laura's performances. Waiting in the hospital. Wheeling her around. Helping her walk. Holding her by the waist. Smelling her hair.

Anthony came over that night, and they talked about the upcoming funeral.

"You want me to go with you?" he asked, pulling the lasagna out of the oven.

"You don't have to."

"You sure?"

She gulped down more red wine. "Yeah. I'll be okay."

When they had sex later, Laura's smells kept coming back. Lilac and rosemary.

Kelsey hadn't seen Laura in years, hadn't spoken to her, hadn't even sent her an e-mail or text message. Once upon a time, they slept in the same bed, shared the same meals, told each other every secret, every smallest detail. Laura had something to say about everyone—if a girl's skirt was too short or her hair too dark, if a guy walked too straight or slouched too deeply. But there was always warmth in her voice, as though she weren't criticizing, but just poking fun, prodding at the quirks and defects, the lovable imperfections. "Now, it's your turn, Kels," she said one night as they lay beside each other. "Tell me what's wrong with me." Kelsey had tried, tried very hard, but she couldn't come up with anything. "You're too perfect," she pouted, and Laura laughed. She said she wasn't, but she knew she was. Kelsey knew she knew.

When Kelsey first met her, Laura had been unearthly in her beauty, as though cut out from a magazine or commercial, every bad hair day airbrushed, every pimple erased. She could wear anything: skirts, jeans, heels, boots, mascara, lipstick. Nothing looked bad. Everything just accentuated her. She was already bright, but she had a way of making herself brighter. You knew she was in the room the second she walked in, all smiles and laughs. She knew you knew.

She loved flowers. She would doodle them in the margins of her notebook, draw them in pink and purple on her arms. Sometimes, she had Alia paint henna on her hands. Other times, she stamped peace signs and smiley faces on her palms and cheeks. She painted her nails red, yellow, and green. She wore her silver rosary around her neck and never took it off.

And the way she smelt! Lilac and rosemary. Always lilac and rosemary. A couple of puffs around the neck, a dollop of moisturizer on each wrist. Those smells followed her around, coalesced, became her. In the dorm. On the stage. By the hospital bed. Like a springtime field wherever she was, however light or dire the situation.

With each recollection, Kelsey's smile inevitably faded. Every memory of Laura terminated with the cancer, the cancer that changed everything, the cancer that robbed Laura of herself. She became Laura with cancer, who couldn't grow her hair because of cancer, who couldn't dance because of cancer, who couldn't finish school because of cancer. By the end, she wasn't Laura at all. She became something less. Like a painting with its colors dulled. Like a broken reflection on the surface of water.

Kelsey was on the highway the next day, radio turned low, wind whistling through the open windows of her car. She recalled what Pete said, how Laura had just fallen suddenly, how the family had shuttled her to the hospital, how the doctors found out the cancer had reemerged. "Kidneys," Pete said. "Liver. Getting to the lungs. She'd been clean, Kelsey. She'd been fine. Nothing for so long, and then it just hit her like a train."

That was how it was in the beginning, Kelsey thought. From one day to the next, practically, as though the cancer appeared from nowhere. As though some power up above realized a mistake had been made and sought to quickly correct it. What did that mean—that Laura herself was a mistake? Maybe not a mistake, but too good. Too unbroken.

When Kelsey arrived at her hotel later that afternoon, she unpacked her suitcase, hung up her black blouse and pencil skirt, put aside her high heels. Everything was ready for the funeral. The funeral. God. How surreal to remember Laura after so long only to bury her again. She fished out the half-pint bottle of liquor stowed away beneath her jeans and twisted off the cap.

She spent that night driving around Laura's hometown of Ranger's Field, trying to restore her mental map of those old stomping grounds. She remembered the town being so much smaller, so much more dirt and crop. A new strip mall was going up. The high school was being renovated. The paved roads outnumbered the unpaved. She and Laura would laze around there during the summers, watching movies, looking up at the stars. The same stars were still out now, still shining. The same stars, but no Laura underneath them. No Laura to look up with her eyes sparkling. No Laura to breathe out in wonder, even though she had seen them a thousand times before. No Laura to help her see Leo and Virgo.

No Laura.

The funeral parlor was packed the next morning. Ranger's Field was still a small town at heart, and Laura's family was well known. Kelsey signed her name in the guest ledger, then looked at the adjacent portraits. Seeing Laura's face was like seeing a literal ghost, an angel pulled down from heaven, a spirit dragged up from memory. The glossy black and shining silver of her homecoming dress and coronet. The silky blue of her graduation cap and gown. The dark red of her flamenco dress and lipstick. The gossamer white of her wedding dress, purple wrap around her pale skull, eyes duller, smile more muted.

Kelsey touched the eyes, traced the lips. Her fingers lingered on the canvas.

A hand found her back. "Kels, that you?"

She turned around. "Pete."

He pulled her into a hug and kissed her cheek. "I'm so glad you came," he said, eyeing her. "You didn't say when I called, so I wasn't sure. But here you are. Almost didn't recognize you. You look terrific."

"You, too," she said. She hadn't seem him in years, but he did look good. Cropped beard, parted hair. His hazel eyes were red, wet from recent tears. A white rose was in his breast pocket.

"When did you get in?" he asked.

"Yesterday. I thought about calling, but I don't know. I guess I wanted some time."

"You should come in. Angela's up front. She'll be happy to see you."

"I don't know."

"You have to. Come on."

He led her by hand into the chapel. The smell of flowers hit her immediately. Red, white, and yellow roses surrounded the casket at the far end of the room. Lilac, too, and moonflowers. Blue and purple light came in through the stained-glass window—Jesus on the cross, dripping blood—and spilt over the white of the casket's interior and the pale face inside. Kelsey kept her eyes away as they got close.

A short, older woman stood at the front pew receiving guests, trading hugs, exchanging kisses. Pete touched her arm. "Angela," he said, "look who's here. It's Kelsey."

Laura's mother turned and stared at Kelsey for a moment, her swollen eyes cloudy and dim. Then they lit up. She took Kelsey's hands into her own and clutched them tightly. "Kelsey," she whispered, another wave of tears sliding down her weathered cheeks. "Oh, my Lord, Kelsey!" Angela embraced her, touched her face, stroked her hair. "Kelsey! I don't believe it!"

"Angela," Kelsey said, just above a whisper. "I'm sorry. I didn't know."

"I called her," Pete said. "I told her to come. That Laura wanted it."

Angela nodded. "She was talking about you. Wouldn't say a word for so long, and then she just started talking. Oh, Kelsey. She just started *talking*. The life came back into her."

"We fought about something," Kelsey said, "and we just—"

"Never mind about that. She didn't care. She was talking about you, sweetie. Smiling and laughing like she used to. She didn't care." Angela brought her over to the casket. "You have to see her. Please."

Kelsey wanted to turn away, leave, but being so close, with the blue and purple light coming down, the scent of the flowers around her, she had to look. Laura lay inside, hair bundled up behind her head, hands clasped over her stomach. Her skin was so pale, her limbs so slim, her face so gaunt. She was so small the blue dress seemed almost like a blanket. She was like porcelain. One touch and she would break.

"She didn't want it," Angela said. "She didn't want the medicine again. She didn't want the radiation. She wanted it dignified. The chances were too small. So, she just wanted to wait. She just wanted it to be over."

"I'm sorry," Kelsey said again. It was all she could say. She didn't feel anything, somehow. Ever since Pete called her, she hadn't felt anything. What was this waking dream, erupting like a volcano and scattering her life like ashes? What was this unearthed grave, flooding and overflowing with water and dirt? Why was it happening? Why to her?

She sat silently through the service. She watched quietly as they laid the casket into a plot at the local cemetery, as Pete and Angela and others threw roses onto the satin pall. Perhaps Kelsey would have been among them with a rose of her own, had she and Laura never fought, never separated. Perhaps she would have wept and wailed, felt something, felt anything. All she could think as the casket disappeared was that Laura was truly gone, not just forgotten, but dead, reclaimed by the earth. Sunbright Laura, then a feeble shadow, now an ashen corpse. No more dancing. No more singing. No more praying. No more.

Pete walked over once the crowd dispersed. "Come by the house," he said. "The reception's not for a few hours. We can talk. You can see Hunter."

"Hunter?"

"Our son."

She followed him to Laura's family home. As with the portraits at the funeral parlor, her memories came to life as they parked in the driveway. The green lawn was as expertly manicured as ever. The single oak tree was as dominating as she remembered, eternally large and imposing. The cherry brick was as warm and inviting as when Laura first brought her to the house during that long-ago spring break. Kelsey would have believed that Laura was waiting for her at the door. She did believe it, in fact, until Pete led her into the orange-smelling foyer, the wooden floor recently waxed, and no Laura greeted her, no Laura took her hand.

"Bernie," Pete called, "I'm back. I have a friend with me."

"We're in here!" In the den, a young woman sat with a small boy. "Look, Hunter," she said, "your daddy's back!"

Kelsey lingered in the doorway and watched Pete take the boy into his arms. He must have been two at the oldest, tiny compared to his father, but with

Laura's hair, her eyes. He stared at her from over Pete's shoulder.

Kelsey looked away. They were definitely Laura's eyes.

"Hey, buddy," Pete said, kissing the boy's brow. "I brought a friend with me, an old friend. This is Kelsey. See her? She was good friends with your mommy. Good friends with me."

The boy just stared. Kelsey cleared her throat.

"I figured you two got married, but I didn't think you'd have a kid."

"You know Laura. She always wanted kids. It was all she could talk about after they gave her the all-clear." Pete paused, struggled to maintain his smile. "Oh, yeah. Bernadette, this is Kelsey Hernandez. I don't know if you ever met."

"I think we did," Bernadette said, shaking Kelsey's hand. "Laura's college friend, right? It's just been so long. How was the burial?"

"It was fine," Pete said. "A lot of people were there. It's going to be packed later."

"No problem. I'll keep an eye on him."

"Thanks. Could you take him up to his room? I wanted to talk to Kelsey for a bit. She's not going to stay for the reception."

"Oh, I'm sorry to hear that."

"I'd like to stay," Kelsey said, "but I'm always so busy at work. You know."

Pete put Hunter down, and Bernadette took his hand. "Okay, Hunter. Let's go play with your toys. Let Daddy talk to his friend."

They went up the stairs in the foyer. The boy looked back at Kelsey. She turned her head.

Pete smiled. "He's something, isn't he? I didn't want to take him over there. Didn't want him to see her. She actually said goodbye to him weeks ago, when she had to stay in the hospital. He didn't understand, and he won't really have to. He won't remember."

"Pete, maybe I shouldn't have—"

"I thought I was going to lose it back there," he said. "I keep thinking I'm going to lose my shit sooner or later, but it hasn't happened yet. I got close the night I called you—the night she went. She was already asleep. At least there's that. No more pain, right? We'd found your number, been thinking about it for a while. She got close, but she wouldn't. She was stubborn about it. Forget it. Whatever happened between you two, it doesn't matter anymore."

He went over to the bar at the other side of the room and pulled down a couple of glasses. "What are you drinking?"

"I really shouldn't."

"Kels, come on. For me."

She sighed. "You have bourbon?"

"Damn. You really took it up a notch, didn't you?"

As he filled the glasses, she regarded the room. Much was the same—the brickwork fireplace, the wildlife decor, the brocade carpet—but there were many more photographs upon the mantel. Beside the pictures of Laura as a child and teenager were now portraits of Hunter. His first birthday. His first visit to the beach. There was again Laura in her wedding dress. There were Pete and Laura exchanging their rings, their vows. There was Angela smiling over her grandson. There were photos of the entire family, so apparently happy that one would never think anything amiss if not for the wrap around Laura's head.

Hidden within some of the photos, hard to spot at a distance, was a small, sweater-clad girl in blocky glasses. Hiding behind Laura's radiant smile. Cowering between Laura and her mother. Laura's little shadow. At one time, long before, her other half.

She paused, raised her head. A scent, faint but distinct. Lilac. Laura's residue, dressing the room like dander. Pete watched her. If he smelt it, he made no sign. Maybe for him, living every day in that house, spending every day with her, the smells and tastes were no longer novel. Oh, he had been lucky.

"Feeling nostalgic?" He handed her drink to her. "A lot changed."

"Yeah. She was happy?"

"Oh, yeah. Happy as she could be." He downed his glass. "You know, I'm really glad you came. I thought it would be awkward, talking to you again, hearing your voice—but it wasn't. It was like nothing changed. And you look so good. So different. Even so much better than when I last saw you. You're so far from that nerdy girl Laura brought down with her that first time. You remember? You were so shy. Always hiding behind her back. I'd take one look at you, and you'd curl up into a ball. Not anymore. Not for a long time. I bet men are the ones who hide now. With just a look."

Kelsey drank her bourbon.

"It hurt," he said. "When you just left. When you stopped calling, stopped answering. I couldn't show it to Laura—I had to be there for her—but, Jesus, Kels, I never thought it would hurt so much. I never thought it would hurt *this* much."

"Pete."

"Was it because of me that you two fought?"

"Pete."

"I have to know, Kels."

She finished her glass. "No, it wasn't because of you. It was something else."

"And did you think about me? Because I thought about you. Every day. Christ, I thought about both of you. It wasn't supposed to be like that. It was supposed to just go away. But it didn't. It hasn't."

Suddenly, roughly, he pulled her close. "You're fucking beautiful." His breath stank not only of the drink he just had, but of the many he had over the last several days. His eyes, no longer watery, but hard, locked on hers. "Like you took it all from her. Like you sucked her dry."

He kissed her hard, ran his hand over her back. He moved the same way even after so many years, took hold the same way. Instinctively, she opened her mouth, pressed herself against him—then stopped. She eased him back.

"Pete, you just put her in the fucking ground."

"You think I'd be doing this otherwise?" The force was gone from his voice. Only a pleading, plaintive whine remained. "I need you, Kels."

"I can't." She wiped her mouth, straightened her skirt. "I'm not the backup anymore. I have a boyfriend. You have a son. We can't."

"Kels, please."

"We can't, Pete. I'm sorry."

He backed away. "You're right," he said at length. "I'm sorry. I just saw you, and it felt like it used to."

What Kelsey didn't say, she thought: Go fuck yourself, Pete.

That night, she drove around Ranger's Field again, stopping finally at the bar she would frequent with Laura, Steely's. It was still the same, and she was grateful for that. Pool tables underneath a persistent haze of smoke. Confederate flag draped across the wall. Jukebox in the corner that played Led Zeppelin or AC/DC. She took a seat at the bar, ordered one beer, then another. She half-expected Laura to appear out of the dark, coming back from the restroom after fixing her hair or makeup.

But it wasn't Laura who eventually, inevitably walked up. No, it was some good old boy in his ten-gallon hat and croc-skin boots, plaid sleeves rolled up, jeans starched stiff. He was young. No one she ever met. No one she would ever see again.

"Hey, there," he said, tipping his hat.

She stifled her laugh. "Howdy."

Back at her hotel room, after they were done, he rolled onto his back and let out a long, drained sigh. "Holy shit."

She pulled on her bra. "Glad you liked it."

"You were like a hurricane. Goddamn."

She almost considered another round, but suddenly, she didn't see him lying there, bare chest covered in a sheen of sweat, jeans like fetters around his ankles. All she saw was the open casket. Jesus on the cross, blood running down his brow. The blue and purple light awash over that soft, porcelain face. That face poised to fall apart at any moment.

"I gotta see you again," the young man said. "What's your name?"

Shakily, Kelsey buttoned her blouse, straightened her hair. Sex was always easy, abundant, reliable—but the casket and lights and smells overwhelmed her. Lilac and rosemary. The glint of the silver rosary around that thin neck. The lurid, oppressive light through the windows when she saw Laura in the hospital bed the first time. The gentle, waning light as she left Laura on the porch after their last conversation. After their one and only true fight.

"My friend died," she said. "Did you know her? Laura Brooks? She used to be Brackett."

"What?"

She imagined touching the porcelain face in the casket, the last image she would ever have of sun-bright Laura. She imagined smudging the rouge and smearing the chalk. But it wasn't just the makeup that came away on her fingertips. It was the skin, muscle, and fat, all of it sloughing off in strings. There was only dull, gray bone underneath—only maggots crawling through the eye sockets, out the mouth, around the nose. She imagined tearing the face away, smashing it, cutting it apart. She imagined poking holes in the portraits, taking out the eyes, ripping out the mouths. Trying to find her. Trying desperately to see more than just her back on that warm-lit, lonely porch.

"Sorry," she said, willing back her tears. "I'm not in the mood anymore."

She left Ranger's Field in the morning, before dawn. Pete tried calling a few times, left a voicemail, but she deleted it. She didn't think anything as she drove. Didn't feel anything. The steel-blue sky waxed on. The crop fields spread to the horizon. The highway snaked ahead.

It was only when she got home, when she dropped her keys, kicked off her shoes, and slid into bed, that the tears came in force. They had been building with each passing day, with each passing hour, but now the floodgates broke. All of a sudden, she was crying, wailing. She couldn't stop it. Her arms convulsed. Her legs trembled. She hugged the pillows, punched the mattress, seized the sheets, but nothing helped. There was just Laura. Laura passing her a note during a lecture. Laura praying at her bedside. Laura dancing under spotlights upon a stage. Laura drawing kittens on a friend's cast. Laura lying beside her. Laura holding her in the dark.

She spoke her name as she once did. Laura. Laura. Laura.

At the most painful moment, her every limb like stone, her chest constricted, the last utterance of Laura's name left her as though it were her final breath, so potent as to be visible, a multi-colored, opalescent wisp, gleaming like a gemstone, that vanished into the air. Drained, exhausted, she fell quickly into a child's deep, unbreakable sleep.

BEFORE THE FUNERAL

2.

Of course, it was raining. The first day of college, the beginning of a so-called new chapter, what everyone said was supposed to be bright and hopeful, the best years of your life. When had anything turned out the way it was supposed to be?

Her father placed a hand on her shoulder. He put on his best, most rehearsed smile. "You want me to go with you?"

"It's okay, Dad."

She knew he wanted to help, but what she wanted more than anything was to just get into the dorm and throw herself onto the nearest bed. The sooner they got it over with, the sooner things could start fixing themselves. Her father came around to her side of the car with an umbrella, and she was thankful she packed light: a couple of suitcases and a backpack. She imagined in her mind a million different fuck-ups, whether they were slipping on the pavement and cracking her skull, losing all her clothes, or getting gunned down by some random asshole. She made that joke to Allison before leaving—"You know, active shooters and all that shit"— and the other girl had just sighed. "When are you gonna stop being so morbid?" she asked, not laughing, not giggling, not even the slightest bit amused. Once, they would have laughed for minutes at a remark like that, but even Kelsey had to admit her heart wasn't in it. Best friends at ten. Acquaintances at fourteen. Strangers at seventeen. Kelsey only called her before leaving because she had no one else.

And, anyway, morbid? This coming from a girl who painted cobwebs under her eyes and wore black lipstick and dyed her hair red? Fuck her. Who was she to judge?

Thankfully, Kelsey didn't trip and crack her head. Her clothes didn't magically disappear. No active shooter put a bullet between her eyes. She just stood awkwardly before the door in her t-shirt and jeans, her big, blocky glasses slipping down the bridge of her nose. Her father scratched his beard, cleared his throat, did everything in his power to delay the dreaded moment.

"I'll call you when I get back," he said. "Let me know how it goes. Who your roommate is. Classes. All of it."

"I will. Bye, Dad."

"Bye, sweetheart."

He moved to kiss her, but she was already dragging water inside, thankful for the rain masking her tears.

The dorm halls were filled with students, all of them nervous and excited, coming in and out of rooms with their luggage, introducing themselves to their new roommates. Kelsey kept her distance, her suitcases nearly dragging across the floor, her eyes trained pointedly on her feet. She trudged up the stairs and took a moment on the landing to look out the window. The clouds were black, throbbing with lightning, and rain swept over the campus. South Texas University ("Stu," as the school was affectionately called) had looked so warm and inviting in the brochures and on the website. Wide, green lawns and plentiful, colorful flowers. Orange-brick buildings and cherry-tile pathways. But today, the storm left the school colorless and sullen. There was something sobering about the view, bleak as it was. Don't get your hopes up, the scene seemed to say. This is as good as it's going to get.

She picked Stu for its supposedly great dental school. Still felt weird to imagine it. Had someone told her years before that she would want to be a dentist, she would have scoffed and rolled her eyes, just like she and Allison had practiced so many times. Teeth? Tongue? Gums? Gross. But housing metal on her teeth throughout high school, watching her horror show of a mouth shift and realign into something genuinely attractive, changed her, awoke some sense of awe or maybe even duty. "Duty" was a funny word, not one she would ever admit in public, but one that lurked on the edges of her cynicism, somehow bright enough to burn through the dark. She could help people, fix them the way she had been fixed. Something in that idea resonated and made her feel proud.

She got to her dorm and stopped in the doorway. Things were only getting worse: the whole left side of the room was straight out of a goddamn catalogue. There was a calendar on the wall with pictures of farmland—the August picture was literally a red barn with a windmill and green grass—and there was an ornamental mirror on the bedside desk and a stuffed caterpillar with a dumb smile on the pillow. The bed had already been made, fitted with pink sheets and a green, floral coverlet. A small, wooden cross hung on the wall over the bed.

Mary Poppins, thought Kelsey. And she's *religious*. It wasn't a pretty picture, and she could only imagine the horror that was to come. Promise rings. Sermons. Plastic red babies. Matthew, Luke, and John. Christ. As in *Christ*. She couldn't imagine how this day could get any worse. Even though it definitely can, she thought. It always definitely can.

She turned her attention to the other side of the room, which was barren and white. The only adornment she had was the plaster mold of her teeth, pre-braces, which seemed fittingly demonic, more a monster's maw than an adolescent girl's mouth. The canines were raised at an angle, as if they were baby fangs, and many of the premolars jutted out diagonally. But as ghastly as the mold looked, Kelsey took solace from it. The mold was her trophy, her lucky charm, proof that one's fucked-up life wasn't permanent, that mistakes made or abuses suffered could be fixed. Maybe God did make mistakes—maybe He and the universe got off on it—but people could fix those mistakes. Regular people. Decent people.

She had nothing else with which to decorate, and sitting there on the bare mattress, cold and heavy-eyed, the mold in her limp hands, she almost didn't have the heart to even put it on the desk. The other side of the room may as well have been the whole room, so complete and oppressive was its pre-school, rainbows-and-cream atmosphere. Was this the way it was going to be? Alone, swallowed up by this bullshit? Eaten up by football and barbecue and big-dick, AK-toting Texas pride? No more late-night movies with her father. No more after-school talks with Mrs. Potter. Not even her ghost of a friendship with Allison. Just this. Every day. For the next eight or more years. Alone.

She lay down and closed her eyes. The sooner it gets done, the sooner it starts to fix itself, she thought. The rain beat down harder outside, occasionally punctuated by a clap of thunder. Fix, she repeated, barely above a whisper. Fix. Fix. Fix.

The next thing she knew, there was a girl in front of her.

"Hello! Are you Kelsey?"

Kelsey looked up. Above her was a radiant, beaming face, one as if from a dream. In fact, Kelsey thought she *was* dreaming. Something about the ocean-blue eyes and golden-blonde hair and rose-flushed cheeks seemed unreal, picture-perfect in the most impossible way. A silver rosary hanging around the girl's neck caught the light from the window.

"I'm Laura," the girl said breathlessly. "Laura Brackett. The posting said I was with Kelsey Hernandez. That's you, right?"

"Uh, yeah," said Kelsey.

"Nice! Well, very happy to meet you!" Laura shook Kelsey's hand and then, akimbo, surveyed the room. "Oh, shit. I got here earlier and started decorating. I didn't even think about what side of the room you'd want."

"That's okay," Kelsey said. "First come, first serve."

"I don't think you believe that." Laura turned and flashed her a sudden, immense grin. "You probably think I'm a bitch, don't you? Another Catholic cunt?"

Kelsey stared at her, wide-eyed. Laura laughed.

"Sorry. Too much? I'm nervous. Just trying to fill the air." She peered out the window. "Looks like this horrible weather's finally clearing up. It was really taking its time."

Kelsey didn't know what to say. This girl came out of nowhere, moved so fast, and damn, she just kept talking. She didn't stop. There she was, talking and talking, plucking the mold from Kelsey's hands without so much as a "please."

"This is bad*ass*," said Laura. "Look at this! Like a vampire."

"It's mine," Kelsey said. "Well, was mine."

"No shit." Laura looked between Kelsey and the mold. "I don't believe it. You mean your teeth were like this?"

"Yeah. Before the braces."

"Well, let's see 'em! Smile big and wide, like this!" Laura grinned as hard as she could, straining to puff out her cheeks and reveal all her teeth. "Come on," she struggled, maintaining that ridiculous face, "this is starting to fucking hurt!"

Kelsey couldn't help it. For the first time that day, she smiled.

That first encounter was a proof of concept for the rest of that week. Whatever anxiety Kelsey felt about her classes—and there was a lot, considering she was taking physics, biology, and trigonometry— was overshadowed by her paradox of a roommate. When she sat alone among a hundred in a dark auditorium, when she stood in line at the campus food court practically invisible to everyone there, when she nested small and unnoticed on a bench and watched footballs fly or listened to guitars strum, her thoughts invariably returned to that ever-smiling, bright-eyed face. Who else prayed fervently before and after bed, clasping her hands so hard around that rosary they could have bled, and yet immediately afterwards joked about cutting her wrists or dumping acid over her face?

The self-deprecating non-sequiturs weren't all. If nothing else, Kelsey thought herself an accomplished cursing connoisseur, but Laura blew past her in that department. Cuntface. Goatballs. Slag-pit. Carpet-munching dickhead. That was only a sample of the colorful expletives that dropped casually from the girl's mouth. If Laura went a full minute without cursing, Kelsey wasn't aware of it. Because she talked, and she *never* shut up. She always had something to say, whether it was a comment or a dumb joke. And when she did stop talking, it was always in anticipation of something she expected the other person to say, something she goaded or perhaps even engineered. The second Kelsey walked into the dorm, there were the damn questions. How was your day? Learn anything? Meet anyone? What'd you eat? Hear about this? Hear about that? She would prod and prod until Kelsey said something, anything, as if she couldn't bear not having some fucking conversation going on. But for some reason,

Kelsey couldn't stop her, couldn't yell, couldn't tell her to go fuck herself the way she would tell anyone else when pushed to her limits. Something about Laura disarmed her, and even if she did insult her, Kelsey knew the insults would be feeble compared to what Laura said about herself. "Yeah, I know I don't shut my fucking whore mouth," she said once. "What can I say? Mama waited a bit too long for the vacuum."

She laughed hard at that one. Kelsey just lay on her bed, too proud to slink out and call her father, too ashamed to simply hear his voice and make him worry that she was alone and homesick and miserable.

That Saturday, with the rain coming down hard again, Kelsey sat alone in the dorm, working through problems in her trigonometry textbook. Getting through the week had been a struggle. She kept thinking of the immensity of the task that lay before her. Long, hard years of work, separated from her home, from her father, from her dog. She had known loneliness, but not like this. Everywhere she turned was alien. Everyone she saw was strange. There was no escape from it.

The door opened, and in came Laura. "Rat's ass," she said, running a hand through her wet hair and shaking off her jacket. "Fucking rain came out of nowhere." She threw herself onto her bed, let out a long, dramatic sigh, lay silently for a minute, two minutes, three minutes. At first, Kelsey didn't register the silence, not even the patter of the rain, but it crept on her slowly, eerily. She turned and saw Laura just lying there, staring at her, smiling.

"You're not gonna talk?" Kelsey asked.

"I know you don't like it," Laura said, "*and* I was waiting for you to notice." She propped herself up on her elbows. "Listen. Couple girls I know got some real good shit they're looking to share. I'm talking about that Mary Jane, bitch. That four-twenty African Bush. Know what I mean, jellybean?"

Kelsey scoffed. "No, thanks."

"Huh. You too cool for that? Not hard enough for you?"

"No, I just have work."

"Ah." Laura came over and lowered Kelsey's textbook. "Well, you know work ain't all good for you, right? You gotta make time to relax, unwind—do things you care about."

"I care about my work."

"Okay, okay. Whatever you say." Laura grabbed her jacket and went to the door. "We'll be in 314 if you change your mind."

After she left, Kelsey tried to study, tried to push out of her head the annoying voice with its hint of a drawl, tried to ignore the lingering smell of lilac. "Bitch," she muttered, putting on her sweater. "Why can't you just leave me the hell alone?"

She didn't like going to 314, didn't like knocking on the door, didn't like the knowing, self-satisfied look Laura gave her. The other two girls, curly-haired Mariah and freckle-faced Chelsea, sat in a circle with Laura on the floor, passing a freshly lit joint between them.

"You're Laura's roomie?" Mariah asked. "Bitch is crazy, right? We've got poli sci with her. She never shuts up."

Chelsea took a puff and passed the joint to Laura. "She give you the abortion speech yet? First day, she was already going at it with the professor."

"Haven't gotten there yet," Laura said. She dragged on the joint. "No one asks to be born. And it sure as shit ain't anyone's right to decide if someone lives or dies—even if they are just a wad of come on some chick's uterus." She passed the joint along, stared expectantly at Kelsey. "Don't worry, girls. Kelsey doesn't like to talk."

"A match made in heaven," Mariah said.

Kelsey snorted. "I just don't like listening to *you* talk."

"*Oooh*," went Mariah and Chelsea in unison, both waiting for Laura's comeback. But Laura merely sat there, those big, blue eyes serene, the lazy, coy smile intact. "Don't look at me," she said. "Give her a taste of that. Can't you see she's drooling for it?"

Kelsey took the joint, inhaled long and hard, coughed and spat. She chanced a look at Laura, saw the same shit-eating grin, and knew she had lost.

The rain only came down harder as the evening wore on. Kelsey lay awake in the dark of the dorm that night, listening to the relentless downpour, shivering despite still being in her sweater and jeans. She stared at the wall, willed herself as much as she could to sleep, but the heaviness in her chest prevented her. This was not her home, not her bed. These people were not her people. This place was not her place. But that wasn't totally right, either. She had no people. She had no place. She knew this, accepted it, but she had never felt it. What she wouldn't have given to curl her arms around her dog Molly's neck and bury her face in that thick, butterscotch fur. What she wouldn't have given for her father to cook spaghetti and say his awful jokes and assure her with his sad eyes that everything was fine, home was home, she would wake up in her bed in the morning, and there would be a tomorrow and many more during which to feel better.

Amid the sounds of the rain and thunder, the covers of the other bed rustled. A moment later, something bumped Kelsey's bed.

"Scoot," said Laura.

Kelsey turned over. "What?"

Laura was shrouded in darkness, only her hair visible in the scant blue light of the window. "Scoot," she said again. "Move over."

"Why?"

"I'm getting in there with you, silly. Why else?"

Before Kelsey could protest, Laura slid into the bed beside her. "*Much* better," she said. "You got it all nice and toasty. I was freezing over there."

"What are you doing?"

"I don't like sharing a room with someone I don't know—and what's the fastest way to get to know somebody besides sleeping with them?" She laughed at Kelsey's nervous silence. "Relax. I'm not gonna eat you out or anything. Don't really like oral. Too smelly."

She drew a breath, closed her eyes, listened to the storm. "I wanted to apologize, actually. For earlier. I kind of forced you to go, and I know you didn't want to."

"You didn't force me. I went because I wanted to."

"Come on, Kels. No, you didn't."

Kelsey was quiet. Laura went on.

"I know I'm kind of overbearing, and I say a lot of weird shit. I don't know why. Well, no, I do know. I get nervous. You know I haven't been able to sleep this whole week? I try praying, counting sheep—I even masturbated last night while you were asleep—but nothing helps. I keep thinking about home. And I know you do, too. You're just worse at hiding it."

"What?"

"I'm saying I know how you feel. I didn't even want to go to college, but my mom, she kept saying, 'You're not gonna be like me, getting pregnant at twenty and having a kid and having some deadbeat man walk out on you.' And I said, 'Mama, I can do a lot of other things besides teaching, like growing a garden, or cutting hair out of the backyard.' But nope! Mama had her way. Like she always does. So, here I am."

"Why are you telling me this?" Kelsey asked. "I don't even know you."

"That's why I'm saying it. You know what makes people stop being alone, Kels? When they get a little bit of courage, and they go up to someone, and they introduce themselves. That's what I do—because I am alone, and I don't want to be, not for one second."

She reached out and touched Kelsey's hair. "So, close your eyes and go to sleep, little jellybean. Because as long as you know me, you ain't ever gonna be alone."

Kelsey didn't know what to say, so she did as she was told. Miraculously, she did sleep.

3.

After that miserable first week, Kelsey puzzled over her roommate. I am alone, Laura had said, and I don't want to be, not for one second. But Kelsey never saw evidence of that loneliness. Wherever Laura went, a crowd of ankle-biters and bottom-feeders followed her. Much to her chagrin, Kelsey often found herself among that crowd. Somehow, she always ended up in Laura's orbit even when she resisted. The girl would urge her, goad her, prod her. Kelsey couldn't take the nagging or joking, and she would finally submit just to get some peace and quiet. Of course, Laura would laugh and smile. Got you, she seemed to say.

In the privacy of the dorm, Kelsey watched Laura for other signs of loneliness, but they were never there. The paradoxical behavior persisted—the praying and cursing, for instance—but nothing that suggested she was alone. For her part, Kelsey thought herself well-versed in loneliness. She never saw Laura moping or reflecting. She never saw Laura get mad or offended. Everything Kelsey did—every irritated fidget and aggravated growl—found no mirror in Laura. *I'm* the one who's alone, Kelsey thought. *I'm* the one who doesn't want to be. But Laura was not like her. If Laura was really, truly alone, it didn't seem to bother her at all.

Another paradox persisted: the late-night confessionals. Too frequently, a different, less abrasive Laura slipped into Kelsey's bed. This Laura was so abundant with apologies and compliments that Kelsey sometimes, occasionally, once in a while, actually enjoyed having her there. At first, she only listened to Laura's never-ending profusions begrudgingly, but in time, she found herself secretly anticipating when Laura would decide next to invade her bed.

And so passed the fall semester. One afternoon in October, the girls sat by a window on the top floor of the university library, couched away in a corner. By this point, Laura had stopped goading, and Kelsey had stopped resisting. Where one went, the other seemed always to follow.

"So, how about it?" Laura asked, nibbling on an eraser, watching the students down on the campus lawn through the window. "Fall break at my place?"

"I can't," said Kelsey, narrowing her eyes at formulae in her chemistry textbook. "I already told my dad I'd be going back home."

"Okay. So, we split it. A couple of days in Ranger's Field, a couple of days in San Antonio. How's that for compromise?"

As usual, Laura wasn't studying, but talking and talking, always with that gentle, dreamy look in her eyes and that sweet, creamy smile on her face. Kelsey had learned to tolerate Laura's attitude in the dorm—even appreciate it, especially during those late-night talks—but in the fucking library of all places, she just wanted to study. Still, she knew any frown or groan or roll of the eyes would be lampooned for the rest of the day, if not the whole week. That was Laura's sense of humor: poke and poke until everything you did was some absurdist joke. And all this from a Catholic.

"Anyway," Laura said, "it'll be nice to have some time off. I'll get to see Pete."

Kelsey looked up. She had never heard the name before. "Who's that? Your boyfriend?"

"Oh, yeah. I haven't talked about him, I guess." Laura shrugged. "We had a bad fight the last time I was back home. He accused me of cheating on him. I told him he was full of shit."

Kelsey closed her textbook. "And did you cheat on him?"

"Kind of? I gave this guy a handjob. Not like I fucked him."

"Why?"

"Why'd I give him a handjob? Why not? He wanted it, I was kind of drunk. It didn't hurt nobody. I don't know. I was mad at Pete. He can get kind of jealous, and I thought I'd fuck with him a little bit. Make him sweat, you know?"

"But he's your boyfriend. You shouldn't do that to him."

Laura laughed. "Oh, Kels. Sweet, baby Kels. Just 'cause he's my boyfriend don't mean I love him. He's got issues. I've got issues. I don't owe him a damn thing." She kept her eyes on the Houston skyline in the distance, clicking her tongue, tapping her pencil. "There was another boy, though. Sweet and smart. Really quiet. Kind of like you, except he wasn't mad all the time."

Kelsey resisted the urge to snap back. Laura went on.

"He moved to town when I was in high school. It wasn't love at first sight. It took a little longer than that. I had to hear him speak up in class sometimes. I had to see him open the door for somebody. And then it was like a switch went off. Next thing I know, I'm thinking about sucking his dick, making him scream in bed—then I'm thinking about having his kids, living with him, just *being* with him. And damn, I was aggressive. I don't think I could've made it more obvious I wanted him. All these other guys after me, including Pete, and I'm only talking to this guy, flattering him, laughing at everything that even sort of sounded like a joke.

"But never, not once, not for a good two years does he make a move. He just looks at me with that sad, sweet smile. And by that time, I guess I thought he wasn't interested in me, so I tried to put the feelings away. I stopped talking to him. I even stopped looking at him. All the other guys dropped off, but not Pete. Before you know it, Pete's asking me out, and here we are."

"So, let me get this straight," Kelsey said. "You're all over this guy, and he never showed *any* interest in you? Not even a compliment?"

"It's not that he wasn't interested," Laura said. "I know that now. Day of graduation, I ran into him before the ceremony. We talked a little bit, and fuck me if he wasn't sadder than he usually looked, more quiet. He said he would miss me, and that was it. Never saw him again. Never talked to him again. I don't know where he went to college. He's gone."

"He's chickenshit."

"Maybe. Maybe he just didn't know what to do. Maybe he wanted to, but didn't think it was right. I don't know."

"Well, you could've asked him out. If you liked him so much, why didn't you?"

"I was afraid, I guess. Afraid he'd reject me, that I'd look like an idiot. But I know better now. If I see him again, I'll go for it. That's what I promised myself after graduation. Even if that means leaving Pete."

Hard to believe, thought Kelsey, that Laura, of all people, could be sentimental. Hard to believe she could be sad or even shy. Laura was always cheerful and upbeat, irreverent and foul-mouthed. She flirted with almost every guy who came to her—they were constant, like cockroaches—but her way was masterful. She toyed with them, gave them hope, quickly smashed it. But she wasn't cruel or mean. On the contrary, Laura was just waving them away after a little bit of fun, sending them down another, more suitable lane once their engines had cooled. Whatever her intents, however popular she was with men, nothing stopped the ever-growing circus around her. At lunch, which Kelsey also took begrudgingly with her roommate, the table seemed more crowded each day. Mariah and Chelsea had been the first disciples, but there were more now, of all colors and stripes. And the core of it all remained Laura, smiling and laughing and talking. Always smiling and laughing and talking.

This enigma of a morose, lovelorn Laura stayed with Kelsey through the next week. Love itself was the biggest mystery of all. There had been boys who asked Kelsey out back in high school—not the jocks, of course, but the "nerds," the guys who played card games or spent their gym sessions on the bleachers instead of the court. On occasion, Kelsey went out with one, to the movies, to dinner. The lucky ones got a kiss, maybe even the chance to fondle her breasts. She hadn't slept with anyone despite talking big game with other girls. She and Allison had competed, bullshitting about who sucked the bigger dick or took it up the ass, but the thought of sex actually made her queasy. However nice or gentle the guys seemed, they always showed their true colors when it came to that moment. Frigid, one called her. Bitch. Cunt. No one else would want to fuck her, anyway. She'd be lucky to get dick the way she looked. The way she was.

The remarks stung, but the confusion bothered her more. Everyone else did it, all the girls, all the guys, like it was simple and easy. You "like" someone. You "love" someone. You think someone's "sexy." You think someone's "hot." You "want" that person inside you. You "need" that person next to you. That's what everyone said, at school, online. That's what you were "supposed" to feel. But no boy or girl ever awoke that in Kelsey. She never felt the supposed pull, never sensed the inexplicable want. She did what she was supposed to do, always wondering when the feelings would kick in. The only thing that remained was the act itself. Maybe that was it? The physical connection had to form before the emotional one did?

In the evenings leading up to the fall break, Kelsey sometimes looked over at Laura, wanting to ask her about all that: sex, love, what either felt like. But she would watch Laura studying or eating, and she couldn't bridge the gap. The curiosity wasn't enough to get over the fear that Laura would judge her, that she would add something new to the long list of things over which she already teased Kelsey. Imagining Laura as some sex fiend was strange, though. Kelsey couldn't reconcile the cheerful, mischievous face with a Laura who could be so dirty, nor could she reconcile sexual deviance with Laura's other face, the one weirdly pained and pensive, somehow fixated on a boy who had never expressed interest at all, whose feelings might have been imagined or projected altogether.

On the first day of the break, they hit the road in Laura's old Chevrolet Malibu. The car was a hand-me-down from Laura's mother, but it felt so distinctly Laura, nonetheless. The interior, like the dorm, smelt of lilac and rosemary. A stained-glass flower hung from the rearview mirror. Clipped to the underside of the visor was a picture of Laura and her mother, both golden-haired and glowing on the day of her high school graduation.

"Gotta admit, Kels, I'm shocked you came along," Laura said as they drove away from campus. "I would've expected you to stay in and study all week as if you're failing your classes or something." Even through Laura's sunglasses, Kelsey could see the laughing eyes.

"Don't get too excited," she said. "My dad wanted me to go with you."

"Uh-huh. Whatever you say." Laura turned on the stereo. "You don't mind, do you? Mariah made me this mixtape. Fuel, Creed, Puddle of Mudd—all the warriors, you know?"

Don't groan, Kelsey told herself. Don't bitch. Just stay calm. Stay. Calm. She didn't have to turn to know Laura's crooked, evil grin had only grown bigger. But despite Laura's joking and head-banging, the distant, sad-eyed Laura from the library still preoccupied Kelsey's thoughts. Leaning against the car as Laura pumped gas, snacking on chips, Kelsey couldn't help but wonder which was real, the cocky, shit-eating Laura, or the Laura pining for some guy she was never going to see again. Was there a real Laura, or was it pointless to even consider?

Perhaps more alarmingly, if there were more than one Laura, were there more than one Kelsey? That was a thought too far. She threw away the chips and steeled herself for more awful, ear-shattering alternative rock.

Ranger's Field was some three hours outside Houston. Laura described it as "homely," but "rural" seemed more appropriate to Kelsey. Literal craters in the streets. High school and movie theater barely breathing after fifty-some years. Kids on bikes. Sneakers hanging from telephone lines. Mom-and-pop stores still around, not because the big chains didn't want to give the effort, but because they didn't even know this place existed. It was like a dream, Kelsey thought. A green and gold place trapped in time, snug in its own hole.

Laura's house was on the north end of town, in a neighborhood lush with overgrown mosses and imposing oaks. Kelsey was surprised at the stateliness of the house, spacious and two-storied, with a speckled walkway leading to a redwood veranda. "I know what you're thinking," Laura said, eyeing her. "Grandpa was a real popular lawyer back in the day. He left the house to my mom."

"It's nice," said Kelsey. She thought fleetingly of the old, mildewed house that stunk of her dog's wet fur and her father's shaving cream. The puny, brown-patched lawn could not compare with the well-kept greenery of Laura's home. The backyard with its weeds and rotted fence seemed now a source of shame. As the girls carried their luggage to the door, Kelsey felt suddenly, sickly, as though she did not belong there, as though she were an invader.

Laura unlocked the door and peeked inside. "Mama, you here?" No response came from beyond the dark foyer. "She's probably in the back with her damn carrots. Here, you can bring that stuff up to my room."

The walls of the house were lined with the stereotypical family portraits. Laura's mother as a child with her sweet-faced parents. Laura as a little girl, her golden hair in ponytails. Laura as a teenager. Laura's graduation portrait. No signs of siblings. No trace of the deadbeat dad. Not even many relatives or friends. By contrast, Kelsey's home was free of any family pictures except one: her father and mother cradling her when she was an infant. There were other scattered pictures of her departed mother and late baby brother, but none of them all together.

At the top of the stairs, a smiley face made of phosphorescent beads marked the door to Laura's room. Kelsey could have guessed the decor: floral wallpaper and pink carpet, ballerina posters on the walls, Christmas lights entwined around the ceiling fan.

"Yep, she's back there," Laura said, pulling aside a window curtain and looking down at the backyard garden. "Fucking around with plants was never my thing. Oh, you don't need to stand in the hall like that! Come on, Kels. Put your shit down and make yourself at home."

Kelsey set down her backpack and suitcase. Standing in the room made her feel anxious, alien. She and Allison used to shoot the shit in their bedrooms, making fun of the popular kids, ridiculing all the fashionable trends. Maybe it hadn't been real, or at least not enduring, but it had been *something*. Now, it was gone, Allison was gone, and Kelsey had no one else besides her father. So, what was she feeling now? Guilt? Regret?

They went downstairs and through the kitchen to the backyard. Like the front lawn, the backyard was spacious and well-kept, the vibrant green dotted with occasional clumps of red and purple flowers. The porch was burgundy wood, recently swept. A wind chime jingled. A birdfeeder smelt of honey.

"Mama, I'm here!" Laura walked onto the grass, thumbs hooked into the pockets of her jeans, her pink shirt suddenly bright in the sun. Her mother was crouched amid a small patch of tomatoes and carrots, dressed in the amusingly stereotypical wide-brimmed hat, boots, and flannel. She rose and beamed.

"Laura, baby!"

The two embraced in the middle of the yard, Kelsey far away, awkward in the shade of the porch. She watched them, suddenly unable to catch her breath, unable to stand straight. She sat on a nearby wicker chair and tried to steady herself. What she would have given to have been home with Molly's snout in her lap and her father's arm around her shoulders.

Laura and her mother walked onto the porch. "When'd you get in?" Laura's mother asked, removing her hat and wiping sweat from her brow.

"Just now. Traffic was shitty, probably 'cause everyone else is heading out, too." Laura gestured.

"Here's my roommate I've been telling you about. Come on over, Kels."

With effort, Kelsey rose and put out a timid hand. "Hello, I'm Kel—"

She didn't expect Laura's mother to sweep her up in a hug just like the one she gave Laura. "Kelsey, yes! Laura talks about you all the time. I'm so glad she's finally got a friend she can talk to."

Friend? Kelsey glanced at Laura, but Laura kept her attention on her mother. "That's enough, Mama. You're embarrassing her."

"I'm Angela," said Laura's mother. "Kelsey, you make yourself at home, and you don't worry about anything. Now, are you thirsty? Hungry? I got some sodas, and Laura loves her pizza rolls."

"Uh, sure," Kelsey said. "I'll take a soda."

Angela led them inside, Kelsey following obediently, if reluctantly. Angela handed her a soda from the refrigerator. "So, has Laura showed you the war room yet, Kelsey?"

Kelsey popped open the can and shook her head. "War room?"

They went into the cavernous den, which was equipped with a brickwork fireplace, aged drapery, brocade carpet, and leather sofa. A collection of trophies, medals, and photographs adorned the expansive mantelpiece, all the photographs of Laura at varying ages, as a toddler ballerina, a pre-pubescent cheerleader, an adolescent dancer. One photo stuck out to Kelsey in particular: Laura in a blood-red dress, hair bundled up, eyes outlined in black.

"My baby's been dancing her whole life," Angela said. "One way or another. Went from ballet to cheerleading to flamenco. Always trying something new. Something different."

Laura was silent. Kelsey looked at her, surprised that in all of Laura's talking and talking, she never once mentioned dancing. But here was proof of yet another Laura, one closer to that sad-faced girl in the library. The Laura standing sharply in that scarlet dress, eyes deep and mournful, seemed about to cry.

Later, around the kitchen countertop, they dipped ham sandwiches into brown mustard and rummaged through a shared bag of chips. "Pete came by a little earlier," Angela said. "He was surprised when I told him you were coming. You didn't tell him?"

"I might've forgotten," Laura said. "Besides, he saw me last month. Ain't that enough?"

"Oh, stop torturing the poor boy. One day, you'll turn around, and he won't be there anymore. You'll have scared him away for good."

Laura shrugged. "What about you, Kelsey?" Angela asked. "Do you have a boyfriend?"

Kelsey shook her head. No boyfriend. No admirer. No crush.

"Well, don't let Laura rub off on you. Men are a lot more fragile than you think. They need reasons to stick around, boosts to their confidence. Otherwise, they find something else they like better." Angela smiled, trying to be wise, but her eyes betrayed something more.

"*Any*way," Laura said, "guess I better see him. You want to come, Kelsey?"

"Me? He's your boyfriend."

"Yeah, but it'll be less awkward. C'mon."

They drove down the main street of Ranger's Field, taking a quick detour to a nearby ice cream shop. In the car, hands sticky and matted with napkins, the girls slurped on their cones. "You got a fucking pistachio Dirty Sanchez going on there," Laura said. "Like you got a damn stomach bug or something." She bit into her chocolate cone and snatched a stray chocolate chip from her lip with her tongue. "Me? I got the ol' traditional."

"I guess you're used to that," Kelsey said, laughing despite the punch to her arm.

When the cones were gone and their hands were washed, they parked outside a small hardware store. Kelsey followed Laura inside, tempted to sneeze by the smells of lumber and paint. A young man was behind the cash register, scanning receipts. Kelsey eyed him from behind Laura. Wavy, blond hair. Boyish, clean-shaven face. Admittedly very cute, definitely better looking than any of the boys she ever fooled around with. He was in a different league.

Laura looked around, saw that the store was empty, and leaned over the counter, back arched, eyes narrowed. There was the Laura Kelsey knew, innocently playful one second, provocatively seductive the next. As much as she wanted to hate Laura's prettiness, her confidence, she was fascinated by the way Laura made seduction look so easy. Not in a million years could Kelsey do the same.

"Pete," said Laura. "Hey."

Pete looked up, and Kelsey thought a spell came over him, such was the momentary softness of his features, the glimmer in his eyes. "Laura," he said. "You're here. Your mom said you were coming."

Immediately, Laura's energy changed. She rolled her eyes. "Of course, numbskull. It's fall break. I'm in for a few days."

"Not all week?"

"Nah. I made a deal with Kelsey that we'd split it between her house and mine."

"Kelsey?"

"My roommate. Maybe if you looked me in the eye instead of at my tits, you'd hear more of the things I say. Come on, Kels. Gotta do another introduction."

Kelsey came forward. "Hi. Kelsey Hernandez."

Pete shook her hand. "Hernandez? You don't look Mexican."

Laura rolled her eyes again. "*Pete*."

"It's okay," said Kelsey. "I have a lot of German in me."

"*Heil*." Pete smiled, soft in a way that wasn't soft at all. "Well, hey, I can probably get off pretty soon. Just need to make some calls. How about we get an early beer?"

"Early," Laura said, "as if you haven't been sipping since ten."

Pete went with them to a nearby bar, Steely's. Pete caught Kelsey's wary look. "Owner knows me," he told her. "We get drinks there all the time. They're not going to card you."

Laura was gentler about it. "You don't need to drink anything. No pressure."

No pressure? Was it that easy for Laura to tell? Just like with the weed? Poor, baby Kelsey. Doesn't drink. Doesn't smoke. Doesn't suck cock. Maybe Laura put on that reassuring smile, maybe she played vulnerable and tender, but Kelsey knew. She was still mocking her behind those laughing eyes. She was still looking for any opportunity to make fun of her, to drag her through the mud.

Laura smiled at her then, a sad smile that reminded Kelsey of the library, of the war room. Kelsey's cheeks quivered. She regretted thinking what she did the moment before. She almost wished she could take the thoughts back.

"So, how's life with Laura?" Pete asked in the bar, sliding a beer between his hands, still smiling playfully. "She drive you nuts yet?"

"Getting there," Laura said. She fiddled with the rosary around her neck. "We still got a lot of year left. I'll get her sooner or later."

"I'll hear it from her, thanks," Pete said. "So. Kelsey. Life with Laura?"

Kelsey thought about her response, distracted by how smoky the bar already was this early in the afternoon, by the goddamn country music coming from the jukebox. There were a lot of things she wanted to say—a lot of frustration she wanted to vent—but then she looked at Laura. The girl's usually chipper face was stern, her hard eyes fixed on Pete.

"She's good," said Kelsey. "She's a good roommate."

"Really? Nothing bugs you about her at all?"

Laura was looking at her now, earnest, maybe even a little confused.

"Well, she talks a lot, I guess. But she's fun, too. Unpredictable. I never know what to expect when she's around."

"Unpredictable," Pete said. "That's one way to put it. She seeing any guys I should know about? Anyone she take to the room?"

Laura groaned. "Oh, for fuck's sake, Pete. I'm barely back, and already with this shit."

"I'm just asking questions," he said. "What's wrong with that?"

"Kelsey, you don't have to answer anything. He's being a jerk."

"It's okay," Kelsey said. "I haven't seen Laura with any guys."

"Huh." Pete shot a glance at Laura. "That's convenient. All this time, and she's behaved herself? That's hard to believe."

"She's your girlfriend," said Kelsey. "Maybe you should have some faith in her."

Pete said nothing, busying himself with the beer. Laura tried to hide it, but Kelsey caught her smile. Kelsey smiled, too.

After they dropped Pete off, Laura raised one of the spare beers they took from the bar. "We're gonna take a little trip, Kels. Hope you don't mind."

They drove to the outskirts of Ranger's Field, Laura drinking as they went, Kelsey quiet and watchful beside her. Once they were clear of the town, isolated in the middle of an empty field, Laura turned the car off.

"Welcome to my quiet place," she said. "Where I come to blow off steam." She got out and climbed atop the car. When Kelsey just stayed in her seat, Laura called to her: "Come on up, jellybean! I ain't gonna bite."

"I know," Kelsey said. "You're not gonna eat me out, either."

She joined Laura on the roof of the car, and the two observed the calm, quiet field and the stretch of blue sky overhead. Kelsey was surprised by the power and cleanliness of the air. A light breeze touched her. The sun was mild, more warm than hot. Nothing like this back home, she thought. Not in that tiny backyard at least. That sick feeling wormed up her stomach again. Another reason to envy Laura, added to a long list already topped by her home, her looks, her confidence, her cheerfulness. But when Kelsey looked over, Laura was no longer smiling. She was somber, maybe even sad. Her haunted eyes seemed unimaginably deep, like caverns within the earth, teeming with sparkling gems and glistening pools. Secret and cool, dark and majestic.

"I'm sorry about Pete," Laura said. "I knew he was going to start. He always does."

"He's an asshole. Why are you with him when he treats you like that?"

"It's not his fault."

"Not his fault? Seriously?"

"Yeah. Just like it's not your fault you're so angry all the time." Laura shut her eyes and let out a frustrated cry. "Sorry. I didn't mean that."

"Sure you did," Kelsey said. "But I guess you're kind of right."

"Fuck, I don't know! I should leave him, shouldn't I? Dickhead. Accuses me of cheating when he's probably out there fingering some bitch! Well, I'll tell you what, his dick ain't all that. A little on the short side if you catch my drift."

She stood up suddenly and hurled her beer away. The bottle shattered on the grass. "Why's it piss me off so much? I don't love him. He could get hit by a car tomorrow, and I wouldn't give a rat's ass! So, why do I feel like I want to strangle the fucker?"

"If you don't love him, why are you with him?" asked Kelsey. "Why'd you even go out with him in the first place?"

"I don't know. Same reason everyone does, I guess. You're supposed to have a boyfriend, right? You're supposed to have sex, you're supposed to do this, you're supposed to do that, yadda yadda yadda. It's all supposed to make you happy. And then you do it, and you don't feel happy. You don't feel anything. And we've got it ten times worse, Kels, because we're a slut if we do, a fucking nun if we don't! Look, I ain't a prude. You want to have fun, be my guest. Shit like that don't matter when you're up in front of Jesus. It's what you believe in that matters. What you do. Least that's what should matter."

She sat back down. Unconsciously, she played with her rosary again. "Ever since I told you about that guy, I've been thinking about him again. I tried looking him up online, and of course, he doesn't have a goddamn profile anywhere. And even if he did, what would I say? 'Hey, remember me? I'm in love with you! Let's make it work'? I mean, am I fucking stupid? I must be, right? Because I'm so afraid I'm gonna forget him. I'm gonna forget him, and then it's gonna be me and Pete. For the rest of my life, me and Pete, and I don't know if I can stand that, Kels. I don't know if I can stand it, and it scares the shit out of me."

Laura wiped her eyes. Was she crying? Actually crying? Kelsey didn't know what to say. Tentatively, she squeezed Laura's shoulder. Laura looked at her in surprise, then laughed. "Oh, shit. I'm sorry, Kels. I shouldn't even be telling you this."

"You know," Kelsey said, "if you don't like Pete, just break up with him. Or work that magic you did on him. You could make him do whatever you want, him or any other guy. They're always around you. You could look at one and say anything. He'd be yours forever."

Laura drank from a new beer. "You're right. It's weird, though. Like, I know Pete. He's not perfect, but he's familiar. I know what I'm getting with him."

"Well, forget the guys," Kelsey said. "You got your mom, too. Your friends at school."

"My mom," said Laura. "She's awesome. Basically raised me all by herself. But we're still different. I love her a lot, but I don't know if I really *know* her or not. It's like, you can't know your parents. You're always separate from them somehow. And the people at school, do I really know them, either? Bunch of leeches and ticks if you ask me. Hell, you'd think I'd have friends here, but they're all gone. They all just kind of drifted away."

Was that true, Kelsey thought, that no one could know their parents? Did she really know her father? And who were her own friends, anyway? If Laura didn't count her hordes of followers as friends, what did it say about Kelsey, neither adored nor envied by anyone at all? All of her so-called friends from high school were gone, having passed on to different places, different passions. Even Allison left her. When did it happen? When did she end up alone?

She reached over and grabbed Laura's beer.

"What are you doing?" asked Laura. "I thought you didn't like to drink."

"I don't, but it isn't fair for you to drink alone." Kelsey drank some and gagged. "Oh, man! How do you guys like this stuff?"

"Don't think anyone likes beer," Laura said. "It's just good for the nerves."

They sat in silence, sharing the beer, enjoying the sun and wind. At length, Kelsey spoke. "You know, it's just been me and my dad forever. My dog, Molly, too. She's a good girl. A big lab. Do you like dogs?"

Laura shrugged. "Don't know. Never had one."

"Well, she loves hugs. My dad bought her when I was a kid. She was there for me after my brother died and my mom left. I don't really remember it too well—I was five—but Molly's been there for me ever since. For me and my dad. I know she won't be around much longer. Kind of a miracle she's lived this long as it is."

"Shit, Kels. I'm sorry."

"It's okay. I'm good with Molly. I don't really talk about the other stuff. I think it fucked me up somehow, you know? Made me this way. Like you said before."

"Oh, Kels, I didn't mean nothing by that."

"No, you're right. I am fucked up. But I wanted to tell you because"—she smiled, almost sheepishly—"maybe you're kind of fucked up, too."

Laura laughed at that. Kelsey laughed, too, harder than she could remember having laughed before.

"That sounds about right," Laura said. "I'm fucked up. Yeah. You hear that, Pete? *I am fucked up*!" She shouted it, let the wind carry it off for everyone to hear. "I am fucked up, and that's okay."

Kelsey smiled. She held on to that mantra, not repeating it aloud until that night, when she lay next to a snoring Laura in her bed, looking up at the plastic stars on the ceiling that glowed a mellow green in the cool darkness.

"I am fucked up, and that's okay," she whispered, breathing in the lilac and rosemary, letting her eyelids fall. "I am fucked up, and that's okay. Because I'm not alone."

4.

Of all Laura's paradoxes, that which captivated Kelsey the most was Laura's ability to morph, chameleon-like, from rustic farm girl to charming seductress. Kelsey suspected the droves of girls who followed Laura admired the same quality. Maybe Laura was right that they didn't just admire—they resented, too, as envious as they were awestruck. If they crowded her, drowned out her light, they might not only destroy Laura, but also take for themselves some portion of her radiance. But testament to Laura's integrity was that she never seemed less despite how many people flocked to her. That was the pride and privilege of the lion, but also the responsibility. Kelsey wondered about it frequently.

One night, weeks after the fall break, Kelsey climbed into Laura's bed, of which she had become a regular guest. She touched Laura's shoulder.

"Hey. You asleep?"

Laura turned over. "Nope. I'm still thinking of that fucker Richardson and the goddamn D on the presentation."

"I told you to check the requirements."

"I did! Asshat just has a thing against blondes, I bet." She yawned. "What's up?"

"I wanted to ask you something."

"Yeah?"

"How do you do it? Be so confident all the time?"

Laura snickered. "You think I'm confident?"

"Yeah. If it was me, I wouldn't stand up to a professor. I'd just take the grade. But you stand your ground all the time. You don't let things go."

"Well, yeah," said Laura. "If I'm right, I'm right. I ain't gonna back down."

"But what's that take? How do you get there?"

Laura lay back. Kelsey saw the metaphorical gears move behind the eyes, the figurative steam leave the ears. The usual insecurities crept up and made themselves heard. Is she really humoring you? Is she really being honest? Is she thinking of a way to turn this on you? But more and more often, Kelsey resisted those pestering thoughts. As strange and discomfiting as Laura's bed was at first, as time went on, she felt increasingly safe in that space—safe enough at last to share what was on her mind and not fear the response.

"I'm not trying to be that way," Laura said at length. "Not everyone's gonna like you. They're gonna think you're a bitch. They're gonna get jealous. You just gotta remind yourself of that. Don't give a fuck about what they think. Only thing you have to worry about is being your best self. The best you can be."

She fixed Kelsey with an interested look. "Why are you asking? You don't think you're confident?"

Kelsey hesitated. "You're gonna make me say it? Isn't that what you're always getting at? I mean, you called me weaselly the other day."

"Oh, shit. I did, didn't I?" Laura smirked and rested her head on her fist. Quickly, lazily, she scanned Kelsey with her eyes, and the other girl couldn't help but shiver. Laura was an observer—to Kelsey's softening chagrin, another unexpected similarity between them—and Kelsey had seen those blue, playful eyes sweep over guys and girls alike, assessing, inferring, judging. Not in a mean way, of course. It was more like Laura saw people for whom they really were. She dispensed with pretenses and false appearances. Even when those flattering mobs surrounded her, she scanned, careful to discriminate between the bigger and smaller leeches, noting where to draw lines, anticipating when to stop inviting or encouraging.

Now, with Kelsey under that analytical gaze, new calculations took place. Musingly, Laura pushed some of Kelsey's bangs out of the way and pulled at the unkempt hair. Unconsciously, Kelsey sucked in her breath.

"All that stuff about what's on the inside that counts?" Laura said. "It's bullshit. That's rule number one, Kels. It's the outside first, then the inside, then the outside again. So, we fix your outside up, and that should do the trick. What do you think?"

Protesting was pointless when Laura's eyes took on their trademark mischievous gleam, so Kelsey only sighed. "I guess I'm at your mercy, huh?"

Laura laughed. "You're the one that brought it up."

The next day, Laura recruited Mariah and Chelsea to tag along on what she called "Operation A Ho is Born." Kelsey cringed at the name, but secretly, she felt an electricity that excited her as much as it embarrassed her. There had been a pride in being off-center and fringe. Being "not pretty" had been itself a badge, one she and Allison had worn shamelessly and with great gusto. Many sleepovers had been spent insulting the perfectly painted nails of the cheerleaders and imitating the practiced gaits and hip swings of the popular girls. Now, as Kelsey followed along in her oversized sweater and scuffed sneakers, she almost regretted the jokes. Being "not pretty" seemed suddenly not a badge, but a blemish, a real source of shame, even if the other girls never said anything outright to that effect. All of Kelsey's manufactured contempt seemed powerless against the critical eye of Chelsea or the perceived sneer of Mariah. Then Laura's hand found her arm.

"Okay, Kels, here's the deal," she said. They stood at the foot of an escalator in Houston's Galleria, their voices nearly drowned out by the latest pop song blaring from the speakers and the collective din of conversations and laughter. The overcast gloom through the skylight rendered the early Christmas decorations—red streamers and wreaths slung through banisters, gilded ornaments hung from rafters—muted and faint. Mariah blew a bubble with her chewing gum, then stuck the pinkish wad to a column. Chelsea thumbed through her phone listlessly. Children rushed past, carrying ice cream cones. Maintenance workers looped decorative lights around railings and potted plants.

"We'll split into teams," Laura said. She pointed at a nearby department store. "Mariah and Chelsea will handle shoes and accessories. Remember, girls, low-key slutty, not full-blown. No hoops or chains or shit like that. I'll take Kels and look at tops, maybe some dresses. We'll meet here in an hour. All clear?"

"Don't I get a say?" Kelsey asked. "No input at all?"

"You wanted my help," Laura replied. She tugged at Kelsey's sweater sleeve. "Besides, doesn't look like you're doing too hot in that department, jellybean. Don't worry. We'll take care of you." With a wink, she swung her forefinger in a circle. "All right, team. Move out!"

Kelsey hadn't been shopping with Laura before—in fact, with the exception of the fall break, she had avoided spending much time with her outside school at all. There was the occasional trip to the grocery store, a one-time midnight run for fast food, but Kelsey had worked hard to keep her distance. Much as she was starting to warm up to Laura, she still couldn't be absolutely sure she could trust her. Laura was too unpredictable and extreme, crass and bitchy one second, saintly and loving the next. She was tonal whiplash incarnate.

For her part, Laura had not pushed the issue too much. Maybe she realized after the weed episode that Kelsey resisted pressure. Maybe she was trying to win her over slowly. But even if Laura had ulterior motives—stop it, Kelsey told herself, stop it—she never let on any sign or hint. Watching her glide down aisles and brandish blouses and skirts, Kelsey actually felt herself having fun and letting down her guard. "You're a twat," Allison would have said back in their heyday. "You're a sheep." But more and more, Laura didn't seem to match that snobbish stereotype they lampooned. Twirling around like a little girl, she didn't seem capable of it.

"Okay," said Laura, dumping a pile of clothes on a chair, "that's one part done. Now, it's your turn, Kels. Park yourself over by that dressing room."

Kelsey did as told, and Laura came over with shirts and leggings draped over one arm and skirts and dresses hung over the other. "I'll tell you what to try, and we'll see what combos work and what combos don't. Got it?"

Kelsey eyed the clothes. "What if—"

"No objections! This is not a collaboration. Look at me, Kels." Suddenly, Laura cupped Kelsey's face in her hands and got close. "This is life or death, okay? You want to die?" She was stone-faced, as severe as the most world-weary news reporter, and then her face broke, and she burst into laughter. Kelsey couldn't help it—she laughed, too. This shit might as well have been life or death. Maybe the start of a new life?

"I know you're married to the hoodie," Laura went on, scrunching up her face, "but it's getting kind of stinky." Then, with a wink, she added, "Trust me, jellybean. We'll do you right."

Trust. She seemed so innocent saying it, eyes and smile wide, probably not realizing at all what was meant by that word. Kelsey sighed. "Okay. What's first?"

Alone in the dressing room, facing the full-length mirror, Kelsey unzipped her sweater. Timidly, she withdrew one pasty, wiry arm and then another. She sniffed the cotton of the sweater and grimaced—not *that* stinky, but probably in need of a wash after months of use. Next came the jeans and sneakers. It was impossible not to see herself in the mirror when it was finally just her bra, underwear, and socks—impossible not to focus on the flat chest, boxy hips, and visible ribs. She fingered a red zit on her shoulder, pinched a flab of loose skin under her arm. Showers were always short for this reason. If she removed her glasses, though, and everything blurred—well, then it was as though the imperfections weren't really there. As though she weren't really there.

She followed Laura's orders. Low-cut blouse with tight jeans. Wool cardigan with floral skirt. Polka dot dress. Denim button-down. With each wardrobe change, she walked out to endure Laura's narrow-eyed, crossed-legged scrutiny. Switch the jeans, she said. Change the top. Tie your hair back. Take off the glasses. Put them back on. Kelsey obeyed at first, but quickly lost her energy, trudging to and from the dressing room, seeing again and again her thin arms and gaunt formlessness in the mirror. Dress-up was nowhere near as glamorous or exciting as portrayed in the romantic comedies she and Allison used to skewer on their weekend sleepovers. Thankfully, when she emerged from the dressing room after what seemed the twentieth time, Laura smiled and saluted.

"Good job, soldier," she said. "We got 'em."

"Are we done?"

Laura's mouth fell in mock shock. "Not with that attitude! We'll try another outfit."

"Oh, come on—"

"That's another! Want to do one more?"

"Laura, *please*—"

"And another! I can do this all day, Kels."

Kelsey groaned. Laura stroked her chin and hummed thoughtfully. "How about that top? We try it yet?"

Bitch is really enjoying this, Kelsey thought, but she grabbed the top nonetheless and returned to the dressing room and the damn mirror.

The torture continued for a few more rounds, Kelsey making sure she didn't let loose even the smallest whimper. Exhausted and annoyed, bristling under Laura's gaze, she jumped when Laura suddenly clapped her hands.

"That's it!" she announced. "We got our top three picks. Now, we just gotta make sure the girls got something just as good. They probably didn't, but nothing I won't be able to fix." She flashed Kelsey a smile. "You can put the old rag back on."

The girls regrouped, and Laura reviewed each of the stores Mariah and Chelsea visited as well as each of their selections. Kelsey was surprised that she actually liked some of the choices—a charm bracelet and heart-shaped pendant, for instance—but Laura shot these down quickly. "Simplify, simplify, simplify," she said. "You're the prize, not some jewelry on your neck." None of the girls challenged her—Laura's reputation as queen bee was well established, and even Kelsey respected her authority. Finally, when the review was over, Laura stood aside, calculating like she did, and then returned to the group with a grin.

"Well, ladies, I think we did it. Here's what each of you need to get . . ."

As they left the mall, Laura triumphantly at the front of the group, Kelsey sucked in her protests and grievances and tried to do the hardest thing of all: trust.

Back at the dorm, under Laura's orders, she shed her sweater and jeans and donned the white-on-black polka dot dress. She quivered under Laura's gaze, but if the other girl thought anything of the thin arms and curveless waist, she said nothing, betrayed nothing. Even her usually laughing eyes were unreadable.

When Kelsey was done changing, she turned around. "So, now what?"

Laura laughed. She brought out her makeup case from underneath her bed and opened it, revealing warm-colored rows of lipsticks, eyeliners, powders, creams, and nail polishes. "Now is the fun part," she said, and Kelsey could hear the cackle before it even left Laura's mouth.

Laura's nighttime makeup sessions were a ritual for them both, one in which Laura participated and one which Kelsey observed. Kelsey had never been one for cosmetics, not just because she had to ironically maintain her own detached appearance, but also because the amount of choice involved made her dizzy. Allison had been heavy into makeup, but of the Goth variety, always sporting black lips, white cheeks, and red-rimmed eyes. Laura was the opposite, fully embracing the mainstream aesthetic, adorning herself in pinks and greens. Occasionally, she went darker if she was trying to be more seductive. "But what about Pete?" Kelsey asked once, and Laura simply looked back at her, deadpan stare saying it all. Of course, thought Kelsey. If there was only one thing both girls agreed on, it was that Pete could go fuck himself.

Did Laura cheat? As Kelsey sat in front of the restroom mirror, Laura standing over her with comb and hairpins between her teeth, hairspray and hairbrush in either hand, she thought about the number of gestures and flirtations that must have reached Laura daily. On the way to class, when she was shopping, when she went out. Subtle advances, practically invisible—definitely invisible to Kelsey. But to the sex-literate, they were probably clear as day. A wink or a touch on the arm. A smile. A passing compliment or even insult. Invitations encrypted in code. The inexperienced boys of Kelsey's past had been free of any guile or game whatsoever. Their advances were obvious even to her. But the world in which Laura lurked? Kelsey wondered if even the toxic back-and-forth with Pete wasn't some kind of demented game. Assuming it was, and Laura was actually happy with him, how could she stay faithful? Statistically speaking, day after day, wouldn't she eventually cave?

Kelsey almost asked, so caught up was she in her thoughts, before looking at herself in the mirror and seeing Laura's handiwork. Her usually unkempt hair was in a modest bun, bangs hanging to the side. With her glasses off, she could focus for the first time on her eyes and the dark eyeliner that encircled them. To say she looked like a different person would have been an understatement—and she both resented and celebrated that fact.

Laura bent her head down beside hers, rearranging a couple of bangs slightly. "Who'd have thought this little hottie was hiding under there? Cute nose."

"Shut up."

"I guess I'm doing a good job." Laura grinned and pointed to a row of lipsticks and lip glosses under the mirror. "I'll let you make the finishing touch. What do you think works?"

Kelsey scanned the options, forgetting all her questions about Laura and fidelity, about love and sex, about prettiness and ugliness. She reached out and took one of the tubes.

"Carmine," said Laura. She considered the pale, newly discovered face in the mirror. "Bold choice, jellybean. Put it on."

Kelsey did so. The dark red on her lips brought to life the deep brown of her eyes, the near-black of her hair. When she smiled, she feared for a moment that the Kelsey staring back at her would not do the same. Her shadow, given its own life, summoned as much from elsewhere as from within herself.

When Laura showcased the made-up Kelsey to Mariah and Chelsea in their dorm, the two girls exchanged incredulous glances. "No fucking way," Mariah said. "You sure that's Kelsey?" Chelsea, meanwhile, pulled and tugged at Kelsey's dress and hair, exclaiming pleasant surprise. Kelsey flushed from their attention, but she was surprisingly glad to have it—surprisingly glad also to see Laura standing aside, smiling smugly, triumphant as always. She glanced constantly at the nearby mirror, mystified by the dark-eyed, ruby-lipped girl who looked back at her. That girl had been hiding under the surface all along.

"Compliments to the chef," Laura said. "But there's still one thing missing."

"What?" asked Chelsea. "She looks picture-perfect to me. A real snack."

"We need to give her a test drive." Laura caught Kelsey's alarmed expression, but only grinned. "The doctor needs data for an experiment—ain't that what Rooker says?"

"That guy is such a creep," Mariah said. "Always feels like he's checking us out."

"Oh, yeah, he's a perverted fuck. But he's got a point about getting results. What do you say, girls—we take Kelsey out on the town tonight?"

"Sounds fun, but I'm going to pass on this one." Mariah lay on her bunk and laced her hands behind her head. "Lot of studying to do tonight."

"She's fucking lying," said Chelsea. "You know Connor from poli sci? Apparently, they've been texting all week."

Laura laughed. "No shit? What about the sisterhood, Mariah?"

"Oh, please! It's been weeks since I've gotten laid." Mariah sat up. "Kels, have fun, but be safe. Don't let Laura use you to get blown out tonight."

Use her? Kelsey turned to Laura, who only laughed. "Feisty tonight, aren't we, Mariah? I guess you really are on edge. Anyway. You in, Chelsea?"

When the other girl gave a thumbs-up, Laura steered Kelsey towards the door. "All righty. See you later—and Mariah, I miss you already, baby! Use protection!"

Mariah had both middle fingers up in the air as they walked out, earning another laugh from Laura. "Still salty I gave that one guy a handjob for the hell of it," she said once the door was closed. "Not my fault the guy was buying me drinks and not her."

Back at their dorm, Laura proceeded to get dressed and apply her own makeup. Kelsey watched from outside the restroom, curling her toes, wringing her hands. She stepped inside.

"Is it true?"

Laura swept on her mascara. "Is what true?"

"What Mariah said. This all some game to get guys? Girls? Whoever you like to fuck?"

"The fuck are you talking about?"

"You tell me," said Kelsey. "Dressing me up, taking me out. That's not for me. When did I pick this dress? Or the shoes? Or the earrings? You did all that."

Laura turned to her, one eye accented in blue, lips a glossy pink. "You don't like the dress," she said, "then don't wear it. Don't like the shoes, the earrings, the bracelets, whatever the hell, take it off. You don't want to go out, don't go out."

"You're just saying that to make me go. You don't give a shit."

"Oh, Lord, when are you going to break through this chick's skull!" Laura sighed. "Kels, what do I need you for if I want to get laid? Come on. I want you to go 'cause I think you'll have a good time.

Maybe *you're* the one who'll fuck somebody. Now, if you want to go, just give me a few more minutes. Or take it all off and study or whatever it is you're gonna do."

Bitch, thought Kelsey. Fucking bitch. I knew it was too good to be true. I *knew* it. I'm not going. I'm not going to be some fucking guinea pig.

Of course, she did go. All it took was Laura emerging from the restroom in her leather jacket and mini skirt, captivating as always. All it took was Laura laughing and swinging her finger around again, all animosity gone, likely forgotten. As she and Laura retrieved Chelsea and headed down to the street, Kelsey wrestled with whether her shivering was due to excitement or anxiety. All those nights Laura had returned to the dorm, exhausted, sometimes sweating, but always grinning and laughing, Kelsey had resisted prying, resisted revealing that she was beyond desperate for details, craving any and every morsel of experience and pleasure. Now was the time. Now was the opportunity. In this new skin, with her red lips, dark eyes, and high heels, she could maybe enter Laura's world. She could partake of the same enticing mystery.

Kelsey wasn't sure what she expected when they arrived at the first club. Dark and cavernous, swelling with people, booming with electronic music, and flashing with multi-colored lights, the club seemed all at once the grinding interior of some noisy, smelly beast. Plastic cups and beer bottles twirled and spun amid bursts of lavender light. Bodies flailed and contorted in ways that didn't seem like dancing, matching rhythm with deep basslines and sporadic vocals. Kelsey stood near the entrance, shoved and jostled by dancers and drinkers, so overwhelmed she barely recognized any specifics of noise or activity. A fleeting conscious thought came to mind: This was a bad idea. A very bad idea. Any thoughts of the new Kelsey she was posing as—the new Kelsey who inhabited her body—fell away. The little flame of that new Kelsey was in danger of being snuffed out. Panicked, hyperventilating, she turned to leave, to run until she came out into open air.

A hand caught her arm.

"Oh, no, you don't!" It was Laura, grinning as usual, eyes gleaming, brow already damp with sweat. "We're dancing, jellybean! Get your ass over here!" She pulled Kelsey back into the sweltering club, onto the writhing dance floor, and within seconds, Kelsey was dancing, spinning, laughing. She forgot any fear of the new Kelsey leaving because she *was* the new Kelsey.

The evening sped by in a blur. The girls danced until exhaustion, and Kelsey, after some coaxing, consented to one beer and then another. They hopped over to another club down the block and a third after that. "I don't know what I'm doing," Kelsey thought at one time, dancing alongside Laura. "I don't know what I'm supposed to do," she thought at another, standing with Chelsea over a toilet as the latter puked out a foul-smelling drink. The rules had always seemed prohibitive—what rules exactly she couldn't say, but she knew they were there—and she had stayed on the sidelines as a result, afraid to take a wrong step, hesitant to put herself at risk. But there was an unexpected, empowering confidence in her black heels and ruby lips. As she sat with Chelsea at a booth in the smoky darkness of the latest bar, watching Laura dance and laugh, watching an arm loop around Laura's waist and a hand rest upon her shoulder, she realized that Laura had figured it out so much sooner. The rules only existed for those too afraid to break them. For everyone else, everyone privileged, there weren't any rules at all.

And yes, thought Kelsey, watching the sweat run down Laura's face, watching the aquamarine eyes dance and glimmer like sparkling stones, Laura was one of the privileged. Not to be resented, but admired. Worshipped. When she sat across from them, panting, emanating heat and beauty, Kelsey forgot every cynical thought and jealous projection. For the first time, she saw Laura as everyone else did.

"Well, that was a hell of a lot of fun," Laura said, nursing a glass of water and picking at the fried pickles and chips the girls had ordered. "Probably should call it a night before Chelsea passes out on us."

"I'm good," said Chelsea, though she was especially pale-faced and soft-voiced. "I just need to sit for a while."

"Yeah, right. I ain't cleaning puke from my jacket tonight."

Kelsey was about to second the suggestion to head back when a young man approached their booth. He was slim but toned, in a form-fitting black t-shirt and jeans. Blue eyes, similar in shade to Laura's, glinted like pale rocks in the dark of the club. "Hey, ladies," he said. "How you all doing tonight?"

"Good," said Laura. "Trying to convince our friend here to go home."

"Oh, really? She good?"

"A little sick. Nothing a good night's sleep won't fix."

"I am *not* sick," Chelsea said. She beamed at the young man. "Do I look like I need to go home? Be honest!"

"You look fine to me," he replied, smiling. He jerked a thumb over his shoulder, and a showy, silver watch slid down his wrist. "Actually, my friends were wondering if you all wanted to have a drink with us before we called it a night, too."

He gestured at a table farther away where three other men sat, all staring at them. Laura surveyed the group, then turned back to the young man. "Appreciate the offer, but I really think we ought to go. Chelsea talks a big game, but—"

"I'm good for one drink," said Chelsea with another reassuring smile.

"That's one vote for, one against," the young man said. He turned to Kelsey. "What do you think? Want to join?"

Suddenly aware of everyone's eyes on her, Kelsey was at a brief loss. I think we're good, she almost said, catching Laura's glare. But then another image passed through her mind: her own dark-eyed, newly revealed face, alien in its forceful beauty, strange in its seductive allure. The lips parted in what struck her as a hungry, animalistic smirk.

"Sure," she said, surprised by the word as it came out of her mouth, surprised by the momentary discomfort on Laura's face. But then the usual, expected confidence overtook Laura's features, and it was as though she never disagreed with the idea at all.

"Go easy on us," she said as the girls rose from their booth. "I don't want to play babysitter tonight."

The young man laughed. "I'm Perry, by the way. Let me introduce my friends."

He led the girls to his table. The men were older than them for sure, easily in their early twenties, all with varying degrees of facial hair, crisp shirts, and jewelry. One in particular, tanned and with a crew cut, met Kelsey's gaze. She looked away quickly, but felt his eyes linger. She found solace in watching Laura, who remained confident and smiling, all the while scanning as she usually did, searching the faces, reading the cues. Oh, if only Kelsey could do the same.

"That's Lucas," Perry said, pointing to the young man at the farthest edge of the table. In glasses, slouched, Lucas seemed the most docile of the group, and Kelsey wondered if Laura thought the same. Perry pointed again—"Here's Clark"—and one last time at the tanned young man who eyed Kelsey—"and that's Michael."

"Hello, boys," said Laura. "This is Chelsea and Kelsey. I'm Laura." When they sat, Laura immediately started talking, asking what the boys were doing, where they were going to school. Chelsea laughed at Perry and Clark's interjections. Kelsey, quiet and nervous, drained of her newfound confidence, found herself beside Michael. She withered under his glances, desperate to have that girl in the mirror reappear, reinhabit her skin, reassume control of her words. She demanded of herself, What the fuck are you doing? You're being a coward. A fucking asshat. This is exactly what you're trying not to be. But she couldn't find the courage no matter how much she berated herself. Across the table, Lucas played her counterpart, equally quiet and nervous. Even as his eyes lingered on Laura, Kelsey knew she would have the best luck with him.

"Well, we were gonna pack it in," Clark said, "but the night is young—what do you all say we get out of here?"

"Let's dance!" cried Chelsea, apparently cured of her nausea. Kelsey watched, waited for Laura to say something. Going back now would be the end of the experiment. She hadn't proved anything, hadn't discovered anything new about herself. Just a little more would be enough—enough to be different, enough to change herself. To reveal that new self in full. She needed that opportunity, whether Laura approved or not.

"We're all pretty tired," Laura said after a moment. "Got classes tomorrow, anyway—"

"Another hour won't hurt," Kelsey interrupted. "Besides, don't we all have afternoon classes? We can sleep in."

"That's right!" Chelsea said. "I'm off till noon!"

Laura looked to Kelsey with interest, an expression she had never given Kelsey before. This was more than the discomfort Laura had betrayed a few minutes prior—this was full-on attention, true acknowledgment. Kelsey had gone against her not just once, but twice? That was a pattern. Kelsey gulped—she could feel the calculations now, the sensors reading her face, her eyes. And then, once again like magic, Laura's face relaxed. She leaned forward and smiled. "Fuck it. I've been outvoted. Where did you guys have in mind?"

The combined group headed outside and down the street. The night air was biting, and the girls shivered in their light jackets and dresses. Kelsey in particular, used to the comfort of her sweater, hugged herself and tried to control her clattering teeth. Ahead of them, an outdoor eatery was loud with talk and music. The smells of burgers and fried foods wafted towards her and made her salivate. Barkers called and passed out flyers. The sidewalks throbbed with new life, and Kelsey lost sight of Laura and Chelsea, their forms disappearing behind an intruding crowd. Suddenly, a hand took her arm—Michael led her back to the group.

"You good?" he asked.

She pulled away. "I'm fine. Thanks." She eyed Lucas, who was also straggling, and sidled up to him. "Hey! They drag you out against your will or something?"

He looked at her in surprise, then smiled sheepishly. "Yeah, they wanted to get me out."

"No shit! Me, too."

"Really?" He looked her over. "You don't look like you're uncomfortable. Cold, maybe."

"I'm freezing my butt off." She laughed, heartened by the exchange. See, she told herself. It's not so hard, Kelsey. Not so dangerous. Don't be a fucking dweeb. She glanced over her shoulder and saw Michael following them at a distance, hands in his jacket, eyes away. The less he looked at her, the better. That was one thing she didn't envy Laura—the attention was nice, but not when it carried with it so much evident hunger, as though she were a meal to be devoured and digested, a bone to be chewed and licked clean.

They passed on a long line to a nearby club and settled for a smaller bar with a live band. The ambience was darker, moodier, and Kelsey settled comfortably into the crowd watching the band. She kept an eye on Laura, who danced with Clark and Perry farther ahead. Barely knew them for an hour at most, and yet Laura was completely at ease, as if she were with lifelong friends. But wasn't that how she'd treated Kelsey? Casting off all propriety within minutes of meeting her, slipping into her bed after only a week—it was like protocol didn't matter. Once, Kelsey might have resented the attention Laura was giving the boys—she seemed to crave that attention for herself more and more—but now, she recognized that if there was a key to understanding everything that confused her, whether boys, girls, love, sex, life, death, it was Laura. Being with Laura could fix her. Being with Laura could show her the way.

Lucas shuffled up next to her. "Good singer, huh?"

"I guess, yeah. All kind of sounds the same to me."

"You not into music?"

"Not really my thing," said Kelsey. "I guess—"

A pale, blonde-haired form flitted across her vision towards the restrooms: Chelsea. Kelsey stared after her as she disappeared into the dim corridor at the back of the bar. "I'll be back," she said before following into the soft-lit restroom. She heard Chelsea retching behind one of the stall doors.

Kelsey knocked on the door. "Chelsea? You okay?"

There was a muffled response, and then the door opened. Chelsea emerged, gray-faced, bile dribbling down her chin. Her mascara and lipstick were smeared from shaky hands. "I think I really need to go home," she said. "Can you get Laura?"

"Yeah. Okay. I'll be right back." Kelsey returned to the corridor. Shit, she thought. Shit, shit, shit. What the hell was she doing there in a bar with sick friends depending on her? She didn't drink—didn't know anything about what to do—just lied and made up stories to Allison and other girls once upon a time. Was Chelsea really sick? Was it Kelsey's fault for making them stay with the guys? Fuck—

Lucas appeared before her. "Hey."

"Uh, hey," said Kelsey. "Listen, my friend's not feeling too good. We gotta go—"

"You like to play hard to get, don't you?" he asked. When she tried to move past him, he shifted to the side and cornered her against the wall. "Teasing me all night, and now you're going to leave? That's rude."

Kelsey stared into his face, which was no longer sheepish, but wolfish. There was just as much hunger, if not more, than what she saw in Michael's face previously. Than what she saw in the faces of everyone around Laura—than what she saw in her own reflection. The corridor was dark, and no one was nearby. Her throat was dry, her chest thick. She fought for words.

"I don't know what you're talking about," she said. "I didn't do anything."

"It's okay." He slid a hand down her arm. "I get it. You want somebody to take it from you. That's what all of you want."

"You need to back off," Kelsey said, but her voice trembled, lacked conviction. "Seriously, I need to get my friend. We need to leave."

"I know what you need," he said, and leaned in to kiss her—

"Get the fuck away from her, you slimy cocksucker!"

A blow sent Lucas reeling away, and Kelsey opened her eyes to see Laura striking him with her handbag as he shielded himself, as feeble and frail as one would have expected. Kelsey found no sign in his wild, fearful eyes of the animal that had just cornered her. It was as if a spirit had possessed him and departed.

"You fucker!" Laura cried, lashing repeatedly, driving him to the back wall. "I'll rip your fucking balls off, feed 'em to you—how's that?"

"What's going on?" Michael was there in the corridor, followed by Perry. "What happened?"

"Put a leash on your friend, fuckface," said Laura, pulling Kelsey behind her. "He needs a goddamn ankle bracelet or something—or maybe a shock collar would be better! Fucking pussy-ass virgin dickhead!"

She spoke to Kelsey without tearing her eyes away from any of the men. "You okay, Kels? Where's Chelsea?"

"I'm good," Kelsey stammered. "And Chelsea—she's in the bathroom. Sick again."

"Jesus fucking Christ. Of course she is. Get her. We're leaving."

Before Kelsey opened the door, Michael spoke to her. "Hey. I'm sorry. I should have been watching—"

"Save it," said Laura. "Kels, get Chelsea. I'm not gonna say it again."

Kelsey looked one last time at Michael's face, no longer hungry, but despondent, disappointed. She went into the restroom and retrieved an aching, swaying Chelsea. Laura pushed them through the crowd and towards the nearest taxi.

An hour later, freshly showered and back in her sweater, Kelsey sat atop her bed and ran her fingers over the plaster mold of her pre-adolescent mouth. She fingered the teeth, rubbed the palate. She pictured in her mind the looks in the young men's eyes: hungry, hurtful, spirited, sorry. She imagined them with as much accuracy as she could muster. She filed them away.

The door opened, and Laura walked in with a dramatic sigh. "Of course, fucking Mariah nowhere to be found! Probably getting plowed by all of poli sci, not just that one asshole. Anyway, I cleaned up Chelsea and put her to bed. She'll be fine." She sat down on her own bed and buried her face in her hands. She said nothing else.

Kelsey licked her lips. She teased the silence thickening between them. At length, she said, "Does that happen often? To you?"

Laura flopped back. She fingered her rosary. "It happens. Even to me."

"I didn't mean it like that."

"Yeah, I know." Laura sat up. After a moment, she joined Kelsey on her bed. "Look, I fucked up. I wanted to get us out of there, but I thought it would be good if you saw what you could do. I mean, that was the whole point."

"What I can do?"

"Yeah. Those guys were all over you. Err, you know what I mean. Captain Turbovirgin Dickhead was getting way too handy, but it's proof that all this insecurity shit is pointless."

"What," said Kelsey, "I should be glad that guy fucking assaulted me?"

"No, of course not. But maybe you'll stop comparing us all the goddamn time."

I don't, Kelsey wanted to say. In fact, at that moment, she wanted to say many things. Screw you. You're the one who compares. You want them to touch you, grope you, rape you. Slut. Whore. Cheater. But Laura looked at her, and her eyes were unlike those of the men, neither ravenous nor remorseful, but pure and serene. Every hateful feeling evaporated.

"I'm with you, Kels," she said. "Remember: with me, you're never alone."

That night, Kelsey lay awake, the mold still in her hands. Laura snored softly across from her. Briefly, Kelsey considered slipping into the bed beside her and leeching from her warmth, but a different thought competed and won. She rose quietly from the bed and went into the restroom. In the low light, she regarded her tousled hair, her stumpy nose, her round cheeks. She pictured again the men's faces, their various looks. She pictured the haunted, animalistic features of Lucas. She pictured her duplicate's face, the one dark-eyed and ruby-lipped and subtly sinister, as dangerous as the men. No—more dangerous. Hungrier.

She picked up Laura's tube of carmine lipstick. That will never happen again, she thought. She uncapped the lipstick and dragged the tube hard over her thin lips, rendering them darker than before. Never again. Never again. Never again.

Light flickered in the deep black pools of her eyes, on the scarlet ridges of her lips. She smiled, revealed her teeth. The face in the mirror was not her own. At least not yet.

Never again. She said it once, twice, a hundred times.

Never again.

5.

The lights in the auditorium dimmed. Chatter waned, and the rustling of programs subsided. Kelsey straightened in her seat, adjusted her glasses. The curtain parted, and Alia clutched her hand. "Exciting, isn't it?" she asked. Kelsey nodded. The dancers appeared on stage, twirling in their red dresses, exposing their bare backs. Laura was among them.

Kelsey had seen this performance before. Time and again, she sat in the gym and watched Laura practice with the other girls. She had watched Laura rehearse the movements in her dorm room, in the parking lot, on the lawn. "My first solo," Laura kept saying. "It has to be perfect. I have to make it perfect."

Two years had passed since the girls met on that lonely, rainy day at the start of their freshman year. Kelsey had dedicated herself to her studies, acing all her classes and preparing rigorously for her upcoming DAT. Laura, meanwhile, devoted herself to dancing classes, particularly flamenco, her passion. She fell in love with flamenco while in high school, but hadn't started practicing again until her second year of college. As her training intensified, so did her schoolwork, involving classroom observations and lesson plans.

Somehow, they stuck together. Even after being placed with different roommates, they studied together, ate together, did almost everything together. Kelsey spent more time in Laura and Alia's room than her own, listening to Laura's incessant talking with a smile, sharing beers they smuggled inside, enjoying the occasional joint. The number of people in Laura's posse had expanded, too, practically quadrupling in size since freshman year. Once, Kelsey had distrusted the endless adulations and fawning gestures. She had resented Laura's cutting jokes and snide comments, been envious of her extraordinary beauty and the copious attention she received. But time had eroded her defenses, and she saw the error of her ways. Laura was Laura—the sad-faced, pining girl in the library and the foul-mouthed, provocative partier were the same person, all the more compelling and trustworthy because of the contradictions. And Laura had kept her word: with her, Kelsey was never alone. She had found a confidant, partner, and sister, and she was more than happy to trail in Laura's shadow.

Kelsey had addressed more than her insecurity, too. In addition to building up her tolerance and even preference for beer—rivaling the steeliest, most experienced drinkers in their circle—she was increasingly attracting compliments and second looks. Funny what flashing the occasional smile or dropping a well-timed joke could yield, and so easily, too! She wasn't as deft as Laura, nor would she ever be, but turning on her charms had become easier and more controllable. Growing her hair, diversifying her wardrobe, embarking on early-morning jogs—all had worked a slow but definite change. The meek girl of her past, so venomous and bitter, yet too cowardly to ever voice herself or take action, seemed stupid and misguided in retrospect. Never again, Kelsey said, looking back at her. The mantra had done its work.

After the main performance, Laura's time alone on the stage finally came. In her red gown and red heels, carnation in her hair, she reminded Kelsey of the many photographs, plaques, and trophies of the "war room" at the Brackett household in Ranger's Field. This was Laura in her element, channeling her paradoxical, enigmatic energy into something more powerful and persuasive. Even though Kelsey had seen the movements of the dance dozens of times— the curling wrists, the thrusting hips, the twirling legs—she could not take her eyes off Laura's lithe form. There was more here than just grace, though. Laura in that striking red, the spotlight upon her, supplemented by the clapping and strumming, seemed especially unearthly, as though divorced from time, isolated from space. Her face most of all, bereft of the usual smile, flushed and dripping with sweat, suggested displacement, transportation. Where did she go? What did she see? Was the Laura who bowed to the audience the same Laura who danced, the same Laura who ate with Kelsey, drank with Kelsey, shared beds with Kelsey? As the audience stood and applauded, Kelsey remained seated, fixated on Laura's flushed, panting face, on the cheeks shimmering with sweat, the eyes glistening with possible tears. Of course, this Laura was the same—Kelsey knew this. But there were yet occasions that made her wonder. She lifted her glasses and wiped her own eyes, and then she joined in the applause.

In the lobby, she and Alia looked for Laura, dodging around dancers and underneath bouquets. As expected, a horde bombarded Laura with hugs and cheers. Kelsey spotted Mariah among them, Luz, Carol, other familiar faces whose names she had yet to catch. Then, before she knew it, Laura broke from the crowd and stood before her.

"So, how'd I do?" she asked, breathless, sweat-laden, hoisting an arrangement of flowers over her shoulder. "Eat shit?"

"You were wonderful," Alia said. "Amazing, even!"

Kelsey nodded. "You kicked ass out there."

"You're just saying that. I know I fucked up some parts. But I tried really hard."

"You did good," said Kelsey. "Really."

The other girls caught up, resumed their cheering. Laura accepted the endless congratulations with smiles and words of thanks. Enough, Kelsey wanted to say. She's tired. Leave her alone. But Laura's attention shifted suddenly. She smiled and moved away from the group. "Pete! What the hell are you doing here?"

Kelsey turned. Pete was there in a sport coat and jeans, holding a bouquet of roses. "Hey, babe," he said, embracing Laura. "Thought I'd surprise you. You were incredible." He handed her the roses, then noticed Kelsey. "Hey, Kels."

"Hey," she said. She felt his eyes on her and shuddered inwardly—the hunger was unmistakable and grotesque.

"These smell great," Laura said, "but you gotta take 'em, Pete. I can't carry all these."

"No problem." He took both bouquets. "Anyway, there any good places to get a bite around here? I'm starving."

"Yeah, we can get something," said Laura. "Let me just—"

"I was thinking it'd just be us," Pete said. "You know, something intimate. Unless you want Kelsey to come. She's good at fading into the background."

Laura bristled. "Pete!"

"Hey, I'm joking! You know I'm joking. Right, Kels?" He winked at her.

"It's fine," Kelsey said. "Laura, if you want me to go, I'm there."

"Sure. Let me just say bye to everyone."

Laura and Kelsey bid farewell to Alia and the girls and followed Pete to his car. The night was breezy, the smell of rain in the air. Even after the performance, Kelsey still caught faints whiffs of lilac from Laura's direction. The smell had once been a source of discomfort at which to scrunch up her face, but now the smell was soothing, like the kiss of spring-time air.

Kelsey tried to focus on that smell in the back of Pete's car. She was used to being the third wheel, largely ignored as Pete talked and talked. Laura was always unusually quiet in his presence, allowed only the occasional affirmation or denial. Sometimes, he did look back and ask Kelsey's opinion on something, and she would offer him whatever was fitting, whether a sheepish agreement or meek shrug. In the side mirror, Kelsey saw Laura playing with her rosary, turning it between her fingers, scratching at the edges.

"Well, this place is certainly cozy," Pete said once they were at the bar and grill. The restaurant was dimly lit, with football on the televisions, cigarette smoke in the air. The trio sat at a booth, picking from a plate of potato skins, egg rolls, and quesadillas.

Pete tipped back his beer. "That was a blast from the past, watching you dance again. You never did say why you took a break from it."

"I thought it would get in the way with school," Laura said. "But that whole year was miserable. I would get so fucking anxious without dancing. Kelsey can tell you. Wasn't I a super bitch freshman year, Kels?"

Kelsey smiled. "No more than you usually are."

Laura punched her arm. "Bitch. Believe me, I was a mess."

"I believe it," Pete said. "You were always in love with that stuff. Me, I don't get it. All that Spanish shit—sorry, Kels—doesn't make a lot of sense to me. But Laura loves it. You should have seen her back in high school. She was obsessed."

"I wouldn't know," Kelsey said. "I have some Mexican in me, but that's it. I can't even speak Spanish. I'm as white as can be."

"What's important to me are the emotions," Laura said, "the feelings you get when you're dancing. More than ballet, which is a lot of precision, a lot of strength. Flamenco has that, but it's looser, more free. It's that balance between feelings and strength."

She was sad-eyed again, looking beyond Pete, looking beyond that night. Kelsey stared into those eyes, dipping into that swirling, flowing majesty, that dark, sparkling ocean of feeling. Then Laura's face changed back to that familiar, easy smile, back to those mischievous, impish eyes. All in a moment, the change probably imperceptible to even Laura herself.

"But it makes sense you wouldn't understand, Pete," she said. "I don't think there's anything in that thick head of yours besides sex and beer."

"I hope you're talking about the right thick head," he said, glancing at Kelsey. She bit her tongue. She wouldn't play his game, nor would she give him the satisfaction of an errant blush.

After a while, he got up. "Nature calls. Play nice, girls."

When he walked off, Laura patted Kelsey's hand. "Hang in there, Kels. I'm gonna convince him to leave in a bit."

"It's fine. It's just what he does, right? Shows up and expects you to cater to him—and on *your* night, too. It's fucking infuriating."

"Hey, it's okay. I'm fine." Laura smiled and broke an egg roll in half, dabbing her greasy fingertips on a napkin. "Actually, now that he's gone, I have to say something."

Kelsey turned to her. Once again, Laura's eyes were distant and dreamy. She pushed her plate around, smashed the egg roll, seemingly determined to waste time.

"What's up?" asked Kelsey.

"I got accepted," Laura said, as if it were an afterthought, "to this dance school in California. I got the confirmation earlier this week."

Kelsey stared at her, unsure if she heard Laura correctly over the din of the restaurant. "You got accepted? To a dance school?"

"I didn't tell you, but I sent out some applications in the fall. I didn't think I would get accepted. I just felt this impulse, and I did it. I even forgot about it until I saw the e-mail. I'm supposed to start in August."

E-mail? August? Was Kelsey hearing this right?

"Kels," said Laura. "Did you hear me? I'm supposed to start in August."

Laura watched her, searching her face for answers, for some hint of understanding or acknowledgement. Kelsey didn't know what to say.

"You're leaving?" she blurted finally. "I mean, you're transferring?"

"I don't know. I haven't decided. I've been going back and forth all week. It's like it's not even real, you know? It's like I'm dreaming."

"You haven't told Pete? Alia? Your mom?"

"No. Kels, you're the first person I'm telling at all."

"Why?"

"Why what?"

"Why are you telling me?"

"Because I'm freaking out. I don't know what to do."

Kelsey bit down on a quesadilla. Slowly, the idea took concrete shape. Laura. Dancing school. August. Laura. Dancing school. August. Laura leaving to dancing school in August.

"You should tell Pete," she said. "You should tell your mom."

"Yeah, I'm getting there." Laura popped her knuckles, blew through her lips. "It's scary, but it's exciting, too. Think about it. Shit, I would have never guessed."

Kelsey was actually happy when Pete returned, a new beer in hand, to break the awkward silence. "What'd I miss?" he asked, receiving only a shrug from Laura. Kelsey sat back, dwarfed by the immensity of the revelation, retreating into the darkness of the restaurant, hearing only the vague, muffled echoes of voices, seeing only blurry, bloated blots of color and static.

She remained in such a state throughout the night, unable to study, unable to focus. In the blackness of her dorm room, beset by the whirring of the electrical fan and the snoring of her roommate Luz, she grasped the fact at last: Laura was leaving. She pictured Laura on some West Coast beach, as radiant as ever, her cheeks their robust red, her eyes their crystalline cyan, her golden hair flailing against a picturesque backdrop of silver city and emerald ocean. She imagined that glowing figure among the bustling streets of Los Angeles or San Francisco, hounded by paparazzi, courted by talent agents. The most enduring image was Laura on the stage of some grand, ornamental theater, alone before an audience of hundreds, thousands, flanked by granite cherubs, garbed in a dress of darkest black and deepest red, bathed in the almost divine glow of a spotlight. Twisting her body, throwing back her head, tapping her heels, her face pointed in such intense, unfathomable focus.

And then it was as if Kelsey were right there, staring at those bright, quivering red lips and into those wet, shaking eyes, losing herself in those portals, those dimensions full of cold, blissful light, those galaxies dotted by glimmering stars, exploding at their farthest reaches in waves of crimson and purple. Suddenly, she could hardly breathe. "Laura," she choked, surprised by the agony, mystified by the tears. "Laura."

She sunk into the bed, unable to move, unable to even speak, exhausted by the pain, but also elevated by the pleasure, the bliss. She couldn't describe it, could process only part of it, but a thought emerged, clear and shining amid the rest of the turmoil, beaming like a neon sign.

Don't leave.

Laura, don't leave me.

Stay with me.

Stay with me.

Her thoughts, audible as though they were words, escaped from her in sparks of shimmering iridescence. Laura. Don't leave. Stay with me. Stay with me. Each utterance a glimmering tendril of red, blue, lavender light, all terminating in a swimming vortex above her head. When her voice returned and the lights faded, she continued to chant the mantra, face buried in her tear-stained pillow, hand clutched to her heaving breast, until the imagined theater, imagined audience, and imagined Laura all washed away in the comforting elision of sleep.

A week later, the girls were studying at their usual spot in the library. "Have you told anyone?" Kelsey asked. Laura sat across from her in sweatpants and a tank top, one leg pulled up, toes wriggling in their sock. She looked a little less flushed, a little less lively.

"No," she said, her thumbnail clamped between her teeth. "I'm nervous, Kels. What's my mom gonna say?"

"She'll support you. You can't do anything wrong by her."

"This ain't the same. She has pictures of me teaching to stuffed animals when I was a kid. She's in love with me being a teacher. And California? I'm all she's got."

"But you want to go, right?"

"Yeah." Laura smiled dreamily. "When I was a little kid, without my dad, without any brothers or sisters, I was always looking for something to do. Something to keep me from being so bored. So alone. Painting, violin, I tried all sorts of things."

Kelsey listened.

"Then, one day, there was ballet, and I was in a studio with other girls, and we were spinning around, tripping over each other. And that's when I knew I found it. And I got this idea in my head. I guess you could call it a dream. I'd grow up, get a lot of money—like, filthy fucking rich—and then I'd open up my own studio. There'd be a place for all the little girls like me—hell, the little boys, too—to be part of something."

"It sounds beautiful," said Kelsey.

"Yeah. Who knows? Going out there might be the start of that."

After they parted, Kelsey imagined that school, imagined a matronly Laura—still just as radiant, no less beautiful—ushering in the children, running them through drills, scolding them, congratulating them. Back in her dorm room, she picked up the plaster mold of her prepubescent teeth. She had a dream, too: fix the mistakes, correct the blemishes. Yet in the light of Laura's dream, her own desires seemed second-rate. She could fix a jaw, repair a smile, but somehow, none of that seemed good enough. Laura was *Laura*, a leader, a motivator, a saint. She changed people with merely a look. Kelsey was just *Kelsey*, unremarkable, cynical, incompetent. She consumed chapter after chapter, toiled over test after test, but still she was no better, no more realized. Laura, on the other hand, was already complete. She carried within her a light and fire against which Kelsey couldn't hope to compete.

Days passed, Laura paler and quieter with each, until one day, Kelsey didn't see her at lunch. Kelsey called her cell phone, but there was no answer. She checked her phone constantly throughout class, hardly listening to the lecture, desperate for a text message, a sign of life. That afternoon, free of classes, she was halfway to Laura's dorm when Alia called her.

"Kelsey, sorry, been trying to find time to call you."

"What is it, Alia? Where's Laura?"

"It happened last night. She just started screaming. I went with her to the hospital—"

Kelsey stopped.

"What? Why didn't you tell me sooner?"

"I'm sorry, I've been trying—"

"It doesn't matter. What hospital? Where is she?"

She was in a taxi within ten minutes, pounding her leg with a fist as the taxi crawled through traffic, clenching her teeth. Laura, she thought, blinded by the harsh sunlight. Laura. Laura. Laura.

When she got to the hospital, she was lost, mute, overwhelmed by the amount of people waiting in the lobby, the number of doctors and nurses passing hurriedly, the humidity, the disinfectant. She paced awkwardly, searching for someone to help her, maybe a nurse, a security guard. Then someone grasped her shoulder.

"Kelsey."

She looked up. Pete stood beside her, for once not smirking like a dickhead. In fact, he was somber, eyes red, nose wet. She couldn't imagine him crying.

"Where's Laura?" she asked, conscious of his hand on her. She wriggled free.

"She's got a room upstairs. Her mom's there. I'll take you."

In the elevator, Pete spoke. "Laura didn't want to call you. Didn't want to worry you. I kept telling her, but she didn't want to."

"Her roommate called me. I came over as soon as I could."

"Yeah." He eyed her. "You're good like that."

Unbelievable. Even now, he had his eyes on her, probably undressing her, picturing her modest breasts, imagining her flat ass. She was getting better at ignoring the constant objectifying and endless fantasizing from men, their emanations so strong as to feel warmly, thickly tangible. The fucking male gaze everywhere, literally and figuratively. But with Pete, no matter how hard she tried to ignore him, her skin always crawled. And especially *now*, Laura in the fucking hospital, who-knows-what wrong with her. He was such a scumbag!

"So, what's wrong with her?" she asked, trying to break his attention. "What happened?"

"Well, last night, Angela got a call from the hospital. Next thing I know, I'm driving her up here. They already had Laura in one of the rooms."

"But what's *wrong* with her, Pete? Is she sick? Was there an accident?"

"There's nothing wrong with her," he said quietly. "You know that better than anyone."

The elevator opened to a waiting area drenched in bleeding, crimson sunlight. Kelsey followed Pete down the corridor to a nondescript room. He knocked very softly and nudged the door open. Over his shoulder, Kelsey saw Angela Brackett at Laura's bedside, silhouetted by that awful, burning light. Laura looked up, caught sight of Kelsey. She turned away.

"Angela," said Pete, "Kelsey's here."

Angela turned. Her weeping face brightened immediately. "Kelsey," she said, taking the girl's hands and kissing them. "Oh, Kelsey."

"Ms. Brackett," Kelsey said. "I'm sorry. I would have come sooner—"

"Never mind about that, sweetie. You're here. You're here."

"Maybe we should give them some time," Pete said. "Come on, Angela."

Hesitantly, Angela moved away, her eyes still locked on Kelsey. Why was she looking at her that way, like Kelsey was out of time, out of place? Kelsey followed that gaze until it was out of the room, but its weight remained, its presence thick in the air. Those hopeless, pleading eyes, and Kelsey powerless to do anything. Useless.

Laura grabbed her hand, with such strength that Kelsey could only stare in surprise. Laura had changed. Something was missing in the pale face, in the dim eyes. Kelsey couldn't name it. The Laura looking up at her was a Laura reduced, a Laura robbed of some portion of her light. Something had sliced off part of her and left it rotting in the dark somewhere, cold and alone, away from its whole.

"Sorry," Laura said. "I didn't want you to come. It was stupid. Really fucking stupid."

Kelsey sat down. "It's okay."

"I didn't want you to see me like this. I mean, it ain't gonna matter. I'm just gonna get worse. Oh, Kels, I'm scared. I'm fucking scared out of my mind."

Her hand trembled in Kelsey's grip. Accustomed to seeing Laura composed and calm, Kelsey herself started shaking. "What happened, Laura? What is it?"

Laura's gaze was out the window, melting into the fiery sky. "My stomach just hurt so goddamn much last night. I woke up, and it hurt like a motherfucker. Like, zero to a hundred. So, they did some tests"—she sniffled, wiped at her eyes—"and it's really bad, Kels. They think it's stomach cancer."

Just as with the dancing school announcement, the words seemed unreal. Stomach cancer. Stomach cancer. Laura going to dancing school. Laura going to dancing school with cancer. Laura with cancer. Laura with stomach cancer.

Then another word took prominence. Think. *Think*. They *think* it's stomach cancer. Kelsey leaned forward. "They don't know. Maybe it's not. Maybe it's not cancer."

"They're waiting on the biopsy," Laura said. "That's what the doctor told me."

"And does it still hurt?"

"Kind of. It's not as bad as it was."

She was quiet. Kelsey watched her, unsure of what to say, what to do. Finally, Laura's lips spread into the familiar wry smile. "One good thing about this. I don't have to make a choice anymore. I don't have to tell my mom about getting accepted. I don't have to do anything."

"I'm sorry, Laura."

Laura just turned her head. Kelsey knew she was crying.

Things moved quickly over the following days. According to the doctors, the tumor had already overtaken a large portion of Laura's stomach, but, fortunately, had yet to spread from the outer lining to any other organs or lymph nodes. Kelsey listened to each of these revelations alongside Angela and Pete, mistaken by not a few nurses to be Laura's cousin, possibly even sister. She was around constantly, tending to both Laura and Angela, studying by the bedside or down the hall in the waiting area. The resident oncologist, Dr. Metcalfe, recommended surgery as soon as possible. No one was opposed, though Laura, silent and grave throughout almost the entire ordeal, seemed less compliant than resigned.

"You'll be fine," Kelsey told her in the hour leading up to the surgery, rubbing her baggy eyes and stifling loud yawns.

Laura lay there serenely. "They're gonna cut my stomach in half, Kels."

"Well, at least you'll never get fat."

Two weeks prior, Laura would have laughed. Now, she just closed her eyes and prayed.

After they wheeled her out, Kelsey waited with Angela and Pete, watching the city lights glimmer through the glass-paneled walls. She was dozing off, her anxiety finally overcome by her exhaustion, when Pete touched her shoulder.

"You look like you could use a pick-me-up," he said. "Walk with me."

She followed him reluctantly to the cafeteria, where he bought them both a soda from a vending machine. They sat in the corner, away from the few occupied tables. Pete opened his can, but didn't drink. He merely stared at it, as if waiting, expecting something to happen.

"You know, I can't remember Laura ever being sick," he said. "She's always been healthy. Not even a cold."

When Kelsey didn't respond, he looked up at her. "Did she seem sick? Did you have any idea this was going on?"

"No. Of course not. I would have said something."

"Yeah. It's just weird. She's totally fine, and then, all of a sudden, there's a tumor over half her stomach? How does that happen? How do you not feel anything, and then just get surprised by it? It doesn't make sense."

Kelsey didn't know. Laura had seemed tired prior to going to the hospital. Not ill, necessarily, but quieter, tamer. She should have known immediately. Laura sad, Laura sick, Laura tired—they were all out of the norm. But as Kelsey watched Pete actually put his face in his hands, actually whimper, she realized she thought the same way he did. Laura couldn't get sick. Laura couldn't get tired.

Laura couldn't die.

"She was gorgeous," he said. "It didn't matter where she was. She was always the brightest face in the room. And she had her—*has* her way. You know. You see it. She gets you on her side. Man, every guy back in high school was into her. That's all we could talk about. Who was gonna do it? Who was gonna wrangle Laura? I wasn't quarterback. That was someone else, Larry Smith. We all figured it'd be Larry, but then, even Larry gave up. It was just me. Shitty linebacker. Not a cent to my name, just the store after my dad's gone. But I kept trying. I was in love with her. And finally, she said yes. She went out with me."

He was quiet, breathing slowly, controlling his tears. Kelsey scoffed. "You say all that, but you treat her like shit. You don't respect her. You act like she's your toy."

"I know, okay?" He stared at her pleadingly. "I know. I'm an asshole. You don't think I hate all the shit I say? I don't want to say it. I don't want to be that way. But it's like I'm not myself when I'm with her. It's like she's getting ready to leave any second, like she's getting ready to take a trip, walk out the door, and then I won't see her again. That's what I feel all the time, Kels. If I don't try extra hard, she'll be gone. She'll go away."

Kelsey avoided the desperation in his eyes. She avoided admitting she felt the same.

"But even if Laura's gone," he said, "it's not as bad as I thought. I get that now."

"What do you mean?"

He was red—embarrassed? afraid?—and then he leaned across the table and kissed her. The kiss was brief, less than a second, and then he was back in his seat, redder than before. She blinked, brushed her fingertips against her lips, trembled. And then she walked out.

"Kelsey," he said, but she was already out of the lobby and in the parking lot, wandering among cars, pacing in circles. Fucking Pete, she thought. Fucking pervert Pete. Fucking pervert asshole Pete—

"Kelsey!" He pulled her aside. "What are you doing?"

"What are *you* doing? You can't just fucking kiss me! Laura's up there, for God's sake! She's up there getting cut to pieces, and you have the balls to get your dick wet? What's wrong with you? You talk all this crap, and then you pull that shit?"

"I'm not thinking like that, I swear! I know Laura's up there. I feel it in me, like it's my own guts getting cut in half. But I can't help it anymore. You're incredible. You're strong. You're not like her—you're not perfect like her—but you're the only one I've ever seen who can compete with her. The only one."

"Oh, God. I think I'm gonna be sick."

Pete took her by the shoulders. "Listen to me, Kels. I've felt this way for a long time, and I know you have, too. I've seen it. I'm not apologizing for it."

"You don't have to apologize," she said, "but, Pete, Laura is sick. She could die. I don't care what you feel. It's not right."

"It *is* right, especially because she's sick. She's going through all this, and we're just sitting around, feeling sorry for ourselves." He leaned closer. "I need you, Kels. You need me. We need each other."

"You're a fucking asshole," she said softly. "You don't deserve her."

He kissed her again, but this time, she didn't resist. In the dark of his car, they lay coiled around each other, Kelsey's bra hanging off her shoulder, her nails digging into his back. "It's your first time," he said, breathing her in, feeling her hair. "I'll go slow. You tell me if you want me to stop, okay?"

She just nodded. Then he was inside her, and she felt surreal, out of her body, torn in two. Laura was somewhere in darkness, weak and frail, suffering, and Kelsey was here, feeling Pete's weight, tasting his lips, smelling his sweat. She hated herself for enjoying it, for wanting it, for fantasizing about it, for having secretly admired his jawline, his chest, his hair. There was a full moon up in the night sky, and she focused on it, wished upon it, hoped that something could pardon this, make it right. For whatever she felt, whatever pleasure or pain, it wasn't Pete she thought of, not his body, not his muscles, not his manhood. She thought only of Laura, the Laura on that stage in red and black, the Laura pained and mournful and tremendous.

In the gray morning light, that Laura was nowhere to be found. Kelsey sat by the bed and took her hand. She found the silver rosary clasped between Laura's fingers.

"I prayed every night," Laura said, her voice thin and fleeting. "Every morning. To see my daddy. For my mom to stop crying at night. He never answered me. I thought, 'That's what faith is. You just gotta believe. You just gotta look for the signs. If you believe, he'll take care of you.' I never missed a prayer. Not till today."

She looked at Kelsey. The wry smile flickered. "Maybe you're right, Kels. Maybe there ain't anyone up there. I'm just pigheaded."

Kelsey crouched down in the hall. I don't want to be right. Please, God, I don't want to be right. Help her. Whatever you do, help her. Help her. Help her.

She heard nothing in response.

6.

Things moved fast after Laura's surgery. The tumor was gone, but given the aggressive, almost instantaneous expansion, Dr. Metcalfe recommended an equally aggressive treatment regimen. It quickly became apparent after the initial battery of chemotherapy and radiation that Laura, feeble and nauseated, occasionally delirious, could not stay in Houston. "We're taking you home, baby," Angela whispered to her daughter at her bedside. Laura said nothing, her eyes forever on the white stretch of ceiling above her head, eternally pleading with the slits of sky through her hospital room's window.

Kelsey was a fixture at the hospital in those early days, but her own schedule soon ripped her from Laura's side. Life went on, as everyone liked to say. Classes required attending. Exams demanded studying. Yet she was restless anywhere but the hospital, as if her real life was there by Laura, and the rest of it— all the classes, even eating and sleeping—was some sort of theater. Nothing felt authentic without the library study dates and the mass congregations in the cafeteria. Mariah, Chelsea, Alia, and the other girls seemed less and less around, and Kelsey realized soberly that Laura had indeed been the lynchpin holding everything together, the axis around which their social and academic lives spun. They were never your friends, she thought, sitting alone during lunch or taking notes from an isolated corner of an auditorium. They didn't really care about you. They don't care about you. They only care about her. They only *cared* about her.

A dark shape slithered into view, something inky and amorphous, purring with a lurid light. Poor, mousy Kelsey, the thing said. Thought you were finally pretty. Thought you finally found a place of your own. The dark shape flashed red eyes that were hers but not hers, licked ruby lips too similar to her own.

(How does it feel? To really be Laura's shadow after all? To be even less than some sick, dying, used-up whore?)

Shut up, she growled. Just shut up.

(Laura, Laura, Laura. You got what you wanted, and you're still miserable. Doesn't matter if she stays here or goes to California. You're alone either way. Always have been. Always will be. Doesn't matter what you try to change. Doesn't matter how much you pretend.)

Shut up!

She punched her pillow at night, slammed her textbooks against tile when studying.

Shut the fuck up. Laura's alive. Laura's still here, and she's alive. That's a miracle, you hear me? That's a fucking miracle.

The shade would slink away, leaving behind a perfume of laughter, a trail of cold.

Not me, Kelsey would tell herself. Not me. Can't be me. But she felt the old demons crowding at the edge of her mind. Laura the slut. Laura the player. Kelsey the victim. Kelsey the misfit. She fought them off, yelled them away, fanning mental flames to keep them at bay, but their taunts floated to her nonetheless on the dark wind and through the abstract smoke. You're happy Laura's sick. Bitch finally got what she deserved. Won't get any more thirsty glances. Won't attract any more hungry stares. No guy will want to touch her. No girl will want to be seen with her. She'll be all yours. Yours to have. Yours to hate.

She made a point to visit Laura as often as possible, even despite the busy schedule, as much to help her as to silence those mocking, violent voices. She couldn't hate Laura—that couldn't be true. She couldn't be happy Laura was sick, no matter the reason. Yet each visit to the hospital only seemed to reinforce that she should stay away. A despondent Laura neither laughed nor cried. A mournful Angela was always recounting this or that tearful story. A lovelorn Pete watched and followed her like a damn dog.

That was another reason to not go to the hospital. She hadn't forgiven him for the night of Laura's surgery—hadn't forgiven herself for that matter. Only Pete would take her fucking virginity in a goddamn parking lot while Laura was sliced open. The guy had no shame. Did she? At night, that red-eyed, ruby-lipped shadow wheedled her. It felt good, didn't it? His big cock? As good as you always imagined it? Or even better? The same cock that fucked Laura. The same cock that probably made her scream. Made her come! Why else would she keep him around? Stupid ape. Dumb gorilla. Good for one thing and one thing only. And not like Laura can get a good dicking right now. Maybe she'll never get one again. That would be a shame, right? Little miss perfect with her perky tits and cat eyes. And not like her being sick or not ever stopped him before. Hell, he used it as an excuse when he fucked you! So, go ahead. Knock yourself out, Kels. The glass is already broken. The ribbon's already cut. Go wild. You know you want to.

She turned over, pressed her pillow over her head. Just a minute of silence. Just one minute. Please. Just so I can finally get some sleep.

In that way, life moved on. The gravity of the world pulled at her. The suggestion of a world without Laura became more concrete every day. The inevitability loomed overhead.

One afternoon, as she cleared out the last of Laura's belongings from the dorm she shared with Alia, Pete found her.

She was packing Laura's leftover clothes away, sorting through what remained of the makeup. The barren wall, stripped bunk, and unadorned desk reminded Kelsey of her own sparse side of their dorm that first rainy day of freshman year. No trace of Laura's distinctive pink and green decor remained, creating a stark contrast with Alia's red drapery and gold-trimmed bedding. Kelsey sat on the bare bunk and closed her eyes, seeking out even the slightest whiffs of lilac or rosemary. This couldn't be the end of Laura. It wasn't right. What had Laura done to deserve any of this?

(Besides be an arrogant, cheating bitch?)

No.

(Yes. Stop denying it. Little hypocrite. Little slut. You're just as bad. You're worse!)

No! Shut up!

"I thought I'd find you here."

She looked up, startled from her thoughts. Pete stood in the doorway, his little grin playing on his face, trying to push out into a massive smile. Instantly, Kelsey sprang to her feet and dashed past him, but he caught her arm.

"Kels, come on. You can't keep running away from me."

"Fuck off."

She shrugged him off and headed for the elevator at the end of the hall. When it was clear that Pete would make it inside before the doors closed, she ran for the stairs. He followed her.

"Can we at least talk about it? This is stupid!"

"No, we can't talk about it! Leave me alone!"

She was halfway across the lawn towards the opposite residential hall when he sprinted and blocked her path.

"Look, I get how you feel."

"The fuck you do. You're a dickhead, Pete."

"I wanted to apologize."

She stared at him, disarmed by the sudden sincerity in his eyes. Was he being serious?

(Obviously not, idiot. Look who you're talking to.)

"Just sit with me for a bit," he said. "Hear me out. That's all I want."

She hated herself for following him to the nearby cafe. Little hypocrite, she told herself. Little slut. But there she was, sitting across from him as he slid a coffee between his hands. The nighttime confessional at the hospital surfaced uneasily in her mind. The shadow wrapped around her shoulders and hissed in her ear. *Is there a round two in your near future, little slut? Why let that good dick go to waste?*

"Remember what I told you before?" he asked. "I'm scared, Kels. I can't lose her."

"I'm scared, too. But what can we do?"

"That's what I can't stand. I can't do anything. Stupid me thought the surgery would be the end, but it just keeps going. Chemo. Radiation. She doesn't get any rest. It's like they want to kill her. They'll do it at this rate."

"Pete," she said. "I know where you're going with this. But we can't. That was a one-time thing. It didn't help anything. It was a mistake."

He shook his head. "You know that's not true. You felt what I felt. Maybe it was wrong, but this whole fucking situation is wrong. Why can't we have something that feels right?"

Kelsey kept her head down. "Okay," she said, struggling to let the words out. "I did like it. But we can't. I'm not the backup."

"I didn't say you were."

"It doesn't matter. You want to do right by Laura? You don't want to lose her? Then you have to take care of her. We both do. No messing around."

He was quiet, watching the trees outside. When he spoke, she was surprised at how genuinely sad he sounded.

"So, that's it? What we have is a one-time thing?"

She stood up. "We don't have anything, Pete."

She returned to Laura's dorm, returned to her seat on the bunk, returned to looking over the clothes and makeup.

(Good on you, girl. You stood your ground. You resisted the urge. Too bad it was too little, too late.)

Shut up. I can't do anything else.

(But he was eating out of your hand, wasn't he? You could have made him done anything. That's how desperate he was. How pathetic. Just like Laura, no? How she can bend guys around her finger? The way she toys with them? Exactly like Laura. You could have made him your pet. Like a doll for you to play with. Could have trained him and everything.)

She looked down at herself, at her thin waist, her modest breasts, her slim legs. The timid girl in the ratty sweater had years before been in awe of Pete. That girl had hidden behind Laura, vulnerable to the slightest of glances, susceptible to even the least titillating of remarks. Yes—she had long admired Pete. She could admit it. The jawline and chest and all that. He was a gorgeous boy. Rotten on the inside, maybe, an absolute dickhead, but gorgeous. It's not like that mattered, anyway. Being rotten. Laura could have anyone, but she stayed with him. Mariah and Chelsea dated asshole after asshole. Always complaining, but then there they were, fooling around with exactly the same type, giggling like they were on gas. Every guy was hiding his inner monster, just like that asshole who felt her up that one time. Did that rule apply even to her father? At least before her mother left? Maybe guys were either broken or not broken, either meek or monstrous, docile or dangerous. Like a setting that got toggled when they came off the production line. One-zero. On-off.

And girls? Just as bad? Worse? Because there was Laura again, pining after that long-lost boy she supposedly loved. She had never spoken of him again, but Kelsey wondered if she thought about him. Was she thinking about him while in that hospital bed, wishing he would swoop in on a white horse and save her like in a fairy tale?

Was it weakness? Weakness that caused eyes to wander? Weakness that made one stay in a toxic situation, waiting for someone from the outside to intervene? Was Laura weak?

(What's wrong? Doubting your friend again? After all that tough talk to Pete?)

I'm not doubting her.

(But you are. And you're thinking about where it puts you. If you're even weaker than the other girls are. If you're worse.)

Was that true? Her eyes drifted over the box of Laura's makeup. She knew Laura cheated at some point. Mariah and Chelsea both had a new guy every week. Could Kelsey do that? If she tried, could she be just as bad? Could she be worse? But that wasn't weakness. There was strength in having that control. Strength in mastering herself and those around her. Maybe there was a way to have the strength and abandon the weakness. A way to rise above it all.

She pocketed the carmine lipstick, snatched some of the eyeliner and eyeshadow. In her own room, she unfurled the old polka dot dress. A test. Yes. A test. She had seen the power of her beauty before, hard as it was to believe. Even Pete couldn't stay away, throwing off the bullshit macho stuff and practically begging for it. A night out without the girls—could be dangerous, but also enlightening.

The dress still fit, even if it was a little looser since she had shed some pounds. The nail polish felt alien on her usually bare, uneven nails. Her knees and elbows, rounder and less sharp, still seemed like bony, unattractive knobs, but if she posed, if she turned them in certain ways, they revealed hidden dimensions of elegance. Without her glasses, her eyes looked watery and weepy, but with a modest darkening of the lashes and selective shading, they took on new confidence. She let her hair, often tied back, fall naturally to her shoulders. She disheveled the ends, parted the otherwise blocky bangs. Finally, she uncapped the carmine lipstick and painted her lips. This last act punctuated the rest—suddenly, she was transformed, or more aptly, unleashed. When she smiled, blew a kiss in the mirror, an old mantra returned to her. Right. Never again. Never again.

As she disembarked from a taxi onto the night streets of downtown Houston, Laura's old warnings came back to her. Number one: don't go out alone.

Number two: always carry something to defend yourself with. Number three: assume everyone's out to get you. And so on and so on. Don't fall for anybody. Don't let anyone else dictate the terms. You don't want that shit to happen again, right? Come on, Kels. Use your brain. Be the predator, not the prey.

Hugging one of Laura's leather jackets to herself, wobbling on little-worn heels, she laughed. She wasn't following any of the rules that night. She didn't want to. She didn't *have* to. Never again. Never again. Somehow, she felt that mantra was protecting her—that if she kept repeating it, some magic would shield her from untoward glances and uninvited advances.

Red-lit bars, pounding with music, that spat out rowdy, foul-mouthed drunkards. Neon-lined doorways, flanked by blue-haired, pink-lipped women, that led deep into dark recesses. Crowded sidewalks that swam with bodies and concealed hungry stares. Loud streets that ran like rivers of burning, searing lights. Her among the congestion, confidence waxing and waning. A blonde head bobbed in front of her, and there was Laura, turning around to look at her, flashing one of her signature shit-eating grins. Kels, come on! We're gonna leave you behind!

Of course, Laura wasn't there. Mariah wasn't there. Chelsea wasn't there. The girls were somewhere else, probably getting blown out by their guys of the week. Laura was in that hospital room, probably in pain, probably alone.

(And you're out here, doing this shit, when you could be there with her. Traitor. Fucking bitch. Hypocrite. How can you live with yourself?)

She paused. This isn't about that. It's about proving this. Making a point.

(Proving what? That you don't need Laura? That she can stay cooped up in that room?)

No. Proving that I can make it if she's gone.

The shadow didn't respond to this last thought. The shadow didn't have to respond.

She pushed herself onward. She was already out there—what point was there in questioning why? As she moved, another of Laura's adages came to mind: a guy's only as good as he can protect you. In an open-air bar, she scanned the tables. There were the typical frat guys either hollering at the obligatory game on television or chatting up nearby groups of girls. There were couples already on one beer too many, the men dour and mean-faced, the women flirtatious and sly-tongued. None of these would do, and she was about to move on when she saw him sitting at the bar, a man with a loose tie and a gray blazer draped over his lap. He was thumbing at his phone, too preoccupied to take more than the occasional, offhand sip of his beer. She quietly sidled up next to him.

"I need a favor," she said. He didn't turn until she pushed down the phone. He faced her, red-cheeked and half-drunk.

"What are you doing?"

"Kiss me. Pretend we're a couple. I'll cover the next beer."

He didn't have time to respond because, much to her own surprise, she leaned in and kissed him. She embellished the kiss, too, drawing on every fantasy and porno she could recall. The boys of her youth had been poor kissers, and Pete hadn't kissed her in his rush to slip her underwear off. But whether or not she did a good job didn't matter as this guy—Scott, she would learn a few minutes later—was hooked. Maybe the alcohol had already predisposed him. Maybe he was lonely and would have accepted anyone, anything. Who cares? She had him after that, and every wink, giggle, and twirl of the hair—all the shit the girls did to express interest—cemented her hold further. But as he talked and vented about this or that annoying office-related bullshit, and she laughed and nodded and ooh'd and aah'd, she realized she was playing the weaker part. The submissive part. That's what Mariah and Chelsea did, always waiting for the man to make the move, always so self-conscious. Laura? She took what she wanted.

Kelsey agreed to go to his place. That was the whole point after all. And she was happy to leave with him sooner rather than later—this obnoxious preamble, the preening, courting, and assessing, was so fucking tiring. Scott kept talking as they drove, as much drunk as he was likely shocked such an average guy like him was getting such an easy lay. He could think what he wanted. It was easier that way. She just needed him to do what he was born to do, what a million years of evolution had expressly designed him to do. Would Laura approve? No. In fact, Kelsey could imagine the dressing-down she would have gotten just weeks before. But that Laura, powerful and commanding, wasn't here anymore. She'd been cut out with that shit festering in her stomach on that terrible night. She'd been cast into the void.

Scott's apartment was small, dark, unimpressive. Through the window, the Houston night beckoned, but that would have to wait. First things first. She accepted the beer he offered her, and they sat awkwardly in the darkness. He talked less, maybe due to nerves, and she realized she had fewer references for this part. Did he move first? Did she? As she removed her jacket, she reminded herself what she was trying to prove. Mariah and Chelsea were the sheep. Laura was the lion. The Laura that was, of course. The Laura that was gone.

"Shit," Scott said, "I don't even know your name."

She came over, draped herself upon him, splayed him across the sofa, the bed be damned.

"Laura," she said. "My name is Laura."

She didn't know what did the rest. Instinct? Fantasy? Or that shadow self, the one who taunted her in her sleep, who longed for the night? Somehow, she knew how to hold his manhood, how to straddle him, how to push and pull her body against his to maximize her pleasure—though within minutes, neither the pain nor pleasure registered, lost as she was to her trance. He didn't last long. She felt his discharge splatter inside of her, felt it trickle down her thigh and calf to her toes. But she didn't stop, pushing and pulling, pushing and pulling, sweating so much her eyes clouded, heaving so heavily her mouth dried. Slowly, realizing she was the only one moving, she rocked gently to a stop. Scott's face was a blanket of shadows, but she heard his snores just fine.

She climbed off him, slightly dizzy, very hot. Sense came back to her. Clarity arrived after its absence. Barefoot, she scampered to the restroom, and in the pale light, she stood in the shower, pulled up her dress, and washed herself out. As she ran the water over herself, the lips inflamed and tender, the water cool and bracing, her fingers found their way inside. She finished what had been started on the sofa. She bit her fist to stifle the moan.

Silently, exhaustedly, she straightened her dress, smoothed out her hair. She strapped on her heels and donned the jacket. Laura's jacket, but then so was the rest of the ensemble. Who had picked the dress? Who had singled out the shoes? All Kelsey owned was the color she chose for the lipstick. Not even the tube itself. Well, she would rectify that. Never again, she thought, smudging the lipstick with her thumb and rubbing the crumbly residue away between her fingers. Never again would she follow Laura's lead. Never again would there be a Laura to lead.

(You don't believe that. She'll come back. She has to.)

No. She's gone.

Back in her dorm, she undressed, showered. Her roommate Luz was gone, so she lay alone in the dark, tempted to reach for the familiar comfort of the plaster mold, but she refused. There was a new comfort now. Many, in fact. One for every night. Maybe more.

She went out the next night, and again the night after that. She didn't always go home with someone, but she nonetheless refined her remarks, practiced her postures. Graceful, she reminded herself, but a word away from dirty. Beautiful, but a moment away from savage. Soft, but only a second from hard. She bought new dresses and shoes, collected her own makeup. A month before, she would have balked at caking herself, and during the day, she indeed did not. But at night, when her other self came out—no, when she revealed all she was, all she hid—she experimented with different color combinations, complementary compositions, contrasting concealers. She changed her voice, adjusted her height, modified her hair. Men looked at her. Women stared after her. And then more. And then more. More, more, more.

Turned out Pete had been good for something after all.

Her new routine had been ongoing for several days when, halfway through painting her lips magenta before a fresh night out, she realized she had not seen Laura at all.

Off with the lipstick. On with the glasses. Returning to the hospital revived all the recent memories she was trying to suppress. Especially the parking lot. Especially the crescent moon in the twilight sky.

Pete was thankfully nowhere to be seen, but when she opened the door to Laura's room, she found Angela sitting at her daughter's bedside, one of her arms over the girl's thin shoulders, their heads nestled together. They were mid-laugh, watching some comedy on the television. Across Laura's lap were a favored pink blanket and a half-eaten tray of baked chicken and boiled potatoes. The scene was too cozy, too private, reminding Kelsey of that spring afternoon when she first met Laura's mother, when she saw the two embrace in the sunshine, participants in a shared, intimate world. An exclusive world, one to which Kelsey had no access and never would have access. A world for which she had no equivalent even with her father.

She closed the door quickly, but Angela called to her. "Kelsey? Sweetie? Come in."

She nudged open the door, and there was Angela, smiling with relief. There was Laura, looking at Kelsey in a strange way, a way she had never seen before. A mix of longing and vulnerability, embarrassment and shame. The closest image that came to mind was that sad-faced, mournful Laura from the library, the one who had mystified Kelsey for so many nights their first year of college. The one who would never again see that boy she claimed to love. The one who would pine forever and wish each day that he would appear, magically, coincidentally, around the corner, in her social media inbox. Stranger things had happened. And yet this would not.

Wherever it came from, whatever it was, the look was enough to make Kelsey forget all about her new nighttime habits. The look was enough to nearly make her go straight home and throw away all the clothes, jewelry, and makeup. To burn it all.

"Sweetie, we've been wondering where you've been," Angela said. She pulled Kelsey into a hug, which should have felt comforting, but instead made her feel cold. "You're so busy, though. Imagine, baby! A dentist. Your daddy must be so proud."

"He is," Kelsey said. "Thank you, Ms. Brackett."

"How many times do I have to tell you? Angela. Hell"—she smiled and hugged Kelsey again—"'Mom' will do. You and Laura are always together as it is." She looked between the girls. "Well, I'll give you some time alone. Do you want anything, baby? Kelsey?"

"No, Mama. Thank you."

Kelsey shook her head.

When she left, Kelsey idled. Laura played with her hands.

"So. A lot of studying?"

"Yeah. You know how it is. You?" Kelsey realized too late what she said, but Laura laughed. Something returned of her old ways, her old confidence. Maybe the old Laura wasn't totally gone—maybe she was just in hiding, and she would need to be coaxed out.

"Oh, I'm super busy," she said. "You know, puking out my lungs. Lying here like a dumbass. My schedule's booked. You're lucky you even caught me."

"I'm sorry. I don't know why I said that."

"You're good. At least one of us has still got dreams to work toward." Laura went quiet. She pursed her lips. "Looks like I'm the real asshole. I don't blame you for staying away."

Kelsey went to her side, took her hand. "Now you *are* being a dumbass. I'm here. I'd never not be."

Laura smiled, but there was none of the usual warmth, none of the typical mischief. "Mariah came by, you know. Looked at me like I was a stranger. Didn't know what to say. Neither did I."

"Fuck her," said Kelsey quickly. "She's always been fake."

"Nah. That ain't it. She just doesn't recognize me. I know you don't, neither."

There was no protest ready. Even reduced, Laura was as perceptive as ever. The gears were still turning, the calculations still running.

She patted Kelsey's hand. "I'll be okay, Kels. Do what you gotta do."

Kelsey watched her face, watched her eyes wander to the window, perhaps pulled to the window, drawn by the same magnetism as she was right at that moment. The night called to them both, singing its sweet lyrics, brandishing its irresistible wares. Cold drink in hand. Sweat on the brow. A shoulder kissed. A thigh touched. Pleasures that were new to Kelsey. Pleasures that were old to Laura. Pleasures that were privileged. Pleasures that were revoked.

"It was fun while it lasted," Laura said. Another smile, this one like a limp flag picked up by a breeze on an otherwise windless day. Like a drop of water in the ocean. Like nothing at all.

What was Kelsey supposed to say? What could she say?

As she left the hospital, as she passed through that tainted parking lot, she didn't bother with prayers like she had before. Why would God listen to her when he ignored even Laura? Or did even God not recognize Laura anymore?

(How funny. The Laura you get to keep isn't the one you want. And the one you want is gone forever.)

That's not true. It can't be. She'll get better. She needs to heal. And I can help her. I can bring her back. Lure her out. She just needs time.

Time. More time. Time, time, time. That's what she told herself, but what if Laura really never came back? What if she was lost somewhere, trapped in a place bordered by sleep, landlocked by dreams? I'll leave my body, Kelsey thought. I'll fly. All the way through space. To Heaven. I'll bring her back. I'll find her up there, wherever she is.

(You really are an idiot. That girl you just fucking talked to? The one you're walking away from right this second? That's Laura, dumbass. Not just what's left of her.)

She sat in a cafe, nervously downing a coffee. She kicked her leg. She drummed her fingers. She scratched her arm. She saw herself as a form of shining light, like a rocket breaking through the cover of darkness overhead. Past that, beyond the atmosphere, light-years away from the sun and its host of planets, among the billions of distant stars, throughout the endless galaxies, the pieces of Laura were scattered. Her arms, her legs. Her breasts, her body. Her nose and her neck. Her eyes and her hair. Each part glowing in the void, radiating its essential heat, calling for reunion. Kelsey just had to follow the trail of warmth in the cosmic cold. Just had to pursue the lilac and rosemary throughout the scentless vacuum. Find her. Find her. Bring her back. Bring her back. Piece her together. Piece her together.

Something rose up in her, something deep and hot, brimming with untold colors, erupting like a volcano from the subterranean earth that was her being.

Find her. Find her. Find her.

The world sparkled like a pearl, as though scintillating pollen had fallen over everything, as though color-swimming plastic had been pulled over her vision.

Bring her back. Bring her back. Bring her back.

There! She saw it. So far away, but clearly visible. A cold, white frontier, like waterfalls suspended in space. Laura was there. Laura was somewhere beyond that barrier.

Piece her together. Piece her together. Piece her together.

She couldn't breathe. Her chest felt ready to burst. She just had to leave this body, this little shell. She just had to launch. She could make it. She knew where to go. Somehow, she had been there before, to that cold, distant place. How? Why? It didn't matter. If Laura was there, she would find her. She would bring her back. She would piece her together if she needed to. Whatever it took. It was worth anything, even herself. Especially herself.

Find her. Bring her back. Piece her together—

"Excuse me? Are you all right?"

A hand on her shoulder. A gentle squeeze. A tanned face. A curl of brown hair across an eye. Kelsey drew a breath—she'd been crying, nearly screaming. She shook with exhaustion, every muscle sluggish, eyelids threatening to close. All her remaining strength was necessary just to stay upright. When she spoke, her words slurred and rolled together.

"I'm sorry?"

"Are you all right?" The woman smiled again, held her shoulder more firmly. "You looked like you were having a panic attack. Do you need something? Should I call someone?"

"No. No, thank you." Kelsey steadied herself. She wiped her eyes. "A friend of mine is just really sick right now. It's a lot to take in."

"I'm so sorry to hear that. There's nothing else I can do?"

"No. Thank you."

The woman offered one more smile, then walked away. Kelsey admired her from the back: the line of her skirt, the curve of her calves, the bounce of her hair. The woman sat at another table, unpacked her bag, unfolded a laptop. As she worked, she shifted her legs, tapped her feet. Her skirt moved. The flesh of a thigh glowed underneath the overhead light.

Kelsey watched. The exhaustion faded, replaced by a rush of adrenaline. That vision of Laura's scattered remnants—that vision of the cold, white frontier at the edge of the cosmos—disappeared completely from her mind. Her shadow peeked over her shoulder.

(She's a lot prettier to look at than some dying girl in a hospital bed. Why bring Laura back when you've got this selection? When you're finally coming into your own?)

But even these taunts hardly registered in Kelsey's mind. The form of this woman consumed her attention entirely. Her own gears turned. Her own calculations ran. She was still so green! How did it take her so long to see when it was so obvious? The hand on the shoulder. The squeeze. The smile. Sitting at just the right table, at just the right angle, under just the right light. Anticipating exactly this scenario. Probably replaying it in the shower, over coffee, at daycare. Improvising. Adjusting. Picking out the target who was not only attractive enough, but also vulnerable enough. Accounting for all the variables. Setting the trap. Waiting for it to spring.

She smirked. It was like seeing a master paint. Like stepping into the ring with a worthy opponent. Here was a challenge she could actually cut her teeth on. No more baby shit. No more child's play.

She stood up, all worry about Laura gone, all concern for those dismembered parts of her soul forgotten. There was blood in the air. There was hunger. There were so many lessons to learn, so many other comforts to unlock. Why wait? Why cry? Take. Take, take, take.

She approached the woman. She bared her own curated smile.

7.

"You're leaving?"

Kelsey turned back, in the middle of buttoning her blouse and smoothing out her hair. Jackson looked so small on the bed, propped up on his elbows, naked except for a pair of dog tags loose around his neck. The way he stared at her, a bit sad, a little desperate, was the complete opposite of how he used to look at her in high school. He'd laughed at her the night she demurred from letting him kiss her. "You wouldn't even know how to handle me," he told her at the time. "You're too tiny, anyway. Who'd want to fuck that?"

She couldn't deny the satisfaction in seeing him this way. Heavier than he had been, with long, unkempt hair and a dirty, little-groomed beard, still living in his parents' house, surrounded by old video games and porn magazines and the stench of beer mixed with that of weed. Fitting for such an enormous shithead.

She put on a smile. "What, you liked it?"

"Fuck yeah. Shit, you're way different than you used to be. Like a different person."

"I think you're exaggerating."

"No, seriously. You look ten times better than you did—no, twenty. You put that other girl to shame. The one you used to hang out with. What was her fucking name?"

"I don't remember." Kelsey looked away, fiddled with her buttons.

"Allison. Yeah, Allison Miller. You talk to her anymore? Last I heard, she was whoring it up at some strip club out of town. Her dad kicked her out."

"I didn't know that."

"Yeah, I guess you were up in Houston. She put on the pounds. Turned into a fucking whale. Her pimp probably keeps her chained up. That's what I'd do."

Kelsey struggled with the last button. Definitely fitting, she thought, for such a massive, outrageous shithead. She hadn't thought of Allison in so long, but now the memories came back. The sleepovers. The shit-talking. The long, silent distance.

"Hey," said Jackson, crawling towards her. "How long you gonna be in town? My parents aren't coming back for another week. We'll have all the time in the world."

"I appreciate the offer," Kelsey said, "but you don't even know how to handle me."

She was back in San Antonio for a brief summer visit. Her second year of dental school was behind her, her third about to begin. Brutal days were spent in lectures and labs, and long nights were spent over books and notes. Still, she had aced most of her classes so far despite the fatigue. There was comfort in so much work, so much routine. Even her moonlighting had become less of a priority with the amount of work on her plate. She could focus without drama or distraction. Throwing off men (and women) was easy when she could just slip out a textbook from her bag or allude to an upcoming exam. The guys and girls in her classes were a different story, and she had fooled around with a few despite her better judgment, more out of curiosity and convenience than actual desire. At least that's what she told herself. The routine was comfortable, but the loneliness was not. She longed for the days spent with Laura, Mariah, Chelsea, and the other girls, or even, now that she recalled it, the carefree time with Allison.

"You got in late last night," her father said the next morning after breakfast. He washed dishes while she dried them.

"I'm a big girl," she said. "You don't need to be waiting up for me."

"I know. Just didn't take you to like the local variety."

She smiled. "Turns out I don't."

That was their way, exchanging barbs, trading jokes, more like friends than parent and child. Ever since Kelsey's younger brother drowned off the coast of Corpus Christi—a day she could barely remember, a day sun-bleached and hazy—and ever since her mother had left them not long afterwards, Kelsey's father had been her guardian, mentor, and confidant. Yet they had grown apart during the years she had been in Houston, partly because of distance, partly because of school.

Partly because of Laura.

He was getting older, evidenced by the graying beard, the balding head. And his "dad sweaters," once unremarkable to her, now seemed funny, even slightly mortifying. Nonetheless, his weary smile never ceased to bring out her own. In that tiny house, the nexus of her youth, there was still a considerable amount of warmth.

"How long will you be staying with Laura?" he asked her later that morning.

"I don't know. A few days, maybe."

"How is she doing?"

"She's doing okay."

Truthfully, Kelsey hadn't seen Laura in months. Over two years had passed since the initial diagnosis, since Laura had been spirited from Houston back to Ranger's Field. Kelsey had tried to visit regularly, but naturally, her visits became more and more infrequent. The last time she saw Laura, in March, she had been recovering in the wake of a recurrence. A routine checkup revealed a small tumor growing on what remained of her stomach. There was another surgery, another volley of medications, another battery of radiation therapy. Laura, knees trembling, unable to stand, unable to even speak—the thought of it made Kelsey's neck shiver.

She kept these details from her father as much as possible. The times Laura had come to their tiny house, joining them around their tiny table, radiating her extraordinary light, had been the only times Kelsey recalled her father having truly smiled and genuinely laughed. In some dark, hidden part of herself, Kelsey hated Laura for bringing that out of him when she could not, but she was also grateful. Laura made them a real family. She made up for something Kelsey never knew was lost to begin with.

She left for Ranger's Field that day. She was glad to have a car of her own after so long. She and her father had given up so much time, money, and energy, but things were finally starting to pay off. School was getting closer to being done, and soon she would be getting her own place and living her life. A light was at the end of the tunnel, bigger and brighter by the day.

She stopped at a motel on the outskirts of Ranger's Field and fetched a bottle of liquor from the backseat of her car. The door to room 105 was already unlocked when she knocked. Pete waited on the other side, holding a bouquet of roses, standing at attention.

"Madam," he said, in a dignified, stately voice.

She laughed and held out her bottle. "I like mine better, asshole."

They kissed, poured themselves each a glass, and lounged on the bed. The motel room was only one of their meeting places—there was the old theater in Houston, the hotel in San Antonio—but it was Kelsey's favorite. Quaint, appropriately sleazy, with floral wallpaper some thirty years old, smelling vaguely of cigarette smoke. Still, the bed was always made, the carpet always vacuumed. No one could ask for a better love nest.

"How was your drive?" Pete asked, twisting her hair between his fingers.

"It was fine. You were right about the tire—good thing I changed it before coming out."

"Of course I was. Maybe I'm not a doctor, or whatever you are—"

"Dentist. And I'm not even close."

"*Dentist*, sorry, but I know some things. Men aren't useless."

"Yeah," she said, putting her glass aside and reaching for his belt. "You're good for one thing, at least."

Pete was a decent lover, better than most of the guys she'd been with, even better than some of the girls. He was great in a mechanical sense, adroit with his fingers, flexible with his tongue, rhythmic with his body—obviously, he had more practice than with just Laura—but he fell into the same trap as all of them: conceit, pride, self-satisfaction. For Pete, sex was selfish, a way for him to make his mark. For Kelsey, sex was just as selfish, but for different reasons. Ever since she invited (discovered?) that other ruby-lipped Kelsey inside her body, ever since Pete took her into his car, ever since she unleashed herself onto the night streets, the integration of that other identity had been ongoing, teaching her slowly, revealing bits and pieces of what it meant to be not just sexual, but also "in love"—yet the storied feeling, which supposedly flooded one with pleasure, which spun figurative butterflies in one's stomach, eluded her. She learned how to smile and wear her hair, how to dress and move her body, but she felt just as apart, assimilating to a role that seemed factory-made and committee-decided.

She was well-acquainted with the orgasm, of course, but something so brief and sudden couldn't be love. She considered Pete physically attractive, but he evoked nothing in her otherwise. Shouldn't there be a more lasting bond between people, she thought, a more enduring feeling? Something that went beyond mere attraction? Something like whatever Laura felt for that long-lost boy, the one with the sad smile, the one she would never see again?

Afterwards, Kelsey and Pete lay together, alternating between the liquor and a joint. "It really is nice to see you," Pete said, stroking her hair, caressing her shoulder. "It feels like it's been forever."

"I've been busy."

"Sure, but you could answer a text once in a while, too."

Kelsey resisted, but she couldn't keep herself from saying what came to mind next.

"How's Laura?"

Pete sighed. "You know the rules, Kels."

"You can make an exception this time. I haven't seen you *or* her."

"She's doing all right," he said. "Getting a little better every day. It took more out of her this time— the medicines, you know—but she's dealing with it."

"She's strong."

"She is." He took her by the chin. "What's going through your head, Hernandez? Do you feel bad about it? Because that's never stopped you before."

"Can't I care about my friend? What's wrong with that?"

"Nothing. In fact, it makes you a hell of a lot sexier."

He kissed her, and then they went again.

Pete left later that evening, and Kelsey stayed behind, flipping through the same five grainy channels on the television, nursing the last of the liquor. She let the shower run hot and humid, breathing in the mist, taking her time to undress. She was "sexy," according to Pete, and, somehow, just slightly, there were more than just mental differences compared to how she used to be. Her figure was fuller. Her features were sharper. Her hair, longer and richer, fell in a more pleasant, sensual way around her face. She couldn't explain these literal, physical differences, so marginal they were only noticeable to someone who lived in that body (shared that body?) day in, day out. She ran her fingers over her skin in the shower, pulled at her hair. A body was "sexy." A body was "wet." But a body was empty. A body was merely a shell, to use and discard.

She touched herself, feeling around, probing, searching. Pleasurable, but unconscious, vacant. She was here, enjoying herself, enjoying what she could tempt from others with this body, this skin. Laura, meanwhile, likely lay in pain and exhaustion, undone by a rotting body, crippled by a corrupt shell. Beautiful Laura—not sexy, but beautiful—housing a dying light in failing flesh. Beautiful Laura. Beautiful, lovely Laura.

In the morning, she drove to the Brackett house. From outside, it looked no different than usual—bathed in sunlight, built of mahogany brick, sporting picturesque green grass and the one tall oak tree. Of course, Kelsey knew the interior was a different story, a den of vague longing, uncomfortably warm, smelling faintly like the hospital back in Houston.

After Laura's initial diagnosis, surgery, and treatment, school had been out of the question—to say nothing of moving to California. Kelsey had watched her tear up the acceptance letter and sprinkle its figurative ashes into the trash. Not a word of it spoken between them again, not a hint of it expressed to Laura's mother, Pete, or anyone else. Laura came back home. She pursued online programs to get her teaching certification like she had wanted. Kelsey had been with her during that recovery phase, visiting as much as possible, helping around the house, trying her meager best to cheer Laura when she was down, but who could cheer Laura, once the cheeriest of everyone? And who could do a worse job of it than Kelsey, so cynical and guarded and two-faced and fucking full of herself?

She let out a breath. Her hands were clenched around the steering wheel, practically glued to the leather. No. Stop. Get over it. Get the fuck over it, you whiny, entitled bitch. You're here now. You're with her. You're with her. And she's with you. You need to take care of her. That's all that matters.

Kelsey carried her suitcase up the walkway and rang the doorbell. She was ready to greet Angela with a hug, but when the door opened, Pete stood there, still grinning like the asshole he was. She dropped her arms and forced a smile.

"Hey, stranger," he said. "You took your time getting here."

"I guess I just had a long night. But you seem well rested."

His grin didn't falter. "There's nothing coffee won't fix." He took her suitcase and led her inside. "I was making some breakfast. Pancakes and eggs. You eat already?"

"No, I haven't."

"Well, you're just in time. Let me get this upstairs and let Laura know you're here."

He left Kelsey in the foyer, and she wandered into the so-called "war room." The den was more grandiose than before, more monumental, the windows draped in perennial black, the mantelpiece decorated with even more photos of Laura, more moments of her dancing, more moments of her with new and old friends alike. But there were other pictures depicting victories and commemorations of a different kind. In one, Laura hung on the arm of her mother, her long, radiant hair replaced by a floral head wrap. In another, Laura was giving a thumbs-up outside a radiation treatment room. Kelsey regarded the photographs, mesmerized by the difference between the Laura of the past and the Laura of the present, tempted to reach out, to touch that healthy, beaming face, to bring it back.

"I look at them a lot, too."

Kelsey turned. Laura's mother, Angela, stood behind her, dressed in stern black, her hair pulled into a bun. Even she looked worse, Kelsey thought. Older, more worn. Lacking her characteristic animating youth, her vivacious zest.

"How have you been, Angela?" Kelsey asked. They hugged, and Angela kissed Kelsey on the cheek, squeezed her hands, rubbed her arms. She was so touchy ever since Laura's first hospitalization, as if desperate to keep whomever there, make sure the person was real.

"I'm good, Kelsey. Very good. You're probably tired of hearing me go on and on about myself. I know I would be."

"No, of course not. I'm sorry I haven't been around as much. With school how it is—"

"You don't have to explain yourself, sweetie. Come on, let's get you in the kitchen. You're eating breakfast with us whether you like it or not."

Kelsey sat at the table, stirring a cup of coffee and making small talk with Angela, when Pete reappeared in the hallway. Laura stood behind him. Kelsey's eyes fell on her immediately, taking in the general pallor, the overall exhaustion. But Laura's smile upon seeing her still made the room brighter, still did away with all uncertainty and anxiety. She was smaller, thinner, a head wrap tight around her skull, but there was light in her yet.

After breakfast, the girls retreated to Laura's bedroom. Kelsey, relishing the familiar lilac and rosemary, savoring the comforting pink and green, fell onto the unmade bed, too relieved to hold back her smile, too relaxed to avoid laughing.

"What's so funny?" Laura asked, lying beside her. "Thinking of me with vomit on my face again?"

"I'm just so happy to see you." Kelsey took her hand. "I didn't know it had been so long until right now, right this fucking second. I'm so sorry, Laura."

"Sorry for what? You're doing your thing. Last thing I want is you pitying me. You don't gotta apologize, Kels. You know that. And I ain't so lonely that I'm crying myself to sleep."

"I should have come sooner. It's just fucking school. It's such a pain in the ass."

"Well, you'll be your own woman soon, fixing cavities and giving stickers with those big, fuck-all teeth with smiley faces to little kids. Living the dream, you know? Hell of a lot more exciting than what I'm up to."

"Oh, so I can't pity you, but you can pity yourself? How's that fair?"

"It's not. But I'm the one with cancer."

They laughed, and then Laura went silent, and Kelsey could only watch her, only try to intuit what dwelt behind those fragile, crystalline eyes. Before, Laura would never have been at a loss for things to say. Now, Kelsey was the one who had to fill the silence.

"So, you going to let your hair grow back?"

"Nah. I think bald is pretty charming. Gives me an excuse to go hairless everywhere." She undid the wrap, revealing the smooth, pale dome of her head. Kelsey wanted to think the baldness beautiful, but it was impossible for her not to take it as a sign of incompleteness. Laura herself must have thought the same no matter how many assurances she gave otherwise.

"I'll donate it from now on," she said. "There's a little girl out there who needs it more than me."

Kelsey imagined a little girl, imagined a whole room of them. Bald little girls. Legless little girls. Little girls in braces. Little girls in wheelchairs. And Laura at the forefront, the way she used to be, no, *more* than she used to be, teaching them, guiding them through a dance only they could perform, a ritual only they could complete. That dream had to live on. No matter what, Laura had to live on.

That thought persisted in Kelsey's mind over the next several days. The girls lazed away the week together, watching movies, taking trips. When they stopped at some out-of-town bars, the men flocked to Kelsey, showering her with compliments, buying her drinks, putting hands on her shoulders, caressing her hair. She received the advances with measured confidence, turning each one away (though mindful of the ones she *would* have taken had Laura not been there). Laura was the one, by contrast, who sat silently, unattended, unacknowledged. Laura was the one who drank nothing but water, who merely nibbled at whatever greasy dish they shared. Laura was the one who looked upon Kelsey occasionally with a hint of regret, a tinge of dismay. Kelsey couldn't bear to meet those eyes, so she drank more, laughed more, danced more. Anything to avoid them.

Later that week, Pete drove the girls into the countryside. Kelsey sat in the back of his roofless Jeep, enjoying the wind in her hair, basking in the sunlight coming down through the trees. All throughout the drive, Kelsey watched Laura's meek smile, listened to her timid laugh. Periodically, the phantom of the old Laura emerged in a robust grin or crude joke, but the ghost only stayed momentarily. Even when they fished, sitting lakeside underneath the twinkling, lavender sky, Laura's hands were loose around her fishing rod, her eyes slack. Kelsey and Pete downed beers, ate chicken wings dipped in ranch and bleu cheese, even lit a joint, but Laura was unmoved. She took her drags from the joint slowly, staring placidly at the darkening sky, the rippling water. Seeing her like that, Kelsey felt for the first time the distance between them, like a yawning crevasse, an impassable gulf. She felt her heart heavy in a way she couldn't understand. So big, so bloated with pain. If she could pierce it with a knife, all of that pain would spill out. If she could do it for Laura, all of that rot eating her up would finally be released.

On the night before Kelsey's departure, the girls sat on the back porch of the Brackett house, admiring the evening sky. This time, Laura watched Kelsey. "You drink a lot," she said. "You notice that?"

"I guess so." Kelsey looked down at her beer. "I like a little wine or something every once in a while. It helps take the edge off, especially when you're up late."

"I just mean there was a time you wouldn't drink at all. When you got nervous just looking at a beer. And the other girls, they'd press you and press you, but you wouldn't do it. You were strong like that. Stronger than me."

Kelsey stood up and poured the beer onto the grass. "Happy now?" she laughed. "You're talking like I'm an alcoholic."

Laura said nothing else. She seemed sicker, Kelsey thought, sicker than ever, just sitting there so still and quiet, fiddling with her rosary like she always did when she was nervous or preoccupied. Kelsey became more aware of the beer bottle in her hand, the texture of the engraved glass, the slickness of the condensation. She put the bottle down and wiped her hands on her jeans, suddenly conscious of how sweaty they felt, how grimy.

"All those girls," Laura said, "they were always there, in school, in college. But after I got sick, they started drifting away. The boys, too. Everyone was around me, and then they were gone. Like they ain't ever been there to begin with."

"Forget them," Kelsey said. "Don't worry about other people, Laura."

"I'm not worried. I get it. I wouldn't want to be around some dying girl, either."

"Hey." Kelsey knelt beside her, took her hand. "You're not dying. The treatments worked. You're okay. You're still here."

Laura smiled, but her eyes were cold. "That's right. I'm still here. Still in this. Don't you get it, Kels? You're lucky. You can do whatever you want. No one can stop you. Me? This is what I have to look forward to every day. And I love it, don't get me wrong. My mom and Pete. You. I love this house, and this town, and the people I do see every once in a while. But there ain't anything more than this for me. I know that. There's not gonna be dancing. There's not gonna be kids, least I don't think. There won't be traveling or going places. There won't be seeing things. And there won't be love. But I knew that. I knew that a long time ago."

"Laura—"

"You know Pete proposed to me? Did he tell you? Probably not, right? When he did, I was so surprised. Why would he want to spend his life with someone like me? And then I thought, it's pity. He doesn't want to feel bad. He's sorry about everything. How he treats me, the things he says. But that's a shitty way to make it up, you know? Because I'm not lasting long, Kels. I'm fucking dying, and you say I'm not, but I know I am. Maybe a year from now, or two years, or ten, but it's gonna happen. And Pete's gonna be stuck with that. Sometimes, I hate him, you know, but I wouldn't wish that on anyone. He doesn't deserve it.

"And then I started thinking, if this is all there is, all there's gonna be, then what do I have to lose? So, I told him I'd do it. I told him I would marry him. Maybe what they say is true—that love grows, that you can water it like it's some sort of plant. It's not a feeling you get when you see someone for the first time. It's not this feeling like you knew them before, that they always knew you. It's more normal than that. Nothing special."

She stopped fiddling with her rosary. Kelsey sat back down, too hesitant to speak.

"But what if that ain't really love? What if it's just settling? And I fought with that for a long time, but I'm okay with it now. I'll settle. I'll settle 'cause life settled with me. My best bet is to take what I can get. All my praying to get better, and Jesus gave me what

I needed. And to think I questioned it. That I doubted. See, I didn't need to get better. I needed to accept it."

"Laura," said Kelsey, "Laura, if you don't love Pete, then fuck him. Cut him loose. You don't have to stay with him."

"It's not about love, Kelsey. Pete's all I got now. He's all I have. There ain't gonna be anyone else, not anymore. No one's gonna save me from this. No one's gonna take me away. I accept that. It's all right. It's part of the plan."

She tightened her hands into fists, clenched her jaw. "And that's why you gotta do this for me. You and Pete have to stop. You hear me? You have to stop, or else it's not gonna work."

Kelsey stared at her, barely cognizant of her heart slamming against her ribcage, her skin tingling, her arms and legs trembling. She shook her head, slowly at first, then more fiercely. "There's nothing going on with me and Pete. Laura, there's nothing going on—"

"Let's not fuck around anymore, Kels." Laura eyes were watery, her voice weak. "I ain't mad about it. I know I'm damaged goods. But he hasn't left me yet. He's had all this time, and he hasn't left me. Why? Because somewhere in there, he must feel the same way. He doesn't want to be alone. Maybe he even loves me."

"Laura. Laura, there's nothing."

"Kels, it doesn't matter. I know I can't give him the things he wants. Even when I was healthy, we all know he'd fool around. Hell, I fooled around. I'm not proud of it. And maybe he felt bad about it, too, but he still did it. Honestly, I don't care. As long as he's here with me, when I need it, that's okay. I just need things to be the way they are. I can make it that way."

"Laura, listen to me. There is *nothing* between Pete and me. There is *nothing*."

"Just promise me you won't see him anymore. Okay? Just promise me that. The other ones, they don't matter, but you're too close to him. Too close to me. It won't work."

"Laura." Kelsey was on her knees, clasping Laura's hands in her own. "Laura, listen to me. There is nothing between us. I don't care about Pete. He's nothing to me. He's an asshole—*I'm* an asshole—but he's nothing to me."

"Kelsey, just promise you won't see him anymore."

"I don't care about him, Laura. Not one fucking bit. I don't care about Pete. I care about *you*. I care about *you*. I look at you all the time, and I think, 'Laura is still alive. Laura is still alive, and that's a miracle. That's a *gift*. That's a gift we should be celebrating every fucking day.' Laura, you are the only person I care about. The only person I really, really care about."

Kelsey gripped her hands tighter, struggled to find words. Something was lifting off her chest and shoulders, something dark and heavy, and from underneath rushed a flood. She couldn't contain her tears, couldn't stop them running down her face and staining her blouse and the wood of the porch.

"I look at you," Kelsey said, "and I hate what I see. Not *you*, never *you*, but what's killing you. I hate that fucking thing inside of you. I hate what it's done to you. I hate that it's making you say these things. I hate that it's taken so much from you. Laura, you have to believe me, if I could take it from you, if I could give myself up, I would in a heartbeat, in a fucking heartbeat. I would give *everything* to make you better. To make you the way you were."

"Kelsey." Laura's own tears ran free. "Kelsey, don't say that. Don't say that."

"It's true. I wish it were me. I wish I were dead. Then you wouldn't be like this. You would be perfect again, you'd be the old Laura, the Laura I—the Laura I—"

She was fumbling, sobbing, oppressed by the tempest raging within her. There was only one way to get clarity, one way to make it stop, so she took Laura's face in her hands and kissed her. She tasted those quivering lips, breathed in that intoxicating lilac, faint as it was. Oh, she could have kissed her all day, every day. She could have embraced her and never let go.

"I love you, Laura," Kelsey said. "I love you. I love you so much, it's like my chest is going to burst. This is what it is, this has to be what it is, because I think about you all the time, I think about being with you, I think about touching you, and talking to you, and helping you—"

Laura eased Kelsey back. "Kelsey—"

"—you're just so wonderful, so beautiful—"

"Kelsey, stop—"

The words were spilling out of her, flowing freely with the tears. She felt so light, so light that she was suddenly, feverishly afraid of floating away, so she held on to Laura that much tighter. She moved in again, eager to kiss those lips and experience that vital shock, like a bomb throughout her body, like a supernova. But Laura's hands, seemingly so fragile, were around her wrists like handcuffs. They were pushing her back, keeping her away.

"Kelsey, stop it," said Laura slowly, quietly. "You're confused. You don't know what you're saying."

"I *do* know. I *do* know. I love you, Laura. I love you, and I want to be with you. And it doesn't have to be anything you don't want, just as long as I'm with you, as long as I'm there."

Kelsey smiled, laughed, trembled. Yet for all her giddiness, she recognized vaguely the trauma in Laura's quaking face. Oh, if she could just kiss her again, she could take away all the pain, all the heartbreak! Why wouldn't Laura let her?

"It's okay. Laura, it's okay. I'm here."

Finally, Laura looked into her eyes. "Kelsey, please let me go. Please let me go."

"It's okay, Laura. It's okay."

"Kelsey, please—"

Kelsey pulled Laura against her more firmly and kissed her once again, slid her tongue into her mouth, let her instincts take control, honed and strengthened as they had been by so many nights in frigid dorms and dark hotel rooms. But then Kelsey stumbled back against the porch railing, shocked by the sudden disconnect, dazed by the cold chill of her sweat, the heavy humidity of the summer air. She looked up. Laura had pushed her back.

"I think you should leave," Laura said. Her words came out in tremors, almost inaudible. "Please go."

Kelsey stood there. She touched her own lips, realized what she had done. "Laura, I didn't mean that. I mean, I did, I did mean it, but—"

"I shouldn't have said anything." Laura turned away, fists shaking, shoulders trembling. "I shouldn't have said anything, not about Pete, not about me. I shouldn't have said anything."

"Laura, don't."

"I'm serious, Kels. You need to leave."

"Laura, don't push me away."

"Just go. Don't make me say it again—"

Kelsey moved without knowing it. She took hold of Laura, pressed their lips together, tried to maintain the kiss. But Laura struggled. She wriggled and writhed, screamed, beat at Kelsey with her fists. "Stop it, Laura," Kelsey said, trying to hold her. "Stop it. Stop it!"

"Let go of me, Kelsey, let me go, let me go, *let me fucking go*—"

"Laura, stop it! Just stop it! *Stop it*—"

Laura fell, knocking over her chair, toppling her glass of iced tea. Kelsey stared down at her. She was so small and feeble with the tea staining her dress, with her wrap sliding down her face, exposing the bare sphere of her head. Kelsey covered her mouth with her hands. The tears that came now were not warm, but freezing.

"I'm sorry, Laura. Oh, God, I'm so sorry." She reached out to help her, but Laura lurched away like a wounded animal, picking herself up slowly, moving sluggishly, drunkenly, as if all her energy were gone. She didn't meet Kelsey's eyes.

"Please leave," she said.

Kelsey stared. She raised a hand. She turned. She opened her mouth. Laura stood, shaking very slightly. The portals of her eyes were shut. The depths and expanses, the great, swimming cosmoses, the vast, majestic seas—all were closed off.

"Laura."

The name hung in the air, a half-finished spell, the closing of a circle. Kelsey watched herself leave. She watched herself wander into the house, shamble through the kitchen, exit to the front yard. She watched herself drive away. She watched Laura stand there, continue to stand there, stand there for all eternity.

When Kelsey found herself, she was sitting in her car in the middle of that empty field, the same field where she and Laura shared beers once, where they proclaimed themselves free, where they took owner-ship of their loneliness. Kelsey stared at the darkening sky, the crumbling sunset, thinking ab-sently that it was raining, her windshield was wet— but they were really her tears. Goddamn it. She slapped the steering wheel, slapped herself. God-damn it. She struck her head, pulled her hair. *Goddamn it.*

She stayed there that night, lying in the back of the car, hugging herself, feeling herself. Her breaths were shallow and choked. When she closed her eyes, she was again in the dorm room that first week of college, entombed in darkness. She was again alone, struggling to sleep, fighting to find ground. Desper-ately, she imagined Laura lying beside her in the car, the old Laura, the perfect Laura. She imagined being taken into those warm, radiant arms.

The orgasm was dry, painful. Asleep or awake, Kelsey was alone in that darkness.

8.

The girl was definitely a looker. Bare, pale arms, toned from what were likely daily visits to the gym. High cheekbones, narrow nose. Slim, pink lips. Wavy, golden hair that came down to her shoulders. A spotlight above her head washed her in light, casting the rest of the bar in shadow. Men approached her, throwing jackets over shoulders, puffing out chests. She waved them away, chatting with her girlfriends, sipping her gin delicately, carefully, betraying her manufactured composure with occasional snorts and adjustments of her bra.

Kelsey watched from afar, simmering in the dark blue of the bar, her eyes gleaming crimson. For the last hour, she sat shrouded in shadow, tapping a heel, pacing her beer. No one saw her, more concerned with the football game blaring from every television, with the dancing, with the smoking and ass-grabbing. Oh, but they couldn't keep themselves from this girl, couldn't resist her perky tits and slender waist. This young, fresh-faced, faux angel. Fuck her, thought Kelsey. Let her run wet and broken in some alley, some ditch.

When Kelsey emerged from the darkness, the heads turned. Their eyes fixated on the ruby lips and marveled at the voluminous hair. They followed the blood-red nails and chased the milky calves. But Kelsey's eyes were solely for the girl, who was unaware of the slim hand until it was around her neck, who was jolted by the lips that brushed her ear, the tongue that teased the canal. The little faux angel was easy after that. The looks she had given the women who passed her, all of them dark-haired, all of them regal and severe, told Kelsey everything she needed to know about what to do and how to act.

Two hours later, Kelsey turned away from the girl's shuddering, whimpering form. She flicked blood and come from her fingers and retreated to the amber-lit restroom. She ran hot water over her hands, nearly scrubbed her palms off. Goddamn it. Godfuckingdamn it. Stupid bitch. Stupid little cunt whore. You deserve it. You deserve it ten times over.

She wrestled her hands under control, but then there was her face collapsing in the mirror. There were her knees going slack. There was her bra sliding down her arm, her panties slipping from around her waist. Why was she crying? Why was she fucking crying?

Ten hours later, she sat in front of her supervisor.

"You look worse for wear," said Dr. Ruth, her lips curling in that smug way Kelsey hated so much. "Even worse than last week."

Kelsey sat immobile in the leather chair all the third-year and fourth-year students bitched about, its upholstery torn and weathered, its frame too big for so many of the meek, little girls looking to be dentists. Even Kelsey felt small in that office, tiny and ragged in her green scrubs and battered canvas sneakers, her hair pulled back haphazardly, her eyes like pits.

"I'm fine," she said.

"Fine," repeated Dr. Ruth. "Fine, fine, fine. Always fine, Hernandez."

How amused she was, how entertained. God, how Kelsey wanted to reach across that desk and rip that fat bitch's face apart. How she wanted to take the photos of the kids and smash them against the walls. How she wanted to throw that whore waste of space out the window and watch her go splat on the cement.

That was one fantasy, at least. There were others. Some with guns. Some with knives. All with this cunt doctor's head rolling across the floor.

"I'm sure you can guess who it was," Dr. Ruth said, leaning back, her double chin folding where her neck should have been. "Stevens."

Kelsey stared straight ahead, unflinching. Nothing changed except the images rolling through her mind, now featuring that dumb bitch Leslie getting tortured and murdered instead of Dr. Ruth. Stupid co-dependent slut couldn't resist running her mouth.

"She wasn't as emotional as the first time," Dr. Ruth went on, "but she claims you were reckless with a patient. Claims you told a patient to 'shut up.'"

"It's not true. That never happened."

"You're saying she's lying?"

"I'm saying it never happened."

Dr. Ruth said nothing, hands entwined, smirk wider and more self-satisfied than ever.

"I believe you," she said. "Shocking, I know. But you've always been cordial with patients. The bed-side manner could use some work, a bit more smiling, but otherwise, you're fine on that front."

Kelsey just stared.

"Send me a statement. Date and time, your version of the events. Then we'll file it away. Avoid the messy business we had to deal with before."

"Why?"

"Why? Because you're not the first kid I've seen get on someone's bad side. You should stop being so emotional. People will stop treating you badly if you do them the favor first."

"Okay." Kelsey stared for another awkward minute. "Is that all?"

"Yes. Just get me the statement by this afternoon. And, Hernandez—keep in mind what I said. We're not running a playground. Keep your hands to your-self."

Kelsey walked out, digging her blood-red nails into her palms, that smirk following her.

A year had passed since she last saw Laura. Well, that wasn't exactly true. She saw Laura everywhere. On the street. On the bus. On billboards. On television. In waiting rooms. In cafeteria lines. In crowded bars. In empty beds. The golden hair and blue eyes followed her always, haunted her like a ghost. The vision of Laura dancing on that ornate stage had emblazoned itself upon her dreams, often the last thing she saw as she dozed off and the first thing she saw when she woke up.

She couldn't find the courage to call, not even to send a text message or an e-mail. The most contact was checking Laura's last remaining social media profile, but it hadn't been updated in two years. The most recent picture uploaded was Laura with her purple headband, smiling against the backdrop of an evening sky. Kelsey had stared at that photo for a long time before breathing deep and sliding her fingers inside herself. But it wasn't enough. Disgusted as she was, ashamed as she was, it wasn't enough. She scrolled down. She kept scrolling. Finally, she found one that scratched the itch. The old, healthy Laura reclining by a pool, wet and shining in a pink bikini, sunglasses slanted seductively across her nose. That one did it. Kelsey had lain weeping afterwards, her thighs wet and quivering.

Pete had called constantly in the weeks after her trip to Ranger's Field. Poor, pitiful Pete. Kels. Kels, please. Kelsey. What happened. What did you do. What did I do. Say something. Say anything. I'm begging you. Don't do this. You mean a lot to me. You mean so much to me. I'll do anything for you. I'll leave Laura. I'll even leave Laura—

Not once the words that really mattered. Not that Kelsey wanted to hear them from him.

"I'm sorry, Pete," she told him over the phone one night, painting her lips and darkening her eyelashes. "We can't see each other anymore."

You were a good fuck, she wanted to say. Well, not really. You're just an asshole. A spineless, selfish asshole. But it didn't seem worth bringing any of that up. Better to let him fade away. Better to let all of that go. Just as Laura had wanted.

He hadn't called since then, thankfully. And Kelsey had taken to repeating another mantra during the night, lying in the darkness of her apartment, feeling the cold of the fan against her bare arms and breasts. No more Laura. No more Laura. No more Laura. I am alone. I am alone. I am alone. And one day, those feelings, once so strong and powerful, once like a miracle, weren't there anymore.

Nothing was there anymore.

Now, Kelsey sat at the back of restaurants, in the shadows of bars. Now, she lingered on the fringes of clubs, on the outskirts of parks. Watching. Waiting. Assessing. All of her training, all of her learning, was for this feast. This slaughter. The young, blonde-haired girls were her obvious targets, but she didn't discriminate. Short, tall, brunette, blonde, black, white. The women she attacked violently, using her teeth, her tongue, her fingers, her fists, so intent on overpowering them that she gave no thought to her own pleasure. The men were usually different, competing with her for dominance, determined to make her small, to reduce her to a passive, docile toy. She would play along at first. They were always so hilariously desperate, thrusting harder and faster and harder and faster, sweating like they were wandering the Mojave. They were never prepared for the turn, to be left groping after her, to pine and whine the way Pete did. Wait, they would say. Please. What's your number? What's your name? But Kelsey only left them with the profile of her face, the cut of her pale nose and red lips. She left them with the outline of that so-called imposter she saw in the mirror years before—the alleged invader whom she realized too late was herself, had always been herself. A monster perpetually hungry, never satisfied. A monster eternally incomplete, never whole.

She would sleep for two hours, maybe three, then wash off the paint and makeup in the shower. Pills, liquor, and coffee kept her going. She would leave the apartment in her scrubs, clean-faced, reeling. After the endless drilling, rinsing, and flossing of her clinical work, she would stumble home, eat, undress, sleep—until the urge came back. And it always came back.

You'll die, she told herself, sitting listlessly on the carpet of her bedroom, nudging the dried remains of some noodles she hadn't bothered to clean up. You'll die and be alone forever. You'll be gone. Yes. Gone. No more. No more Kelsey. No more Laura. No more anything.

Months passed.

She sat at the edge of the university cafeteria, watching lazily the smiling faces, the animated chatter. Her eyes wandered to the table where, once upon a time, she and Laura and all the other girls had sat. Beautiful, glowing Laura, surrounded by her devotees. But Kelsey looked at the table now and recognized it no more than she did any of the other tables. She recalled no vivid, pleasant memory. She only stared.

Someone pulled out one of the chairs at her table and sat down.

"Hey," said the young man. "Is it okay if I sit here?"

She looked at him. He was young, dark-haired, slim-framed. A dog-eared book was folded in his hand: Jean-Paul Sartre's *Being and Nothingness*. She smirked. Be alone. Be nothing.

"What's funny? That I want to sit here?" He waited, then raised the book. "Or do you mean this? You ever read it?"

"No."

"Okay."

He waited, looking at her expectantly. She resumed staring, not at him, but at the cafeteria, beyond the cafeteria. He opened the book.

"I'm going to read, then."

A few minutes later, she stood up and walked away. The young man watched her leave.

The next day, when she sat down to eat a small sandwich, he was there. Again, he asked if he could sit. Again, she said nothing. Again, he sat and read. Again, she stood up and walked away. Again the next day, and again the day after that. She sat, he read. He read, she sat. The same ritual, day after day. The same sandwich. The same staring. The same cafeteria. The same bars. The same mirror. The same ruby lips. The same milky calves. The same fake angels. The same shower. The same staring. The same cafeteria.

The same face. The face that was not her own. The face that was entirely her own.

Eventually, the young man put the book down. Kelsey turned.

"The long game," he said. "And it wasn't worth it."

"What?"

"The book. It wasn't worth it. Camus is better."

Kelsey picked up the book, turned it over. "What's it about?"

"A lot to say in a sentence. Basically, we're all playing roles. We stay trapped in those boxes instead of being who we really are."

"Sounds fun."

"It's philosophy."

"Oh. How wise." Kelsey slid the book back to him. "Let me guess. You're taking an intro class and think you're hot shit because you're reading some hipster garbage. I mean, look, the thing's falling apart. So authentic, right?"

He smiled—turned red, in fact. "Almost right. Missing a bit."

"Oh, yeah?"

"There were two long games. The first was the book. The second was you talking to me." He extended his hand. "I'm Tony. Well, Anthony, but everyone calls me Tony."

She shook his hand. "Kelsey Hernandez."

"It's nice to officially meet you, Kelsey."

The ritual changed after that day. Kelsey would sit, and Anthony would talk, first about his books, but later about himself. He brought the aforementioned Camus, then Beauvoir: the "Frenchies," he called them. Yes, he was taking an intro philosophy class, but he had been dabbling for years, picking up names and suggestions from online reading circles. "My parents, too," he said. "They're both teachers. Mom's a professor."

"And you're from Houston?"

"Born and raised."

Anthony himself was less sure about what he wanted—he was a third-year history major, he liked reading, but he couldn't imagine himself in front of a classroom or a conference audience. "I suck at writing," he told Kelsey. "It takes too long. I've never been patient enough."

Kelsey listened mostly, but she did let slip the occasional backhanded compliment or subtle insult. They were halfhearted comments, she hated to admit. She didn't want to push Anthony away, or at least, she couldn't muster the energy to do so. He was good at taking her comments in stride, making them a million times worse, deprecating himself with more creativity than she ever could. The behavior reminded her of Allison. Of Laura.

He asked her about dental school, about her family, her friends. She never said much. "My dad raised me," she told him once. "Him and Molly."

"Who's Molly? Your step-mom?"

She smiled. "My dog. *Was* my dog. She died a long time ago."

Another memory buried away. The tiny, frigid backyard. The tiny, damp hole in the ground. The stiff fur. The limp ears. Amid darkness forever.

"I'm sorry," Anthony said.

"It's okay. She lived a long time."

Thinking about Molly made her think about her father's tiny house, about the many Christmases with their tiny tree and its tiny red and gold ornaments, its tiny, flickering lights. She thought about Molly's rich, chocolate fur and her cold, wet snout. She would lap coffee from her father's mug when he wasn't looking. Laura would let an old, aching Molly lick her hands, her face, remarking that she wished she had a dog so devoted and sweet.

During the long nights, Kelsey repeated her chant more fervently. No more Laura. No more Laura. *No more Laura.* But when she stopped chanting, the silence filled up again—filled up with Laura's laughter, her little drawl, her breathing. Breathing beside Kelsey in the dark of their dorm. Breathing in the moments between their kisses. Those apocalyptic kisses she recalled time and again, simultaneously basking in them and wishing she could take them back.

She hovered on the edges of bars, amid dim, blue smoke, but she did not take anyone unsuspecting to a hotel or alleyway. She simply watched, thinking vaguely about Anthony, what he would think of her, what he would say.

As they were leaving the cafeteria one day, he to a journalism class, she to another clinic, he touched her arm. "Kelsey. I wanted to ask you something."

"Yeah?"

He was red again, red the way he got when his questions became slightly too personal. "Are you seeing anyone?" He didn't meet her eyes. "You know, like dating them?"

"You fucker," she laughed. "You can't do that. It's illegal."

"What do you mean?"

"Talk to someone for months. Trap them emotionally. Then spring the question."

When he said nothing, she only laughed harder. "There's no game in that, Tony. It's cheating. Like rigging the deck and knowing what cards you're going to pick."

"Okay," he said, "but if I'd asked you that when we met, would you have been honest with me? Would you have even thought about it?"

She shrugged. "Probably not. But maybe that says more about you than me." She reached for his phone. "Anyway, here's my number. Call me when you want to do something."

"But you didn't answer the question."

"Tony, if I'm giving you my number, what do you think?"

She walked off, careful not to show him her smile.

That Saturday, the night of their first official date, Kelsey committed fully to her ritualistic preparations. Fuchsia lipstick, rose nail polish, maroon dress, black jacket. She curled her hair, let it fall over a shoulder. She downed a glass of whiskey, crushed ice between her teeth.

Anthony met her outside the apartment building, dressed in an outsized blazer and dusty jeans. His eyes went wide at the sight of her.

"What's wrong?" she asked.

"Nothing. You just look so different."

"Isn't that a good thing?"

"It's not a bad thing." He fumbled with the plastic container in his hands. "Here. This is for you. I hope the color's nice."

Kelsey laughed when she saw it. "A corsage? Are you taking me to prom, Tony?"

"I didn't know what else to get." There was that redness again, noticeable even in the chilly dark. "And it looked pretty."

"It's okay," she said, opening the container and fastening the snow-white corsage around her wrist. "I didn't go to my prom."

They rode in Anthony's Cadillac Seville, an heirloom passed down from his father. Kelsey pulled at the corsage, ran a hand over the leather seat. Laura's old Chevrolet Malibu, red as a cherry. Laura's old Chevrolet Malibu, crashed into a tree. The girls caught in the headlights, laughing, Mariah, Chelsea, Kelsey—Laura the loudest of them all.

When they pulled into the nearby burger joint, Kelsey smiled, but said nothing. She played along, letting Anthony pay for their meal awkwardly, letting him choose their booth. All the while, everyone stared at her: the girl counting bills at the register, the mother of four preening in the corner, the freckled kid mopping up a spilt milkshake near the exit. All stared except Anthony, who had trouble raising his eyes, who had difficulty forming his words. She had never seen him so nervous. He had always been so self-assured before, so cutely kind-of funny, but now he was limp, even shaking.

"I know it's not five-star," he said, watching her chew into a burger. "I don't get paid until next week."

"It's fine," she said through a mouthful. "Really. I'm just happy it's not ramen again."

Little else was said the rest of the time, and then suddenly, they were back in Anthony's car in front of her apartment building, as if they never left. "Well, that was fun," he said, clearing his throat. "I had a good time."

Kelsey just sat. When she didn't leave, when a full minute passed without her so much as budging, Anthony turned. "What—"

She grabbed his thigh. "I want you to come up to my room."

He opened his mouth. She squeezed.

"Don't talk. Just follow me. Yes?"

He nodded.

In the cold, barren blackness of that bedroom—for there was nothing, no television, no photographs, no decorations, just stark gray and black—he alternately stood and sat, stood and sat, removing his tie, shedding his blazer. Kelsey appeared in the doorway holding two glasses.

"Whiskey," she said. "It'll calm you down."

He drank too fast, almost spat it out. She smiled.

"Is a beer better?"

A few minutes later, they sat on the bed, he drinking a beer, she drinking the whiskey—first her glass, then his. "So," she said, "who goes first? Me or you?"

He took a moment to respond. "What?"

"Do you want me to undress first, or you?"

"I don't—Kelsey, stop!"

She was already standing, unzipping her dress from the back. She sighed and turned to him. "Tony. You're making this harder than it has to be. You're sitting in front of a Christmas present. Open it."

"You're not a present," he said. "You're not a box with wrapping on it." He set aside the beer and stood up, paced. "How can you be so casual about it? Like it's nothing?"

"Tony." She stared at him, and even in the dark, her gaze made him shiver. "Tony, you're the one who came up to me. You're the one who asked me on the date. I didn't do anything."

"I know."

"So? This is what you wanted. To fuck me. To put your dick inside me. Make yourself feel good or strong or whatever it is you need today."

He didn't answer. He just kept pacing, kneading his hands, placing them on his hips.

"Tell me I'm wrong," she said. "Tell me it's not what you want, and we'll stop."

"It's *not* what I want!" he snapped. His raised voice surprised even himself. "I mean, it is, of course—but not like this. I would look at you every day in the cafeteria. For weeks, Kelsey. I just stared at you, and I wanted to talk to you, and I didn't know how. And my friends, Rick and J.C., they kept pushing me, and one day, I did go to your table. You remember that."

She was quiet.

"Sure, I thought about it. I thought about it a lot. What it would be like to touch you, to kiss you, feel your hair—of course, I thought about it. That weird girl who'd just sit there every day, eating the same thing, never saying anything, I *wanted* her. I can't explain how much I wanted her or why. But the more I got to know her, the less I wanted *that*. The less I wanted her in that way. Not that I don't want her—I do, I really do—but—"

Kelsey took him by the shoulders, placed his hand on her breast, kissed him, pushed him onto the bed. Suddenly, his shirt was unbuttoned, his belt unbuckled. Her fingers lingered over his torso, caressed their way towards his waistline. "She wants you, too," she said between kisses. "She wants you, too—"

"Then where is she?"

She stopped. She hunched over him, both of them breathless, both avoiding each other's eyes in the dark. He asked again. "Where is she? Where's Kelsey?"

"She's right here."

"No. I would know if she were here. I would know."

Kelsey climbed off him. She wandered to the doorway. "I think you should leave."

"No," he said, more firmly this time. "Not until I see her. Not until I know she's here."

"I don't know what to tell you."

"Kelsey. Come on. This isn't you."

She laughed. "Maybe it is me, Tony. Maybe it's the part of me you didn't want to see. Maybe it's the part of me you *couldn't* see."

"I just want you to talk to me."

"You want me to talk," she said, "and then you want me to fuck. But you don't want me to fuck. You want me to talk. Well, I'm talking, Tony. Is that what you want? Because what was the point of all this, then? Why are you wasting my time?"

"I'm not wasting your time," he said. "I love you, Kelsey."

"Oh, for fuck's sake."

She laughed, laughed and laughed, laughed until she coughed and spat and clutched her stomach. "You love me, huh? You know that's the worst fucking thing to say to a girl? Tell me what that means, Tony, philosophy man. Tell me what that means."

"It's not philosophy. I've felt it for a while, but I didn't know what it was. Now, I do."

"Oh, I'm happy for you, Tony. Really, I am."

"And I know something else, too. I know Kelsey feels the same way. I know she does."

"Wow. Everyone just loves each other, don't they?"

"It's not a joke. I don't know why you're acting like this."

"It *is* a joke," Kelsey said. "Don't your philosophers say that? Here's the truth, Tony, if there's such a thing: Kelsey's never loved anyone. Just her dad who's getting old, crying himself to sleep every night. Just Molly, who's in that hole now in the backyard, cold, probably wanting her blanket. Just her mom who left her, just her brother, and he's been dead for years. Just Laura—just Laura, and she may as well be dead!"

She cried cold, rough tears. Anthony watched her.

"Who's Laura?"

"It doesn't matter." Kelsey wiped away her tears, smearing her hands and cheeks with blue and purple. "She's gone. There is no more Laura. There's no more Laura anywhere."

Anthony took her hand. "You never told me about your mom. Or your brother."

"I didn't want to tell you. You wouldn't understand."

"Maybe that's true. I don't have any brothers or sisters. I didn't have a dog. But I have my parents. I have my friends. I had a girlfriend—I told you about her. Alexis. I loved her, too."

Kelsey gripped the corsage tightly. "I've been with people, Tony. A lot of people."

He didn't say anything for a long time, then finally, "That's okay. It doesn't matter."

"You say that, but you don't know."

"Kelsey."

"You don't want to know. *I* don't want to know."

"Kelsey, stop it. Don't talk anymore."

She stopped. They stood quietly beside each other, he holding her hand as though inviting her to dance. At last, she squeezed back. "Come to the bed with me, Tony."

"Kelsey—"

"Don't talk, remember?"

She led him back to the bed, where they sat and held each other's hands. "I don't know what to do," she said. "I don't know how to be with someone. I don't know how to love them."

"Me, neither," said Anthony. "Alexis and I never got this far."

"You're a virgin?"

"Uh. Yeah. Yeah, I am."

"And you loved her?"

"Yes."

"Shit. I hated the guy who took my virginity. But it felt good, the way he looked at me, the way he made me feel. It felt so good."

"Kelsey," Anthony said, stroking her face, "we can just go to sleep. We can just lie here."

"And you won't go? You'll be here when I wake up?"

"Absolutely. I promise."

She smiled, genuinely smiled, and she did lie with him, allowing him to wrap his arms around her until the darkness of the bedroom became complete, listening to his breathing until silence overtook her. And there was silence, silence and darkness—neither laughter, nor the mischievous flash of those blue eyes, but a quiet peace. For once, there really was no Laura.

9.

Anthony became a fixture in Kelsey's life. They spent what they could of their free time together, he talking to her about his books—he started reading biographies, Bob Dylan, Theodore Roosevelt, and so on—and she listening, less interested in the material than simply the conversation itself. It was good to have someone talking again. Good not to be alone.

He helped her clean and decorate the apartment. Almost overnight, there were posters on the walls, plants in the corners. "Mom always says cleaning is like therapy," he told her, wiping down a drawer, working the rag around the knobs. "Keeps your head clear."

"Well, I didn't have a mother to tell me that," Kelsey replied, popping open a beer. "Dad tried his hardest, but I guess I'm just too lazy."

"No good female role models. That would explain a lot."

There was one, she wanted to say. There was one.

She did talk about Laura, but selectively. She told Anthony only that Laura had been a good friend of hers from college with whom she fell out of contact. No mention of Pete. No mention of the cancer. No mention of the disastrous kisses shared between them or the shameful nights Kelsey spent pleasuring herself to old pictures and fantasies. Lying with Laura atop her red flamenco dress. Losing herself in those mournful eyes.

Anthony didn't pry much. "You should call her," he said one night as they shared a hamburger. "If you were that close, what's the harm?"

"I can't," she said. "I just can't. Nothing more to it."

He wasn't replacing Laura, as if Laura could even be replaced. Anthony was too different. Even at her lowest, Laura was more confident than him, more powerful, more self-assured. The more time Kelsey spent with Anthony, the more she saw the hidden indecision, the secret anxiety. The pressure from his parents to pick a field and stick with it, whether that was law or education or something else entirely. The dread of a college career running out, leading him closer and closer to an adult life without the comfortable framework of a classroom. The nervousness with which he touched her, kissed her. It's not going to fucking bite you, she wanted to say one night. There aren't any teeth down there. It doesn't spit out acid. Time and again, she led his hand, guided him through the movements. Time and again, she coached him, comforted him. Slowly, he got better, but she had to admit she missed the gross, misplaced confidence of literally every other guy, all of them beating their chests and bragging about the size of their loads. Yet there was something charming about Anthony's feeble, anticlimactic orgasms and the unimpressive splotches of come he left on her stomach and her back. "That's cute," she said once, and even in the darkness, she saw his face redden.

Outside the bedroom, however, the farce was usually on full display. At breakfast: "Two percent? You should be drinking soy." Before going out: "You're going to wear that?" In the library: "Balance is the key. At least according to Aristotle." Always a smart comment at the ready, a pithy lesson to dispense. She thought of the acts put on by every guy who bought her a drink or took her to his place. Every aspect of the transaction controlled, dominated. She thought of Pete, the biggest asshole of all, silencing Laura again and again. Oh, but he loved her. Oh, but he couldn't live without her. He just needed to be understood. He just needed to be forgiven. Men didn't change, no matter the size, age, or background. All seemed intent on conquering you. At least with women, Kelsey felt she was on more equal ground. She felt there was a common experience, a shared understanding of what each party wanted. She herself had exploited that understanding so many times, in a way worse than the men, worse than some of the women. She betrayed that shared trust, betrayed it viciously.

But she couldn't think like that anymore. Anthony could be an overcompensating dickhead, but he could be sweet, too. He could be charming. At least he was there, and he talked, listened, and did things boyfriends supposedly did. Boyfriend? Yes, she thought. Her first. Her first honest relationship. Not some lurid affair conducted amid red, black, and blue.

At least he's there. Didn't she rail on Laura for saying the same damn thing?

"There were guys," she told her father on a visit. "I didn't tell you about them."

He smiled, eyes more tired than ever, beard fuller and grayer than she remembered.

"I knew that. I'm just glad you found one worth telling me about. Better late than never."

"I'll bring him down one of these days. I promise."

They sat like they usually did, at a table made for four, alone.

Meanwhile, Anthony wasted no time introducing Kelsey to his parents. The father, wide at the waist, bearded with glasses, like a jovial sage or wizard. The mother, slender and wraithlike, with long, sinewy white hair. A professor, prolific in her circles, smarter than everyone else in the room. "Anthony was a C-section," she said at the candlelit dinner table, in a dining room that may as well have been a library, lined as it was by bookshelves and paintings.

"I could never forget that. I think my spirit left my body at some point because I remember looking down at myself while they worked. Really, at forty, it was a miracle nothing went wrong—even Tony was fine besides that. But the whole experience was not something I could repeat. Having another child would have killed me."

"I think that's enough morbid talk," Anthony's father chuckled. "But if I'm being honest, it was scary as hell. Thank God it wasn't me on that table."

"And you, Kelsey?" Anthony's mother sipped her wine. "Plans for any children?"

"Probably not for a while," Kelsey said. "Maybe when I'm forty."

"Well, I don't recommend it. I didn't have the luxury of doing it young. You'll save yourself some grief."

The ensuing awkward silence, punctuated by the intermittent clinking of cutlery, was broken by Anthony. "Kelsey's going to be a dentist. She'll be done with school soon, and then she'll be able to practice."

"That's the plan," added Kelsey with a dry smile.

"I'm glad one of you has a plan," Anthony's mother said. "If you're going to get married, you can't be living like kids forever."

Kelsey glanced at Anthony, who was quiet, his eyes on his plate. She thought about defending him, but said nothing.

When the dinner was thankfully over, the two of them driving away, Anthony smiled. "I think that was a success. She likes you."

"Is she always so charming?"

"I'm the only child. And I might've talked you up a bit."

"She's kind of a bitch. No offense."

"Not untrue. But she is my mom for better or worse."

Maybe it's good mine's dead, Kelsey thought. Wouldn't have to put up with that shit. But she knew, of course, how misguided that thinking was. All the hours spent looking at photographs. All the time wishing someone was there to answer her questions, explain the nuances. Her father meant well—she loved him to bits—but he could not fulfill that role. And the one woman who had been a mother to her, Angela Brackett, was lost to her, lost long before the fight that drove her from Laura. Lost ever since that fiery evening at the hospital. Ever since Laura lost the ability to ever be fully Laura again.

One afternoon, while they sat in the corner of a cafe, Anthony reading, Kelsey looking absently out the window, a man approached them.

"Kelsey? That you?"

She looked up. The man was in his late twenties, tall, toned—almost the complete opposite of Anthony. He grinned at her. "Do you remember me? Kent?"

She racked her brain, trying to place the burnt-orange beard and thick-framed glasses, and then finally, she remembered: meeting him in a bar months ago, sleeping with him a few times, leaving him one cold morning, moving on.

"Yeah," she said. "I remember."

"I almost didn't recognize you. You look so different. Not that it's bad, just—different."

She waited for him to say more.

"You know, I wasn't sure I'd see you again. I must've gone by that bar two, three times a week hoping you'd be there." He gestured towards his table at the other end of the cafe. "I'm not here with anyone, just having a coffee. Do you want to talk, or—"

She looked to Anthony, who up until this point had been silent, his eyes low. "Sorry," she said. "This is Tony. My boyfriend."

The word had an immediate, almost supernatural effect, dragging Anthony's head up and wiping the smile off Kent's face. The latter cleared his throat, registering for the first time the young man sitting across from her.

"Sorry about that," he said. "I don't know what I was thinking. Have a good one."

He returned to his table. "Talk about desperate," Kelsey said.

"Yeah." Anthony tapped a finger against his book, kicked the floor. "Is it okay if we leave? I don't really feel like being here anymore."

"Okay. After you."

As they drove out of the parking lot, Kelsey turned to him. "Are you seriously doing this right now? Forget that guy."

Anthony said nothing.

"Tony, give me a break. Are you really going to give me this shit?"

When he still said nothing, didn't even look at her, she scoffed. "Okay. Silent treatment it is, I guess. World comes to an end if a guy so much as looks at me."

"You were looking at him."

"What?"

Again, he was silent.

"What the fuck did you say?"

"I said you were looking at him. He wouldn't have noticed you otherwise."

"Jesus Christ, Tony. That's rich. I *looked* at him. Holy shit."

"You were looking at him, and you didn't even notice it. You were looking right at him, eyeing him like he was a steak."

"I didn't even know he was there. How could I have been looking at him?"

"You *were*!" They were at a stoplight, Anthony's hands clenched around the steering wheel, his breathing fast and heavy. Kelsey watched him. It was rare to see him actually angry. For a moment, she imagined his hand coming off the steering wheel and striking her, but it was a quick, silly fantasy. You idiot, she thought. He didn't have the balls, among other things.

"You invited him with your eyes," he said. "I saw it."

She laughed. "What the fuck are you talking about? Do you hear yourself?"

"You do it all the time. You don't even know it. You look at them. Men, women. You don't think I see them, too? The difference is, I'm looking at *you*. I'm trying hard to look at *you*. But when we're together, it's like you're not there. You're just looking for your next catch."

Kelsey stared at him. Fuck you, she wanted to say. I'm here. *I'm here*. But she said nothing, instead letting the silence simmer, letting the passing buildings and people and fading light take her away. They drove. At last, they got back to her apartment building. She reached for the door handle quickly, practiced as she was by the countless car rides with overeager men and desperate women, but then Anthony spoke.

"He didn't even see me."

She gripped the door handle. "You're pathetic. Who are you really angry at, you or me?"

"How many?"

"What?"

"How many have you been with?" He looked forward, avoided her eyes. "How many? You're still doing it, aren't you? Going out at night?"

"I don't need to tell you a goddamn thing. Have a nice life, Tony."

She left the car, small in her scrubs and frizzy ponytail. In her bedroom, she hit the wall, screamed, caressed her bruised and bloody knuckles. And then she stopped. She ran the shower. She washed off the blood, rinsed out her hair. She shaved her legs and painted her nails. She donned a black dress, a pair of black heels. She colored her lips red.

One week passed, then another. Once again, she prowled the streets. Once again, she hovered outside restaurants, in the dark of bars. She looked at men and women alike, attracting them to her, telling them what they wanted to hear, touching them in ways they didn't know they wanted, robbing them of control. Anthony never called. She went out. She came back. She resumed her ritual, exchanging her dresses and skirts for her scrubs and sneakers, doubling down on her clinics, studying for her remaining exams. It was a relief to have him out of her life, a relief to focus again on the soul-crushing, mind-numbing essentials. A relief to be alone.

Then one night, as she pulled into the parking lot of her building, he was there.

"Kelsey," he said. "Hey."

She stared at him. "What do you want?"

"I looked for you in the cafeteria. I should've figured you'd avoid it."

"Tony."

"I'm sorry. I'm sorry I said those things. They were wrong, and I shouldn't have."

"Tony, I don't give a shit."

She walked past him, but he spoke again.

"I don't know how to do it," he said. "I don't have experience with this. Alexis, she—she got fed up with me somehow. Like I wasn't doing what she wanted, or I wasn't doing it right."

"That's because you never touched her, Tony. She's not a doll to look at."

"Okay, but that's what I want to learn. I want to be like you. I don't want to be scared of it. It's not about getting people to like me, or want me—maybe it is, I don't know—but I do know I don't want to be scared anymore. I want to be better. I want to be a man, I guess."

"What do you want from me?" asked Kelsey. "Teach you how to fuck? Pick up girls?"

"It's not that. I want you in my life."

"Tony—"

"But I want to be on your level. I don't want to be an afterthought or a shadow."

A shadow, Kelsey thought, remembering Laura, the way she would light up a room, the way people of all ages and sexes followed her. She remembered Laura lying in a hospital bed, first with hair, then without. She remembered Laura silent and docile, eyes glazed, sitting listlessly, whether at a restaurant, on the shore of the lake, on the porch. Where was she? What was she doing? Who was she talking to? Was she happy? Was she safe? Was she alive?

Sun-bright Laura, now a shadow. Now a corpse?

"Kelsey?"

"I'm okay." She wiped her eyes. "Really. I'm okay."

"I shouldn't have come," he said. "I'm sorry. I'll go."

"Tony, hold on. I'll show you. I'll show you."

"What do you mean?"

"I'll show you what it's like for me."

He followed her to her car, and they drove into the night. "Where are we going?" he asked, but Kelsey offered no explanation, keeping quiet until they were at the back of a bar. The familiar haze of smoke. The clack and clash of pool. All that was missing was the Confederate flag. Even then, stronger than ever, she expected Laura to come out and sit beside her, talking as usual, laughing as usual.

"Don't say anything," said Kelsey. "Just listen to me. Follow what I say." She pointed at a couple sitting near the entrance, an older man in rolled-up sleeves and jeans, and a young woman, probably only twenty, blonde-haired and green-eyed. Anthony turned and looked through the smoke.

"See her?" Kelsey asked. "She's hard to miss, isn't she?"

"I—"

"I told you. Don't say anything."

He nodded.

"That girl," Kelsey continued, "there's thousands just like her in this city. Millions of her. Good-looking. Sweet. Inexperienced. Maybe only been fucked by a couple of boyfriends. And now this old creep is trying to woo her with money, status, who knows."

The man rose to retrieve some beers. While he was gone, the girl propped her head on a hand, scanned, jumped from person to person—met Kelsey's gaze.

"I could have her if I wanted to," Kelsey said. "The guy's an issue, but he wouldn't need to know. Just whisper in her ear. Make her question things. Get her excited. Get her curious. She'll follow your lead. She'll make an excuse. He might have money, but he's vanilla. She doesn't care about vanilla because she *knows* vanilla. She *is* vanilla. She wants something else. Something she's afraid to ask for, something she'll *never* ask for. She's scared to even think about it because if she does, it's a betrayal—of her parents, her friends, her whole life."

The man returned to the table, and the girl turned back to him with some reluctance. Kelsey smirked. "You can tell she's disappointed. She'll want to look back over here. She *will* look back over here, especially when she's leaving. She'll keep thinking about it, about what could have been, about the little taste. That's lesson number one, Tony. Leave a taste. You're not excited about the meal after you eat it."

"What would you do," he said, "if you did have her?"

"That's easy. I'd make her never want it again."

"Why?"

"Why what?"

"Why does she deserve that?"

"She doesn't deserve it. I just want to do it to her. The same way you want to be with me? Whatever you fantasize doing from all the porn you watch? Well, this is what I want to do all the time. And not just to people like her. You see that guy over there, hitting on that girl like he's the best thing since sliced bread? You see that woman by herself? I'll take them, too. I'll make them feel worthless. I'll make them feel ashamed. I'll do it without a second thought."

She wiped away a fresh set of tears. "You want to know why, Tony? Because I'm a piece of shit. Because I can't stand seeing them act that way. Like they're better. Like they're not bad. Bullshit. They're filthy. And they'll never admit it."

They sat for a while in silence after that, Kelsey shaking, Anthony with his head down. At length, he looked up. "Can you stop it? Stop doing this to people?"

"I did stop," she said. "When I was with you, I did stop."

"Kelsey, nothing happened. We can go back to how it was."

She smiled. "You say it like it's easy."

They ate and drank in silence. Eventually, the girl did leave. Kelsey didn't watch her. Instead, she watched Anthony. What was it that allowed him to think like that—to approach her after his fuck-up, to act like nothing happened? And why was it working on her? She had a right to be angry at him, but that right seemed so pointless in the face of what he was suggesting. Nothing happened. What had been done could be undone. Things could be fixed.

"My dad wants to meet you," she said as they walked out. "He seemed excited."

"Okay. If that's all right with you."

"It is."

That night, lying atop her bed under that endlessly spinning fan, she held up the plaster mold of her mouth from so many years ago. She felt the grooves, ran her fingers along the ridges. The teeth were sharp enough to draw blood, the contour ugly enough to scare away even the most intrepid, the plaster cold enough to raise the hairs on her arms. But those teeth had been real once. They had belonged to a little girl yet untouched by the world. No matter how misshapen or imperfect, they had been part of her, part of her potential, part of her beautiful, blessed miracle. Holding it reminded her of those things, reminded her of her ambition. She could still make good on the debt she owed that little girl. She was not filthy. She was not wrong. There was still time.

Fix, she thought, for the first time in years. Fix and make whole. Fix and make right.

She slept peacefully in her scrubs and sneakers, the mold snug in her hands, not thinking of anyone or anything, not repeating any mantra.

In the years between then and Laura's funeral, Kelsey found some semblance of security. Anthony was, above all, a comfort. She finished school. She secured a position within an office, eventually co-established a practice. Time and life did their work, erasing in their way the disastrous kisses and their aftermath, papering over the other, invasive shadow self that lurked in the mirror and at the edges of her mind. The nights on the town felt like someone else's life. They never happened. None of it ever happened.

Until Laura came back.

AFTER THE FUNERAL

10.

The morning after returning from the funeral, Kelsey woke up feeling surprisingly calm. The overwhelming surge of emotions from the night before was gone, as if evaporated. She rubbed away the dry tearstains on her cheeks. Dreaming. Remembering. All those nights spent with Laura, the time they spent in that dorm, at the library, with the other girls—she had pushed so much of it away. She had sunk by degrees into this present life. Each day, she had fallen deeper and deeper, her every movement, every breath, becoming sluggish and protracted. Waking up now, after that surreal return to Ranger's Field, was like coming up for air.

Light flooded the bedroom. Too much light. Had she overslept? She yawned, stretched—and then screamed.

Lying beside her, sleeping gently, was Laura.

Kelsey tumbled from the bed and backed against the wall. For a long moment, she sat in stunned silence, staring at the sleeping face, the rising chest. She pinched her arm, tugged her cheek. Was she still dreaming? She shut her eyes and counted down— five, four, three, two, one—but the room was still there. The bed was still there. The woman was still there. No matter how many times she closed her eyes and counted down, the woman was still there.

Hesitantly, she approached the bed. There was no doubt about it. Years had passed, time had skewed her memory, but the face was that of the portraits at the funeral parlor, that of the corpse in the casket. But whereas that face had been gaunt and pale despite the rouge and chalk, this face was full and flushed. A mane of shining, golden-blonde hair crowned the head. And, yes, hovering over the woman were the unmistakable scents of lilac and rosemary, mixed together in that quintessentially Laura way. Not pungent, like those flowers desperately crowding the casket, but strong and clean, as from a freshly blossomed, springtime field.

"Laura," said Kelsey, neither a question nor declaration, but an incantation, something beginning. And as the name left her lips, the woman's eyes opened.

"Good morning," she said, rising, her hair falling down her bare shoulders, across her collarbone. Kelsey watched her, awed by the sheen and color. Never had she seen Laura's hair like that, even in the touched-up portraits. Never had she seen the eyes filled with such unprecedented vibrancy. Without knowing it, Kelsey's hand rose. Her fingers extended.

"Kels?"

The voice brought her back.

"Kels, you okay?"

She lowered her hand. "Laura?"

"Who else would I be, silly?" The woman smiled. "There a reason you're looking at me like that? You feeling all right?" She felt Kelsey's forehead. "You feel cool. What's going on?"

Kelsey shivered from the touch. "I don't get it. How is this possible?"

"How is what possible?" Laura looked around her. "Oh, you mean why I'm here? I think I just crashed on the couch for a bit and came in here without realizing it. Just like old times, right?"

She shook free of the sheets, revealed a breast, a stomach. "Don't remember taking my clothes off, but maybe I got hot?"

"That's not what I mean," Kelsey said, rubbing her eyes and drawing a long breath. "You can't be here. This can't be happening."

"What are you talking about? I got in last night. We've been talking about this forever."

"Talking about *what*?"

"My visit," Laura said. "It's been so long since I saw you. At least a year."

"That's impossible." Kelsey turned away, faced the blinding light of the window. "I hadn't seen you in years. Oh, what am I saying, you *can't* be here, you're—"

Dead? For some reason, the word didn't feel right. True, Kelsey had gone to Ranger's Field, stood above the body, looked upon the face. She had watched the casket descend into the earth. She had watched the roses fall. Laura was gone, soon to be dust, less than even those portraits now. Kelsey knew that. She *knew*. But this woman in her bed, this bright, smiling ghost, was no dream. She was here. She was real. She was flesh and bone and blood—or was she?

"Where *are* my clothes?" Laura pulled aside the sheets and peeked under the bed. "Weird. You mind if I borrow some, Kels?"

"What?"

She was already in the closet, sliding on a pair of jeans, slipping on a t-shirt. "Our sizes are still the same. Shit, you might be smaller. You do look like you lost weight."

The reality of the woman could not be denied. She moved. She spoke. She was a perfect duplicate at a glance, but there were minor differences Kelsey noticed once she watched and listened closely. No matter how much time passed, there were aspects of Laura that were unforgettable. The little drawl, the stray moles on her neck. This Laura had none of those imperfections. Her accent was clearer, the moles gone. Perhaps the biggest differences of all were how healthy she looked, how quickly and confidently she moved. Even if Laura were still alive, she would be frail and exhausted. The cancer had taken so much from her.

Now, the woman was in the kitchen, preparing a pot of coffee, hooking up the toaster. Kelsey watched. She knew this was wrong, knew it was fake. But this woman really *was* in her apartment. This woman really *was* spreading jam on toast. This woman really *was* humming. And so there were two possible options: Kelsey was crazy, hallucinating all of this, or, maybe, the past decade had been some type of hazy, muffled dream. Maybe she had awoken finally from that dream into her real life, one in which she and Laura never fought, never separated. Or maybe this was hell, a punishment for the mistakes she made—

She took a bottle of liquor from a nearby drawer and drank from it. It was all she could do to keep from collapsing on the spot.

"Thought we were saving that for tonight," Laura said, "but if you really want to get shit-faced, I'm up for it." She grabbed the bottle from Kelsey and took a swig. "Long drive up here. Could *not* sleep on that bus for my fucking life."

"You came on a bus?"

"Yeah. Car's been in the shop. I thought I told you?"

"I'm sorry. I'm just trying to understand."

"Understand what?" Laura eyed her. "Kels, what is going on with you?"

"I don't know. This just doesn't feel real, you being here. It doesn't feel like *I'm* here."

"I know what you mean. It's been hard to find the time to see each other, but guess what? I'm here, and everything's gonna be great. We're making the most of this week, you hear me?"

"The week," said Kelsey.

"Yeah. And today we're going shopping, remember? Girls' day out."

"I have work—"

"Oh, bullshit. You told me last night you took a few days off."

She had taken the days for the funeral, that much was true—but she never told this woman these things. She never discussed shopping or planned a week-long stay. You have a son, she wanted to say. A boy. Hunter. He has your hair and your eyes. Don't you remember? Don't you want to see him?

But she didn't say those things. She didn't ask those questions. She didn't know if her reality was still real. She didn't know if this was only a powerfully lucid dream, one ready to break at any moment.

So, she went. She watched. They ate out for brunch, admired the view of the city in the clear, noonday sun. They shared a bottle of wine, Laura talking and talking like she always did. Kelsey listened, occasionally sipping from her glass, cross-checking what she heard with what she knew. Teacher, yes. Still in Ranger's Field, yes. But no mention of Pete. No mention of Hunter. No mention of the cancer. And much of it said as matter of fact. You know this, Kelsey. You know that, Kelsey. Remember that one time? Remember this other time? Kelsey did not remember—because so few of those things actually happened. But the way this Laura spoke, excited and breathless, made Kelsey doubt herself. She almost believed this woman had been in her life all along, animated and joyful throughout.

Maybe I really have been asleep, she thought. Dreaming this whole life.

They shopped. Laura tried on blouses and jackets and pants and shoes. She posed and modeled. Straight out of a romantic comedy, thought Kelsey with a tiny smile, forgetting her present, remembering the past when she and Laura would do exactly this, and Laura would be exactly this way, and Kelsey would just watch and nod and smile at the different outfits, the reds and blues and yellows. Laura could wear anything, after all. And Kelsey was always happy enough to bask in the light, happy enough to be in the shadow. Happy enough to be the shadow.

"I am *beat*," Laura said when they got back to the apartment later that afternoon. She yawned and rubbed her eyes. "Real grateful to you for covering me, Kels. I could have sworn I brought money with me. I'm gonna have to call and cancel my card if I can't find it."

Kelsey put down the bag she was holding—a blouse and skirt she bought at Laura's request—and studied the woman standing before her. She looked genuinely confused. Not disturbed, as one might expect from someone mentally unwell, but just confused, absentminded, making rationalizations for her missing clothes, her missing wallet. There aren't any clothes, Kelsey almost said. There isn't any wallet. But every time she felt the urge to deny this fantasy, to speak out against it, the words caught in her throat.

"I think I'm gonna take a cat nap," Laura said, flopping onto the sofa. "Just plain ate too much. Why didn't you stop me? Now I'm gonna look fat in front of your boyfriend."

"Excuse me?"

"Your boyfriend. What's his name? Tony? You said we were having dinner with him."

"I did?"

"Yeah, before I came. Don't you remember? We must've talked on the phone for hours. Shit, Kels, what's up with you? You've been acting weird all day."

How could she know about Anthony? Kelsey had said nothing of him—had thought nothing of him, in fact. It was bizarre to hear this Laura look-alike mention his name. The break between the past and the present had been too clean. Laura didn't belong here, but neither did Anthony belong in the distant memories of boys and bars, autumn and spring, lilac and rosemary.

"Dinner," said Kelsey. "Right. I'll call him."

On the phone, Anthony was skeptical. "A friend? What do you mean you can't say?"

"It's better if you see for yourself. I don't know how to explain it."

He paused. "Well, I should get out by 5:00. I'll head over there."

It's Laura, she wanted to say. *The* Laura. The Laura that's dead. Only it wasn't that Laura, not that porcelain doll amid the blue and purple light, not that gaunt shell now deep in the earth. She looked over at the woman reclining on the sofa, whose feet were in the air, whose toes were wriggling, and wondered once again if she was dreaming.

When Anthony arrived, Laura embraced him. "Never thought I'd see the day! Kelsey got herself wrangled. By a real looker, too."

It was true, Kelsey thought. In the years since she met him, Anthony had refined himself, taking his diet more seriously, running cardio at the gym. He sported a trimmed beard now, as well as a regular rotation of plaid shirts and khakis. Kelsey mocked his attire regularly, but now, this phantom of Laura fawning over him, she felt oddly charmed by the simplicity of the look.

Laura took hold of the ID card hanging around his neck. "Well, damn! Kels didn't tell me you were a teacher, too. We're on vacation right now, but I guess not for you?"

Anthony had been silent during this time, shifting his gaze between Kelsey and Laura, probing for answers. At last, he said, "Sorry, but Kelsey didn't say you were coming."

"I ain't surprised. Apparently, she forgot we had this whole week planned out. I'm the famous Laura Brackett." She shook his hand. "Bet you've heard a lot about me."

Anthony turned to Kelsey. She returned his incredulous stare.

The evening passed like the afternoon. Around a restaurant table, Anthony joined Kelsey in listening with quiet astonishment as Laura described her life: her passions, her students, her travels. Anthony shared details of his own—his decision to teach in the spirit of his favorite professors, his interest in philosophy—but his words and thoughts were dim sparks compared to Laura's fire. At some point, the look of confusion on his face became one of wonder. At some point, in spite of himself, he believed in her being there just as much as Kelsey did.

That night, after a couple of beers at Kelsey's apartment, Laura took her leave to the guest room. "*Adieu, adieu*," she said. "I'm more beat than I thought. And I figure you two lovebirds need some alone time, anyway. Just keep it down, you hear?"

After the door closed, Anthony spoke. "Laura Brackett? *The* Laura?"

Kelsey drank. Her voice shook. "Yeah."

"There's no way. You said she died."

"She *did* die." Kelsey handed him the program from the funeral. He looked it over, slid his thumb over the embossed lettering, over the glossy portrait of a pre-cancer Laura.

"They're the same," he said. "She could be her twin."

"When we were in college," Kelsey said, "we slept in the same bed together sometimes. It was just something we did. It made us feel less alone. And when I woke up this morning, she was there, sleeping next to me. Like nothing changed. Like we were back in the dorm."

She recalled the patter of rain and the crash of thunder. Feeling so achingly, despairingly alone. Then the kick against the bed. Scoot. I'm getting in there with you, silly. Like nothing. Like they had known each other for years when it had only been a week. In retrospect, such a Laura thing to do. Such a Laura thing to do before the cancer, before everything changed.

She almost told Anthony, almost described for him every vivid detail, so clear was the memory now in her mind. But his eyes were clouded, his fists clenched. She hadn't seen him like this in so long. Insecure. Afraid.

"It's not possible, Kelsey. It just isn't possible."

"Tony, she's here. You saw her yourself. She's *here*."

He paced and wrung his hands. "She has a sister—"

"No. Laura was an only child."

"—and she's playing a joke. She's fooling around."

"She was an only child."

"Then a cousin. She has a cousin—"

"No."

"Then someone's pretending to be her! They're trying to get money, trying to extort—"

"Tony, it's *her*. It *is* Laura. Look at the face. You can't deny that." Kelsey held up the funeral program and stared into those old but familiar eyes, their oceanic depths, their inner reaches. "I know it's not possible. I know it's crazy. But, somehow, she's here. She's alive."

Again, she stared at the miniature portrait. Again, she made to touch the face.

"Kelsey." Anthony drew her back. "I don't think you should stay here tonight. Who knows who she is? It's not safe."

"What is she going to do?" Kelsey asked. "If she wanted to kill me, she could have done it last night when she got into my bed. But all she did was sleep. Whoever she is—whatever she is—she's not going to hurt me."

"How do you know that? You don't know what's going on here."

"No, but I know Laura."

"Laura's dead! You said it yourself. That is not Laura, Kelsey. That is a stranger sleeping in your apartment, right across from your room. That is a con artist, or a fraud, or—or something—"

"Just stop, Tony." Kelsey held the program out to him. "Take another look. It's the same face. There's no surgery there. It's not a twin, not a cousin. It's her."

He looked again at the program. She felt the urge to ask him if he experienced what she did. Do you see it? Is she calling to you? Can't you tell it's the same Laura? But how could he? Anthony had never met Laura back then. Even the Kelsey he met had been the Kelsey from afterwards, the Kelsey who lurked in the dark and vetted her prey—the Kelsey she was trying so hard not to be. It was foolish to think he would feel the same magic from the picture, but he should have believed her at least. Hadn't she proven herself to him?

He turned the program over. If he did hesitate, she couldn't tell.

"Fine," he said at last. "But I'm staying tonight. In case anything happens."

"All right. If you want."

He took the couch despite her protests. Yes, he was acting like he used to act: insecure, defensive, childish. She hid nothing from him. The Kelsey from before and the Kelsey from afterwards might as well have been different people, but she never hid anything from him. "This is what you're getting," she told him once. "This is what's left of me."

Perhaps she hadn't told him everything. She never told him about what happened, never explained why she was broken when he found her. She barely mentioned Laura, to him or anyone else. Why talk about the past? Why invite ghosts? Laura had banished her, after all. Laura had commanded her to leave. Never once had Kelsey considered disobeying. Not until now. Not until Pete's phone call summoned her to Ranger's Field. Not until this phantom appeared in her bed and brought Laura back to life. The wall she erected between the past and present was breaking.

Later that night, Kelsey left her room and stood for a long time in the hallway. The ceiling fan whirred coolly and quietly in the darkness. The soft blue light of the coffee pot's digital clock illuminated the vague shape of Anthony on the couch, his back to her. Okay, she thought. It's okay. Everything's okay.

Gingerly, she nudged open the door to the guest room. Although difficult to see in the darkness, Kelsey could make out Laura's form, her long hair, her shoulder. It could be like it was. One step forward. Two steps forward. She could fix it. She could make it right. Slip in beside her, wrap her arms around her waist, nestle her cheek against her back. Apologize for everything. Beg for a second chance. Plead for forgiveness. Fix it. Make it right. Then make it wrong. Punish her. Squeeze her. Pinch her. Choke her. Slap her. Make her cry. Make her bleed. Make her feel the years. Make her feel the loneliness.

She stepped back. She clutched herself. God, no. Not to her. Please. Don't hurt her again.

Back in her own bed, she felt the gloss of the program portrait under her thumb. She closed her eyes, and this time, she did not resist the torrent of memories that swept her away. Her waking dream—because this could not be real, she kept telling herself, simply could not be real—bled into a genuine dream. For the first time in many years, she enjoyed genuine, restful sleep. A miracle, she thought as the darkness swept over her. The prayers answered at last.

11.

"I'll be back soon," Kelsey said on the phone to Brooke, her main receptionist. "Don't worry about the appointments. Dr. White can handle my load. Reschedule the rest."

"It's just a long time to be out."

"I know. It'll be soon. I promise."

She said that, and then she looked over at Laura eating cereal at the counter, and she honestly felt no desire to go back to work at all.

Days had passed since she awoke to Laura alive and well in her bed, days she had tried vainly to rationalize and understand. Being around Laura again after so long was unreal—dreamlike, even. That was the best way to describe it: a dream she had entertained long ago of the two reconciled, of the dreadful evening at the Brackett house, the forbidden words Kelsey uttered, her transgressions, all wiped clean. Now, the dream was real, and the way this Laura laughed and smiled, talked and moved, brought back more and more memories. Studying in the library. Sharing a joint. Fishing at the lake. Each resurgence proved more pointed and palpable than the last. Kelsey felt as though her life had resumed after years on pause, and she herself was reinitialized, revived from a long slumber. This wasn't a dream, but life itself.

Laura was alive.

Obviously, there were questions. How did this happen? Where did she come from? Why aren't you concerned? Why aren't you doing anything? But each question, so significant at first, lost its potency quickly with just a glance from Laura, just a single word. Kelsey knew the discrepancies in Laura's stories should have raised red flags, should have driven her to seek understanding. The mere fact that she was alive, even if marginally different, should have been enough. But Kelsey was content to hear the voice, happy to meet the eyes. In fact, she was surprised at how happy she was to spend time with this Laura—so happy she was almost scared.

Anthony called and messaged her constantly over that stretch of days, demanding answers, stressing caution. Kelsey responded at first, emphasizing her safety, deflecting his concern, but eventually, she stopped. Just a week prior, his nagging would have sent them into a shouting match, but now, his presence felt more and more like an afterthought, not even a nuisance. You should feel bad, she told herself. He's just trying to help. He's just looking out for you. But Anthony was *always* trying to help. He was *always* trying to look out for her. Ever since that first day they met at the cafeteria, he was still the smarter one, the one with all the answers. The philosopher. The disciplinarian. No amount of years could change that.

"He's sweet," this new Laura said the day after their dinner. "Cares about you a lot. I can tell." Sure, thought Kelsey. I'm supposed to love him. I should love him. He's put in the time and effort. He's earned it. Isn't this what a healthy relationship looks like? But no matter how many times she willed herself to touch him, forced herself to take him inside her, she didn't feel anything. She wasn't alone when she was with him, but she wasn't in love.

There was guilt—had been for a long time. Laura being there helped her see it. Anthony brought stability, but Laura brought peace. Kelsey hadn't realized how accustomed she became to the lack of peace. The pressures of school, the frustration of loneliness, all had consumed her for so long. To be around Laura again, even if it wasn't real, even if it wasn't exact, was like an antidote to all her problems, all her secret anxieties.

They sat around the coffee table in the dim light of the apartment, wiping the grease of pizza off their fingers, knocking back beers. "Problem is the lack of discipline," said Laura, tearing off another slice of pizza. "Girls nowadays are too wrapped up in boys this, clothes that. They don't want to dance. I tell 'em, 'You think a guy's gonna like you prattling on about stupid shit?' I don't really say *that*, but you know what I mean. They look all bug-eyed. No fuck-ing guy really cares about your purse or your jewelry. They just want to see your cunt. And even that won't last too long. So, you need to work on your-self."

Kelsey nodded.

"Maybe it's a generation thing. Yeah, I screwed around when I was their age, but I also had an idea about what was important. I dedicated myself to dancing. Now, it's like every kid can't focus. You don't read up on conspiracy theories?"

"Not really. I know about some."

Laura took a bite of her pizza. "Well, let's say low attention span is something the government wants. So, every year, kids are less and less likely to actually make something of themselves. They're on their phones more, playing video games, all that. I don't know if I buy it, but it makes you wonder. A kid with a future and a goal can do a lot. It's scary. Are they gonna be good? Bad? How do you control that? You can't. So, you take it away instead. No future 'cause of debt and loneliness. No goals 'cause of dis-tractions."

"I never took you to be so cynical."

"You think it's cynical?" She chewed, swallowed. "Maybe. Doesn't make my job easier. Can't teach a kid how to read if they can't sit still. Can't teach a girl to dance if her heart ain't in it. I guess I'm invested."

"The girls who work at the office are aimless," Kelsey said. "They talk a lot about partying and drinking, just like we used to. But they're young, and it's not like I really have a right to tell them how to live. Who's got it figured out, anyway?"

"That's true. I guess I'm just looking for an excuse to bitch."

Laura went silent, holding her pizza at an angle, dabbing at her collar with the fingertips of her free hand. She did this for one minute, then two. Kelsey watched her. The fingers searched for something, finding only skin. Then the eyes came alive again.

"My rosary," she said. "I don't have it."

"You haven't been wearing it."

"That's not right. I always wear it." Laura stood up, her eyes no longer calm, but frantic, scared. "How long haven't I had it?"

"Since you got here," Kelsey said. She stood as well, alarmed, and reached out to take Laura's arm. "Listen, it's not a big deal—"

Laura slapped Kelsey's hand away. The wild look in her eyes was more aggravated, and when she turned to Kelsey, it was as if she stared at a stranger. Kelsey returned the look with one even more frenzied. She had never felt afraid in Laura's presence before.

"Who are you?" demanded Laura, whirling around, retreating from the apartment's very walls, its furniture. "Where am I? What the fuck am I doing here?"

"It's me. It's Kelsey."

"Kelsey? You're not Kelsey! Kelsey's gone! I haven't seen her in years!"

"Laura, I'm standing right here. It's me. It's *me*."

Laura pulled at her face, her hair. Her anxious eyes were glossy, looking but not looking, seeing but not seeing. There was no recognition in them when she turned to Kelsey.

"Mama," she said. "Where's Mama? Where's Pete? Where's Pete and—and Hunter?"

Kelsey heard her utter the last name with a chill. Suddenly, immediately, she was again in that old foyer that smelt of orange polish, watching the little boy with his golden hair and ocean-blue eyes disappear from the room. That little boy with his quiet, mournful loneliness, the same as that of his mother. Her loneliness inherited, bequeathed.

"Hunter," Laura repeated, sitting back down on the sofa. "Hunter. Hunter."

She hugged herself, muttering his name again and again. Kelsey knelt before her.

"Laura. Sweetie. He's back home. With your mom. And Pete. Hunter's safe."

"He's home?"

"Yeah. And you're here with me. Kelsey. You came to visit. We'd been planning it."

"Planning?"

"For a long time. Forever. That's what you said. Remember?"

"Oh." Laura rubbed her eyes. She laughed. "Oh. Oh, shit. Kels, I'm sorry. I don't know what the hell that was. Maybe I'm tired, or—"

"It's okay. You can go to sleep. We'll talk about it tomorrow."

"Yeah. Yeah, that sounds good. I'll do that."

She lifted herself slowly, and Kelsey helped her to the guest room. She stiffened upon touching Laura's waist, her shoulder. She bit her lip. Laura sat silently on the side of the bed, her face half-empty and dazed. Kelsey stood in the doorway.

"Let me know if you need anything. I'll be right outside."

"Okay. Thank you."

Kelsey tossed and turned throughout the night, hot and suffocating. Even at full speed, the fan did nothing for her. The fucking fan. She wanted to throw something at it, rip it off the ceiling, tear it apart. Again and again, she pulled up her phone and agonized over calling Pete. Didn't he deserve to know? The prick. The fucker. Laura barely in the ground, and already he wanted to get his dick wet. No, he didn't deserve to know. But Angela. Hunter.

Growing up without a mother—what did that do to someone? Kelsey was tempted to blame the way she was, the detachment, on her lack of a mother. She could barely remember the woman. Long face. Dark eyes. Bobbed hair. She could recall an outline, the most basic of visages, but the image was a blur otherwise. Gone. Left after the death of Kelsey's younger brother, who drowned off the coast. "She wasn't the same after that," her father often said. "We both lost Dylan, but she lost more." Did she? Enough to abandon her family? Her father had carried that burden all of Kelsey's life, always with that sweet, sad smile, always with the lame jokes. And yet he seemed always moments away from tears. The same loneliness in him was in her. They could never cure each other of it.

Would Laura's son grow up the same way? Deprived of his mother, living in a home too large for three people, forever wondering what his life would have been otherwise? Alive or dead, would Laura have passed on that loneliness? Was Kelsey doomed to that same fate? From Laura's mother to Laura to Hunter. From Kelsey's mother to Kelsey to her own future child. From their progeny down through the generations until there were none left.

She smiled despite herself. A child—with whom? Anthony? She tried hard to picture a small face, a head of dark hair, but just like the memory of her mother, the image remained hazy and indistinct. Did she even want to be a mother? What else were you supposed to do? Get the degree, get money, get married, have kids. Maybe she was still on the way, not yet done with the plan. Maybe that explained the distance, the melancholy.

In the morning, Laura was herself. Eating cereal. Laughing and talking. Kelsey regarded her. The face was slightly thinner. The breasts were seemingly larger. The hair was longer, more luxuriant. Minute differences in isolation, but enough altogether to signify something distinct from the original. Prettier, maybe. Sexier. More sanitized. But not the same.

"Last night," said Kelsey, "do you remember what happened?"

"What do you mean?"

"You freaked out. You couldn't find your rosary."

Laura was quiet. "I hadn't thought about it. You know, my great-grandmother gave that to my grandpa, and he gave it to my mom. I was fifteen when she put it around my neck. 'Laura, don't you ever take this off. It's gonna protect you.' And I never did. So, I don't know why I don't have it now. Maybe I took it off and didn't realize it. Shit. Where's my head, you know? My clothes, my wallet. Where is everything?"

"You don't need those things. You have everything you need right here." Kelsey smiled. "I'm going to check on Tony today. Fulfill that girlfriend duty. Remember? You talked about that a lot with Pete."

Laura's brow furrowed. "Pete. I ain't seen him in so long. I mean, seriously seen him. Once in a while at a store or on the street. But ever since I turned him down"—her face clouded further—"since then, it's like we never went out at all. Like we were never together."

She paused. "That doesn't seem right. Turning him down. Not being together. That doesn't seem right at all."

"It's true," Kelsey said softly. "He asked you to marry him, and you refused. You didn't want to spend a lifetime with someone you didn't love."

"No, I didn't. Why waste it on him? Why settle?"

"Some people do it so they won't be alone," Kelsey said. "Because they don't think there's going to be anything else."

As she left, she felt a warm, private relief. No memory of marriage. No mention of Hunter. For now, Laura was okay.

It was Saturday, so she found Anthony at his apartment alternating between grading essays and reading books. He was working through psychology texts, the last she heard, a break from the usual philosophy. When she came inside, he looked up from the sofa and seemed more confused than anything. Perhaps more sad.

"How long's it been since you used that key?" he asked.

His bookshelves were increasingly expanding. At least one whole wall was occupied now, some of the shelves practically bursting. She looked over the titles briefly, wrinkling her nose at the thinkers he liked so much: Sartre, Camus, and the other "Frenchies." There were other names she didn't recognize, authors who felt faintly familiar from the one literature class she took years before—a class shared with Laura, incidentally. Shelley. Byron. Dead white men indistinguishable from one another. She couldn't be bothered to keep track of them, much less care about the ones who captured Anthony's interest at any given moment.

He sat up and set his papers aside. "Why haven't you been answering your phone? I've been worried."

"You're always worried. You can handle it."

"You came to fight?"

"No, I didn't." She sighed. "I've been a bitch. I'm sorry. It's just been a really strange few days. I'm sure you can appreciate that."

"Your dead friend came back to life. Sure. I appreciate that."

"Is that a joke?"

"You don't know who that person is. Maybe she is your friend, somehow. Maybe Laura really is alive, and she magically appeared to you. But you can't just act like that's nothing. And you can't just cut me out."

"Jesus, Tony. Always so dramatic."

He ignored this comment, looking at the bookshelf, scanning names, making connections. "Robbed graves made people think of vampires. Eventually, we got zombies. Even Jesus came back from the dead."

"She's not a fucking zombie."

"You know what doppelgängers are, right? Supposedly, if you see your doppelgänger, it's bad luck. It might even mean your death. But if Laura had a doppelgänger, why would she appear now? Why to you?"

Kelsey half-listened, recalling suddenly the preoccupied, vacant look Laura had the night prior. She focused on the terror that permeated the otherwise beautiful features, the loss and displacement that overshadowed the brightness. She had never seen Laura so discomposed, so fragile, but the look was nonetheless familiar. She had looked like a doll divested of its animating force. Like a statue. Like porcelain.

"Thought-forms," said Anthony. "That was the last thing I looked up. Entities you create from your mind, emanations projected into existence. Tulpas and jinn. Giving life where there wasn't any before. What if that was real? What if we could create something not in our mind, not as a hallucination, but that was flesh and blood?"

"What are you saying? I made her?"

"I don't know. People don't just appear out of nowhere, Kelsey."

"Tony, I don't care why she's there. She just *is*—there's no explaining it. I don't know why or how. Maybe it means there's a God. Maybe it means there isn't one. The only thing I know is that there's something wrong with her. Something is starting to happen to her, and I have to help her. I have to protect her."

"What do you mean?"

"She started talking last night. About Pete. About Hunter."

"Who are they?"

"Pete was her boyfriend. Uh, husband. They got married, and they had a son. This was after we stopped talking, so I didn't know any of it until I went to the funeral. Laura never loved him. He's an asshole, a dickhead. But she was talking about him last night. She acts like she was never married, so why would she mention him and her son?"

"She doesn't know, right? That she's supposed to be dead?"

Kelsey shook her head.

"You can't keep her there. Her husband and son deserve to know. I would want to."

Kelsey was mum. She kept picturing that lost face. That lost, lonely face.

She went home. Laura said she felt better. That evening, they shared dinner and talked. Nothing about the previous night or the morning. Nothing about Pete or Hunter or even Ranger's Field. Nothing about the past at all. A resumption of the dream. More and more, Kelsey drew towards this woman who shared Laura's skin and hair, face and voice. She leaned towards her. She inclined her head. She breathed in the familiar, haunting scents of lilac and rosemary.

That night, a scream awoke her. Sweating, breathless, she could not move—her limbs remained wedged to the bed sheets as though by cement. Her voice was trapped in her throat, leaving her mouth only in hoarse, wiry moans. Then the weight was off her, and she shot up amid the dark and cold. Another pained, tearful scream tore through the apartment. She rushed into Laura's room and found her writhing atop the bed, clutching her stomach.

"Laura?" Kelsey pulled her into her arms. "What's wrong? What's happening?"

"It hurts!" Laura said between exhausted breaths. "It hurts so goddamn much!"

She let out another shriek, and then she whimpered and cried, kicking her feet, clawing at her arms and face. Kelsey cradled her. "It's okay, Laura. It's okay. I'm here. I'm here." She caressed the hair, stroked the skin, kissed the cheeks. "You're okay. You're okay." As they rocked, the whimpers died down. The energy faded. The women slept.

What woke Kelsey next was not a scream, but the hiss of the showerhead. Through the doorway, she could see the pale light of the restroom across the corridor. "Laura?" she called. "Laura, are you in there?"

She found Laura huddled in the corner of the shower, naked, hugging her knees to her chest. The water drenched her.

Kelsey lingered in the doorway, afraid to cross the threshold. "What are you doing?"

Laura gave no response, overcome once again by that vacant look, that absence of self. Kelsey felt the water and recoiled. The water was scalding.

She snapped the shower off and stood there, neither angry nor frustrated, but expectant. Laura was like a wounded animal, vulnerable and pitiable, at the mercy of the world. She reminded Kelsey of meeting her dog Molly at the animal shelter—an old, distant memory—when the dog was only a scared, shivering pup. Kelsey felt the same, sudden desire now as she did then: to take the poor thing into her arms, kiss it, protect it. Only with Laura, she felt desires less innocent, things as unspeakable as they were sublime. She restrained herself.

"Laura," she said.

Laura raised one of her hands, turned it, regarded the droplets of water upon the skin, regarded the wrinkles and creases, the fingerprints, the nails, the knuckles. "I keep thinking I'm asleep. Like I'm in a dream, getting scared and thinking I'm going to wake up in my bed. But I hit myself. I pinch myself. And I just stay here. Nothing changes."

Kelsey watched her.

"I keep seeing him. I close my eyes, and I see him. I turn a corner, and I see him. A sweet little boy. A sad little boy. I feel like I know him. I *do* know him. Hunter. He's my son. Even though I've never seen him before, I know that he's my son. And I feel I should love him. I feel I should love this sad little boy I've never seen before in my life. But I don't have a son. I don't."

"Laura."

"His little face, Kels. I can't get it out of my head. He's in my house. My grandpa's house. My mama's house. He's there. Bernie was watching him. Pete's cousin. She watched him for us all the time, watched him because I—because I—"

"Laura, you're tired." Kelsey knelt on the wet tile, and took Laura's hands. "You're tired, and you should go to sleep."

"*Did* she watch him?" Laura kept talking, murmuring to herself, oblivious to Kelsey altogether. "She must've. She was playing with him. She took him upstairs. Took him upstairs because Daddy wanted to talk to his friend. His old friend."

Kelsey watched her eyes, watched for recollection, recognition. Dreaded it.

"Pete and I got married. But I don't remember that. I don't remember the ceremony at all. I don't remember the vows. I don't remember the ring. See? I don't have a ring." She looked at her hand again. "There ain't nothing there. Not even a mark. Married for years, and not even the slightest fucking mark."

"Laura. Let me take you to bed. Let's go back to bed."

"My vows, Kels. My fucking vows. Why wouldn't I remember that?"

"Laura. Laura, listen to me—"

"Why can't I remember, Kels? I know we never married. I turned him down, like you always told me to. I cut him loose. You remember? You always told me. You wanted me to be happy. You said you'd give anything. You'd give anything for me to be the way I was."

"Laura." Kelsey's throat was dry, her heart heavy. "Please. Let's go back to bed."

"I'm here with you," said Laura, "but I haven't seen you in years. But I see you all the time. I talk with you all the time. So, why do I feel like I never see you?"

Kelsey couldn't say anything because she was crying, crying and unable to stop.

"I don't feel right," Laura went on. "Ever since I woke up next to you. I just don't feel right. I thought it was nothing at first, but it ain't. It's like I'm not here. Like I ain't supposed to be here. Like I'm supposed to be somewhere else."

"Laura." Kelsey sobbed, she shuddered. "Laura, I'm sorry. Baby, I'm sorry."

"Why are you crying?"

"Because I left you," Kelsey said, her hand over her mouth. "I left you, Laura. The one goddamn person that made me feel like I was where I belonged. My whole life, I'm like an imposter in my own skin. I'm like a shadow. And then I found you. I found you, and I could be with you. I fit with you."

She took Laura's face in her hands, brushed aside her slick hair, cupped her wet cheeks. "I love you, Laura. I love you so much." And then she kissed her, feeling again after so many years that electric shock, that atomic bomb. Feeling the hair on her arms bristle. Tasting that saliva, sweet as honey.

When she pulled away, Laura simply stared at her, lonely and lost. "I love you, too," she said. "I feel like that's true."

Kelsey hardly heard her. She kissed her again. And when they lay together in bed, wet and cold,

Kelsey felt as though she were in Laura's bedroom of old, settling in the cozy dark, looking up at those luminescent stars, falling asleep without a care in the world.

12.

The morning after, Kelsey lay in the soft light, look-ing at the woman sleeping beside her, admiring the fine features and rosy blush. Not a porcelain face at all, but one full of life.

Tulpa. Doppelgänger. Thought-form. The words came back to her now. Laura was dead, so this wasn't Laura—but she *was* Laura. Barring the few physical differences, so much was alike. So much was better. Kelsey ran her fingers through the golden hair, marveling at the softness, the veracity. Even the light sheen of sweat on the forehead seemed doubly authentic. Wait. The sweating. The screaming.

A sudden chill replaced the warmth running through her. Was the cancer here after all? Had this miracle come with strings attached? Kelsey regarded the face, so peaceful and content, and vowed that it would be different this time. She would not aban-don Laura again.

As she made a pot of coffee in the kitchenette, Laura emerged from the hall. She looked around herself, touched her arms, felt her hair. She seemed even more beautiful to Kelsey in the morning light, but also so much more vague and ethereal, as if she would fade into that light and disappear forever. Kelsey struggled to keep from embracing her right then and there to keep her on this mortal, material plane.

"How are you feeling?" she asked. "Does it still hurt?"

"No. I don't know. The pain didn't last long. It just came and went. Like a ghost." She looked up. "Something is wrong with me, Kels. It's like I'm losing my mind."

"Tell me. What's happening?"

"Hard to describe it. I remember coming on the bus, least I remember that I remembered that—if that makes sense? It's almost like the last few days ain't real. Like they were some sort of dream I'm waking up from."

"What do you remember about me?" asked Kelsey.

"You?" Laura mused on this. "It's like you've been there and not been there. I remember you being in my life all along, but I can't nail anything down. The things we would've done, like birthday parties or weddings or those things, they aren't there. It's like I'm getting the forest instead of the trees, seeing the big picture, but not the little pieces."

"Laura. Do you trust me?"

"What's that mean?"

"If you remember something bad," Kelsey said, "will you trust me? Whatever it is?"

Laura smiled. "Why wouldn't I trust you? You're my best friend, Kels. Of course, I trust you. No matter what."

"Thank you." Kelsey hugged her, holding her tight, breathing in the scent of her hair, her skin. "I love you, Laura. I mean that. I won't leave you to this. I promise."

They shared coffee and eggs. Laura talked little, so it fell to Kelsey to make up the difference. There was difficulty not seeing in this new Laura's place the sickly, frail Laura from so long ago. Cancer-stricken, weak and melancholy, the original Laura would often go silent, as though leaving herself. She would laugh, and then stop. She would smile, and then stop. Kelsey always thought this eerie, afraid that Laura would not come back, that she would stay in the dark place to which she retreated. The same, quiet deadness pervaded now, hanging over them like a fog. Kelsey's attempts at conversation ended again and again in failure. At last, she simply took Laura's hand. She had done exactly the same many times before, always powerless to lift the pall.

She invited Anthony to lunch. They met at a hotel restaurant, a favorite of theirs, its ceiling high and gilded and its walls glass-paneled. Kelsey arrived first. She pulled at the white tablecloth with her fingers, stared with dread at the Houston sprawl below. When she ordered a second glass of whiskey, the waiter looked on, probably tempted to caution her otherwise. She nearly laughed. She needed the drink. She deserved it.

She was so focused on her glass, beyond her glass, that she didn't notice when Anthony set down his satchel and removed his jacket. He almost leaned down to peck her on the cheek, but thought better of it and sat down.

"Are you okay?" he asked.

She looked up, betraying what must have been desperation or anxiety because his face softened. He took her hand.

"I don't know what's happening, Tony," she said. "There's something wrong with her."

She withdrew her hand from his. Anthony sat back. "What is she doing?"

"She started screaming last night. Her stomach was hurting. I thought maybe I'd have to call an ambulance, but then she was okay. Or seemed okay." She drank her whiskey. "You know, Laura had cancer. That's what killed her."

"You told me."

"It was stomach cancer. From one day to the next, it seemed like. She just had it all of a sudden. And the doctors had to operate, and she just wasn't the same after that. And now I remember how she talked about finding it—waking up, screaming. I can see it in my mind, crystal clear."

The waiter returned and took Anthony's drink—just a water. Afterwards, Anthony looked at Kelsey's glass. "How much have you been drinking lately?"

"What?"

"You're drinking a lot. So, that must mean you started slipping again, too."

"I can't fucking believe you," Kelsey said. "I'm here about my friend, and all you can do is bitch about my drinking. And then you accuse me of fucking around? What is your problem?"

"She's not your friend," Anthony said. "You don't even know who that woman is."

"Of course, I do. She's Laura."

"Laura's dead, Kelsey."

Kelsey grinned. "You know, maybe this is what I was waiting for. An opportunity to finally tell you to go fuck yourself. Every time I'm with you, I feel like shit. But I don't need you anymore. I don't need you telling me off, and I don't need you trying to make me feel guilty. You know who never made me feel shitty? You know who always had my back? Laura. And she needs me now, whether you understand or not."

She downed the rest of her whiskey and stood. Anthony watched her.

"If she really had your back," he said, "then where was she all this time? Why could you never even talk about her?"

Kelsey spun around, her face in his, eyes burning, nostrils flared. "You say another word about her, and I'll break your face in. You hear me? You don't have the right. You don't have the goddamn right. Who the fuck are you to judge us?"

Heads turned. The waiter watched from a few tables away. Kelsey met each gaze, ready to challenge, to demand what the fuck was so funny, what the fuck was so interesting, this was her friend, her friend who was suffering and sick and needed help. But she contained herself. Trembling, teetering, she contained herself.

"I guess I won't be needing this anymore," she said after a pause, removing Anthony's key from her purse and slamming it onto the table. "See you around. Or maybe not."

She left, surprised by her careening stomach, her sweaty palms, her teary eyes. Out on the street, she wanted to scream, throw bricks at storefronts, take poles to windshields. Instead, she stopped at a store, bought a six-pack, and took refuge in the nearest parking garage, where she sat in her car and drank. How dare that motherfucker, she thought, wiping her mouth with her sleeve, sucking in the taste of beer. How dare he say a single word when he never even knew her, when he never even saw her alive and smiling and eternal. The *real* Laura. The Laura everyone left behind and buried.

She paused. The Laura she left behind. The Laura she buried.

Halfway through her second beer, a fresh volley of tears overcame her. The real Laura—as though this one screaming in the night was not in pain, as though this one huddled in the shower was not tormented. She *is* real, you stupid bitch. She hit herself, again and again. You dumb bitch. You stupid whore. She *is* real. She *is* real. And she needs you. She needs you. So, get your shit together. Fucking get it together.

She dumped the remaining beers in the trash. In a restroom, she washed her hands, rinsed out her mouth, splashed water over her face. Laura on the porch in the burning light, begging, pleading. Laura in the shower under the scalding water, questioning, despairing. Both the same. Why the same? Why was it happening again? Why couldn't she goddamn *do* anything?

When she got back to the apartment, Laura wasn't in the living room or the guest room. Kelsey entered her bedroom and found Laura sitting cross-legged on the bed, surrounded by disarrayed shoe boxes and bags. The pink, embossed funeral program lay before her.

Kelsey looked at Laura, and then she looked at the program. She didn't say anything.

"I had a feeling you were hiding something," Laura said. "So, I snooped. Sorry."

Kelsey remained quiet. Her eyes watered. She stilled her trembling hands.

"Laura Brooks, née Brackett," read Laura. "Something about it don't seem right."

"I can explain," said Kelsey.

"I don't think you can." Laura flipped through the program. "I was thinking before, somehow, that maybe I wasn't Laura. Crazy, but I was thinking it. Like when you suspect something and don't want it to be true, but you know it is. It's been creeping around in me the whole time I've been here. Everything felt all right at first—nothing was confusing, nothing didn't make sense—but the little things kept bugging me, like my clothes and my wallet. And then I thought about my rosary, how I never take it off."

She touched her bare collar. "I keep reaching here, thinking it'll be there. I keep trying to picture my students, and I can't do it. I think about what I was doing before I woke up here, but I can't. The bus is fuzzy and vague, like it never happened, and if I try to push more, it's scary how blank it is. It's like I wasn't doing anything. Like I was never anywhere before this."

Kelsey wanted to speak, but only a tiny croak left her throat. The pounding between her ears must have been her hammering heart. Please, Laura. The words formed themselves in her mind, but they couldn't come free. I can explain. Let me explain.

"They buried it with her," she said at last, hardly above a whisper. "Buried it with *you*. The rosary. I think it was part of the arrangement."

"Makes sense. I'd want it."

"Laura, I can explain—"

"You said that. So, explain it, Kels. Tell me."

"I got a call from Pete," Kelsey said shakily. "It was the middle of the night. I hadn't talked to him in years. You asked me not to talk to him, and I didn't, I swear to you. I cut him out of my life. I made good on that. But he found my number, and he told me— he told me—Laura died. He said the cancer came back. They thought it was gone, but they did a test, and it was all over. Not in the stomach anymore, but everywhere. She didn't have a chance."

Laura waited for more. Kelsey fought to keep from flinching.

"I went to the funeral. Your mom was there. Pete. Hunter, your son, he was at your house. And then I came back, and I went to sleep, and when I woke up, you were there. You were just *there*, Laura. It was like a miracle."

"Just there," repeated Laura. "Why? How?"

"I don't know. I opened my eyes, and you were there. I swear I'm telling the truth."

Laura sat there, absorbing, processing. Kelsey climbed onto the bed beside her. "Why does it matter?" she asked, taking those soft hands, kissing them, rubbing them against her cheek. "You're here now. You're alive. The rest is nothing. It's nothing."

"It's not nothing. She had a family. She had a little boy."

"He won't remember," Kelsey said, kissing the hands again. "He's so young. He won't remember. Pete said it himself. Pete said it himself, so why—"

"He's her *son*." Laura drew herself away. "He's *my* son. And I need to see him."

"What good will it do? They think you're dead. Let them think it. You're free. You can go wherever you want, be whatever you want. We can be together. Finally, we can be together! Don't you want that? I won't leave you! I'll stay with you! I'll do whatever you want me to do, whatever you need me to do, I swear!"

Laura shook her head. "It ain't right, Kelsey. I shouldn't be here. God—"

"Who gives a fuck about God?" Kelsey shouted. "Fuck Jesus! Fuck what anyone else says! They don't know you, Laura! But I do! I knew you from the first time I saw you! I was so stupid, fighting it and fighting it, because I didn't want to admit what I felt! I didn't want to believe it! But it's the truth, the goddamn truth! It's the only thing that matters!"

She stumbled towards Laura, arms outstretched. "I know you! I can take care of you! I can do all of it!" She took Laura into her arms, aimed to kiss her. "I love you, Laura! I love—"

She fell back against the bed. Laura stood over her, those sad eyes somehow sadder.

Kelsey looked up at her. "Don't. Please. Don't push me away. Not again."

"You can't explain it," said Laura, "but I can. I know it in my bones. You brought me back, Kels. You wanted me, and you got me. I know it because you're in my head."

"I don't understand."

"You're in my head," Laura said, matter-of-factly, as if it made perfect sense. "What you think. What you feel. It's all there, mixing around with the other parts of me that belonged to Laura. I see my mom, and then I see your dad. I see Hunter, and then I see your brother Dylan."

"Dylan?" Kelsey hadn't heard the name in so long that it felt dry, alien. "What?"

"You can't explain me," said Laura, "but you brought him back, too."

"What are you talking about?" Tears streamed down Kelsey's face, snot bubbling in her nose, spit dripping from her lips. "Dylan drowned! He was walking with my mom, and the water came and just—just took him away! That's what Dad always said—that it just took him away!"

Laura nodded. She was crying, too. "And your dad swam out for him, but the waves were too strong. Your mom was kneeling in the water, screaming for him to come back. Everyone was watching. You were watching. You were so little, you didn't even know what was happening. You didn't know what it meant."

"Why are you saying this?"

"Because it ain't right! He shouldn't have come back! *I* shouldn't have come back!"

"He never came back! The water took him, I already told you!" Kelsey stood up, breathing so fast she thought her chest might burst. "You want to hurt me. I know. I deserve it. I left you. I shouldn't have left you. Laura, please, *please*, you have to believe me, I wanted to be with you, I wanted to see you, I would've given anything, *anything*, to make that happen! I wish it could've been me! I wish it *was* me!"

She reached for her again, groping, crying, but Laura was faster. She stepped aside, and Kelsey plunged to the floor.

"I'm leaving," said Laura through her own quiet tears. "I'm leaving."

Kelsey clutched at her ankles as she walked past. "No, please! Don't go! I'm begging you, I'm begging you—" She turned over, shuddering, weeping.

When the door shut, she let out another moan. "Laura, please come back! Don't leave me alone!"

Minutes passed. Her cries grew softer, dimmer. She curled up into an exhausted ball, whimpering, until finally, she slept.

13.

Laura wandered, no particular destination in mind, just walking along streets and through alleys. The city felt familiar, not because it was—*she* hadn't studied there, she reminded herself, the real Laura had—but because something deep inside her resonated with the darkening sky and swimming lights. She passed restaurants and bars at which she was sure, somehow, she had once eaten and drunk. Sometimes alone, but at other times with men, with women. Frequently, there was a morbid impulse to steal away into one of those dark corners and wait for *something*, something she couldn't place, but wanting it, needing it desperately.

She had no money, no coat. She stood absently on street corners. She idled nervously under storefront awnings. Men watched her. Women, too. She gazed into the glass of a display window and searched for what they saw. Face pale and ghostly. Hair light and soft. Eyes blue and faded. Beautiful, but not hers. Stolen, the features yearning to return to their rightful owner. Yearning so badly she felt as though she were bound to lift up at any moment and dissolve into the air. She pictured her dislodged particles spiraling into the vacuum beyond, eventually disappearing altogether.

That night, she slept on a park bench, curled, cold. There were no stars to see, so she imagined them, willed them into being upon the blue-black canvas. She liked looking up at the stars. No. She only thought she liked it. She remembered liking it. But she had to tell herself, again and again, that her impulses were not her own, her feelings lifted and appropriated, her skin and bones and thoughts grafted onto a faceless, lifeless mannequin. The fire of her life imparted by an artist's loving kiss and gentle breath. But still not her own. Nothing her own.

She watched the next morning's rain from inside a coin laundry, wringing out her wet hair, trembling in the sweater and jeans she had borrowed from Kelsey. The machines whirred warmly, soothingly. She needed a jacket, a hat. A woman sat across from her. She smiled. Laura smiled back, but if she smiled too long, the tears welled up. Did at least the tears belong to her? She couldn't tell. When she thought of the real Laura, she felt exhaustingly sad, miserably so. She saw that Laura standing alone. She felt a kinship with her. She felt she would give anything to be with her, absolutely anything.

In the shadow of an underpass, her stomach flared with pain again. She held through the first spasm, nails digging into the concrete wall. The second spasm sent her to her knees. She breathed deep, taking in the real, freezing smell of rain and the imagined, rancid stench of blood. I'm in a hospital, she thought with sudden, inexplicable clarity. I'm about to be cut open. God ain't watching me. No one's watching me. The pain felt almost unreal, somehow hyperbolized, like the pain dreamt up by a sympathetic observer. Each ache, burn, and throb felt simulated, estimated, intensely agonizing but nonetheless inauthentic. When the spasm finally passed, she pulled at her hair and laughed. It wasn't falling out. Thank God. At least it wasn't falling out.

The next day, the hunger was too much to bear. She waited in one of those familiar bars, practicing the right smile, rehearsing the correct laugh. It was surprisingly easy. Her body knew what to do. Eventually, a man sat next to her, and then another after him. She waited for the right one, and then he was there, suit jacket over his shoulder, sleeves rolled up. She told him she had forgotten her money, how dumb was that, and he laughed and paid for her beer, her meal. Did he know he was being tricked? Did he care? She was careful to let him drink more than he could handle. When they were back at his apartment, red light burning through the bedroom window, he thankfully fell asleep during the handjob. She felt disassociated the entire time, as if watching from above, such was the easy, secondhand way with which she seduced him. Walking out into the night, she felt a lingering disquiet. No, more like a disgust. At him? At herself?

She was lost and tired. In need for somewhere to rest, her feet carried her.

Anthony found her outside his apartment building.

He couldn't believe his eyes at first, staring at her through the windshield, her ghostly visage revealed intermittently by the wipers before being washed away by the rain. There and then not there. There and then gone. He got out and held his umbrella over her. Those lost, mournful eyes did away with all his doubts and suspicions. Watching her tremble, he felt only tenderness, as if she were a dog with its tail tucked between its legs, thrown out by its owners, nowhere to go, no place to be.

He made coffee while she wrung her hair with a towel and dried her face and neck. She drank heavily from the ceramic, her tongue burning, her nostrils sizzling. He refilled her cup.

"I didn't know where else to go," she said.

"How'd you even find me?"

"I just knew. Because it's what she would've done."

She sat on the sofa, hands wrapped around the cup, head bowed. She explained what happened: the transient, excruciating pains, the fleeting, irreconcilable memories, finding the funeral program, leaving

Kelsey screaming and crying on the floor. Floating. Fragmenting. Not knowing whom or what she was supposed to be.

"It's unbelievable," Anthony said when she was finished. "That you'd just be there."

"She called me here. I know it's crazy, but it's true. I know it's true."

Anthony nodded. "I think I believe you. I've never seen Kelsey act that way. All this time I've known her, and she's been distant. I'm always fighting to get something out of her—*anything* out of her. But with you, she's different. She's got life in her I've never seen before."

"That's why I can't be around her," Laura said. "She won't let me go. And I need to go. I *want* to go. I want to see my baby again."

"Your son?"

She nodded. The faintest of smiles formed on her lips. "I can't explain it. I don't know if I'm really his mother, but if there's a place for me, it's with him."

"You think that'll work?" Anthony asked. "You think you can be with him?"

"I don't know. But at least I can see him for myself."

Anthony watched her, struck by her earnestness, her nakedness. Something in her, something weak and fragile, seemed out of place in his apartment, especially so in the world at large. He almost felt like he wasn't talking to a person at all, but something far more elemental, something more deserving of being helped by virtue of its simplicity, its purity. In the back of his mind, the usual suspects were screaming. What are you doing? Are you crazy? Weren't you convinced this was all a hoax just a day ago? But something stirred in him he could not have expected. He reached out and took her hand.

"I'll take you," he said. "We'll go together. We'll find your son."

She looked up at him, so full of reverence and devotion, practically glowing. Not a person, he thought. No one real was capable of that brightness.

That night, lying atop the sofa under the moonlight from the window—he allowed Laura the bed—he thought of Kelsey. More accurately, he thought of his relationship to her, so tenuous and dreamlike. Her explosion at the restaurant had been on his mind, not necessarily because he was hurt, but because the outpour of emotion had been so uncharacteristic. Her puzzle had layers he didn't know existed, layers he likely would never reach, let alone solve.

Remote. Cold. Those had been his mother's words. "You can do so much better," she told him constantly. "She's pretty, but she's cold. You don't want to live with someone like that. They'll wear you out." You would know, he wanted to say, exchanging knowing glances with his father. But his father always urged understanding and forgiveness of his mother. She only wanted him to succeed, to be happy, to have everything she never could. That had been the same story for as long as he could remember, the same story meant to justify the lectures, insults, and manipulations. Maybe that was why the remarks from Kelsey and his friends stung so much. Controlling. Obsessive. He couldn't get away from his mother. She was always with him, in each of his own elitist comments and snide insinuations he regretted, but couldn't suppress.

Compared to his mother, Kelsey took little interest in him at all. She was like mist, like smoke. Her skin always felt cold, her breath frost-ridden. Was there really anything between them? He remembered seeing her so long ago in the cafeteria. She sat like a statue, unassuming, unfeeling. She didn't belong in that place, he thought at the time, and she was failing at playing along. Is that what drew him to her? What still drew him? All logic and reason argued otherwise, that they weren't working, probably hadn't been for a long time, but he felt authenticity in her distance, reality in her transience. The night she revealed herself to him, however briefly, simmered in his memories. They could have that again, couldn't they? Or did only he want that?

His father pulled him aside at one of their yearly family barbecues, standing with him in the dark of the yard while cousins and aunts and uncles chatted inside, clinking wine glasses, alternating between laughing and biting their tongues. "You really want to marry her?" his father asked him, so tired-looking in his khaki sport coat with its tweed patches, white-haired and gray-bearded. Anthony watched her through the window as she mingled in the dining room with some of his cousins, on her third or maybe fourth glass of wine, laughing a rehearsed laugh, smiling a practiced smile.

"I think so," he said. "What else can I do?"

"When the table takes the first five-hundred, you don't have to give them the second," his father said. "You always have time, Tony. Don't feel like there's a rush."

"It doesn't feel like there's time. It feels like I already blew it."

In the morning, a hand shook him awake. Laura stood over him.

They stopped briefly at a thrift store before heading out. Laura chose a handful of blouses and pants. Anthony watched her. Supposedly a mirage of a person, but so lifelike, so real. Somehow, she could smile at the pinks and reds she held up for him to appraise. She could grimace at the washed-out jeans. She tried on a pair of cowboy boots, tipped a Stetson hat to him with a wink. In that moment, he could see clearly the playful, charming girl who once captivated rooms. But when she came up to him, her smile vanished. The light faded. They both remembered what she was and what she was not.

They spoke little on the road. Rain fell in occasional bursts, pelting the windshield, making gray the passing prairies, wind turbines, and ranch houses. Anthony drove with clenched hands and stiff shoulders. He looked over at Laura, who sat watching the landscape, her eyes cloudy, her lips sullen. She looked about ready to break apart, to trail through the cracks and crevices of the car in wisps of smoke. He couldn't think of anything to say.

They ate dinner while parked at a gas station, chewing on cold sandwiches, listening to a local countdown of 70s hits. "Poetic," Anthony said, hearing the opening notes of "She's Gone." He turned off the radio, and they finished their sandwiches amid the muffled sounds of the trucks pulling in and out of the station.

It was early dusk when they checked into the motel outside Ranger's Field. Laura stood in the parking lot, looking up at the decaying doorways, the sagging shingles. "Kelsey's been here," she said. "Been here a lot."

Anthony didn't respond. He retrieved their bags from the trunk. Laura came around to him. "You mind staying with me? Stop me from going anywhere or doing things I wouldn't do?"

"Sure. Whatever you want."

She smiled that sad smile, laid a gentle hand on his arm, then started towards the motel. He stared after her, listening to the crunch of her footfalls on the gravel, watching the sweep of her hair in the late wind. As real as anyone he had ever seen, as anyone who had ever touched him. But somehow from air. From nothing at all.

Inside their room, he ran the shower, checked the sheets. "It'll do," he said, removing his shoes, shuffling off his watch. "You can take the shower if you want. I think I'll skip it tonight."

"Okay." Laura idled in the doorway. "You know, I haven't thanked you yet. For coming with me. Putting up with me."

"It's all right. I think I'm just riding it out. Seeing where it goes." He sat on the edge of the bed and rubbed his eyes. "If I'm being honest, it feels like all this isn't even happening. It's like I'm asleep."

She smiled. "Is there some philosophy thing in there?"

"I thought you would say something like that. Because Kelsey would, right?" He could hear the unsettled nerves in her lack of a response.

"Sorry," he said.

"You're fine."

As she showered, Anthony spread a blanket over the carpet and lay with an arm behind his head, scrutinizing the cracks in the ceiling, searching vainly for an explanation that would provide order to the sur-real play his life had become. What was he doing, taking this ghost woman to see a family who thought her dead, who had buried her? Who would believe him or even entertain his story? Not a single sane person. No one who presumed to understand with some certainty the mechanics and orientation of the world. He had been such a person just days prior. Student. Teacher. Supposedly interested in knowl-edge, learning, but as he lay there and felt for the first time a vast loss of faith in science and rationality, he realized he was more disturbed than curious. "There's nothing the human mind can't solve," his father told him once, adding with a wink, "with some good, old-fashioned curiosity."

But he wasn't curious about this woman. He wasn't curious about what she heralded or implied. "Oh, God," he said, closing his eyes, trying to silence the thoughts, trying to sink into the comforting, muffled sound of the shower. He wasn't chasing a cosmic mystery with the childlike innocence cham-pioned by his father. He was chasing Kelsey, miring himself in a mystery that was both infinitely more mundane and infinitely more multifarious. That woman was a cosmos in and of herself, a self-contained universe with as many perplexing contra-dictions and unknowable truths. He thought of the pale, baggy-eyed girl in scrubs sitting listlessly at the cafeteria every day, more dead than alive, more spirit than body. He had been chasing that mystery for years, and for what?

"Nothing," he said, turning over, willing himself to sleep. "Nothing at all."

After he had fallen asleep, Laura sat idly on the bed, tugging at her wet hair, clutching a towel to her damp flesh. Not mine, she thought. Not mine. She curled into a ball, challenging herself to dream. Something mine. Something mine. Anything mine. Her fingers roved her collar, searching unconsciously for the comforting presence of the rosary. The real Laura would have prayed. She would have turned to God for answers. Maybe she wouldn't have needed answers. Confidently, powerfully, she would have figured it out on her own. Or was that only the impression Kelsey had of her? Didn't Laura seek in Kelsey comfort of her own? Wasn't she terrified of being alone?

She turned over and faced the ceiling. "Dear God," she breathed. "Help me. Show me."

The dark above her remained silent. Even when she wept, the space yielded nothing.

In the morning, they ate breakfast at the nearby diner. Anthony paced a second cup of coffee. Across from him, Laura chewed on bacon and egg yolk. She wore a pair of cheap, store-bought sunglasses, a last-minute recommendation from Anthony. "If people see you, they're going to ask questions," he said.

She had just laughed at him. "Ain't every day you see a ghost. Probably most exciting thing that ever happened to this town. Laura Brackett, back from the dead." She had slanted the sunglasses down her nose, smiled, summoned all the powers of seduction at her disposal—and he could tell they were many—but something in her eyes was missing. Every word was stolen. Every laugh and gesture was borrowed. Both knew it, and anything convincing in the facade was fading fast. Increasingly, Laura went silent. Her eyes glazed. She stumbled on her words.

They drove down the picturesque main street of Ranger's Field, past the sleepy storefronts and into the lush neighborhoods. Even the town was out of place, out of time, Anthony thought. Laura said nothing throughout the drive, peering out the window, staring with no discernible interest at the buildings, the trees. Recollecting, maybe? Pining? He didn't know.

At last, they came upon the Brackett home. Cherry-red and accentuated by a shaved lawn and speckled walkway, the house seemed to Anthony even more surreal than the rest of Ranger's Field. Beside him, Laura removed her glasses and snorted. "Don't think too much of it. The money's running out."

After she said this, the property's blemishes became suddenly apparent. The lawn's cut was not as precise as he first thought, and the green was patchy, broken by squares of withered yellow and brown. The speckled walkway was cracking. The roof was missing scattered shingles. The house was impressive at a glance, but time had done its work and would continue to do so.

"Let's go," Laura said. She stepped out of the car and was halfway to the porch when Anthony caught up to her.

"Wait a second. These people—your mother, your son—they think you're dead. No thought about what you'll say?"

"I shouldn't need to say anything. Not if I'm really Laura."

Before he could protest further, she rang the doorbell. Anthony prepared himself for the confusion and anguish, maybe even the fury. Laura had been dead, what, two weeks? Less? What would that look like on the faces of these people? How would they react to this ghost on their doorstep?

Another thought intruded: he knew nothing of the Brackett family. He didn't know about Laura's mother or son. He didn't know the husband. Kelsey had never mentioned anything about them. Standing there, about to upend a family's life, he wondered if he was wrong to have brought Laura. Maybe this *was* a grift, but not the one he initially thought. The grift was of their collective grief and goodwill, a swindle of their need for closure and reconciliation. Maybe some god up high—not benevolent, but sinister—was guiding their strings as he thought amusing, arranging their pieces in ways unintended by nature.

Or maybe there was no god, no puppeteer. Just need. Just desire.

Kelsey's desire. For Laura?

When no one answered the door, he touched her arm. "We can come back later."

Laura was quiet, surveying the porch. She nudged aside one of the potted plants under the windowsill. A key lay underneath. "Laura's memory," she said, unlocking the door. "Or Kelsey's. Maybe it's the same now."

"You're going inside?"

"It's my house, isn't it? You can stay in the car if you want."

Reluctantly, he followed her into the foyer. The house was silent save for the creak of the wood under their feet and the chime of the grandfather clock at the base of the stairs. "Orange," said Laura. She sniffed the air. "Never used to smell like that. Not before."

She moved distractedly, her gaze lingering on each feature of the house long after her body had turned to the next. She ran her hand over the stucco walls, the brocade upholstery. She gazed at the paintings of sun-bathed wildlife and scenic countryside. Anthony followed her, watching her with the same intensity with which she reviewed the den. Was she appraising? Cross-referencing the inventory with her mental ledger? He almost asked her when both their gazes fell upon the mantelpiece. An array of gold- and silver-framed photographs dominated the space, and each featured the same head of blonde hair, the same pair of blue eyes. Anthony and Laura studied in time-lapse the maturation of the little girl in a tutu to the young woman in a flamenco dress. They watched the radiant smile widen, grow smart, grow self-assured, and then diminish into a more pained, wistful face. They saw the head of long, leonine hair suddenly vanish, replaced by head wraps of purple and pink. They studied the faces of mother and boy-friend, husband and son—and one other, one that was unfamiliar, that of a grim-faced, short-haired, stout-nosed girl in blocky glasses and ratty sweater. This girl also changed across the photographs, shed-ding the sweater, growing the hair, substituting the grimace for a smirk.

"Kelsey," Anthony said. "And Laura."

Laura plucked the final photograph from the line and wiped away the light sheen of dust. She traced with her fingers the shape of the woman's face under the glass—traced the shape of the baby boy's face beside that of the woman. She sat down and stared at the pair of faces.

"Is that him?" asked Anthony. "Your son?"

"Her son," she corrected him softly. "I never held him like that. I don't remember it."

"Maybe we should leave."

Silently, she placed the photograph back in its place, careful to arrange it just as it had been. Almost reverentially, she stepped back, took in one last time the arc of a life. Anthony waited for her quietly at the doorway of each room as she explored the house. She felt the granite countertops of the kitchen. She pressed her feet into the carpet of the study. She paused before the sliding doors that led to the back porch, and then she proceeded up the stairs and through the bedrooms. All throughout her tour, she assessed everything with a keen, watchful eye, as though afraid of missing a single detail or overlooking a salient clue.

"This was Laura's room," she said, staring into the dark of what was now a guest bedroom. The walls were bare, the bed stiff. "Used to be pink, with glow-in-the-dark stars. Do you smell it?"

Anthony shook his head. "What should I smell?"

"Her. The lilac and rosemary. What Kelsey always smelt."

Next, she paused at the door to the master bedroom. "Where Mama slept. And then where Laura slept? With Pete?" The certainty left her voice gradually with each room until finally, peering into the sunlit, cream-colored nursery, she had no words at all.

The nursery was small, furnished only with a white, wooden crib and a plain, pine dresser. Plastic stars were arranged in uneven clumps across the ceiling. A stuffed giraffe and zebra lay among a wreckage of scattered letter blocks and an overturned toy train. Laura looked at each item, and though her lips moved, her words were whimpers.

"Are you all right?" Anthony asked. "We should leave. Go back."

"I don't remember this," she said. "This room. I've never been here. Oh, Jesus. Sweet Jesus. I've never been here. I shouldn't be here."

He had her halfway towards the stairs when they heard the front door open below. "I've got him, Pete," came a tired, matronly voice, at first distant, then close, coming up the stairs. "I'll put him to bed. You put the bags away."

"That's Mama," said Laura breathlessly. "Tony, that's my mama."

Angela Brackett reached the second floor, swathed in all black, hair unkempt and half-gray, a baby boy asleep against her shoulder. When she saw the pair across from her, she did not scream. She stared with muted confusion, eyes hazy, mouth limp. Slowly, in phases, the wrinkles of her face pulled together. The eyes watered. Her voice left her in discordant jumps. "Pete! Pete, come up here! Come up here now!"

"What's wrong?" sounded another voice from downstairs, followed by a thundering up the steps. Just like his mother-in-law, Pete made it to the top and froze. He stared with the same bewilderment, the same pain, but his legs betrayed him. He crumpled, sobbing, balled fists over his eyes. His son, roused, nearly cried from the distress, but then he also saw the face of his mother, alive and pristine, more stunning than any photograph or painting could ever hope to match. Laura remained quiet and still. Anthony was at a loss.

"Look, Hunter," said Angela softly, stroking the boy's hair and kissing him. "It's your mama. It's my baby. I told you. I told you she wasn't gone. I told you she'd be with us again." Angela approached, whispering into the boy's ear, her eyes never leaving the phantom of her daughter. "My baby," she said, again and again. "My baby. My baby."

Laura stared into the glimmering, gray eyes of the old woman. She stared into the clear, cyan eyes of the young boy. She drew on all the knowledge of the Laura Kelsey knew, the Laura who calculated, the Laura who studied and assessed. Keen and sharp, that Laura would be able to tell if she was this woman's daughter, this boy's mother. No, she would know. It wasn't a question of perception, but intuition, a recognition between souls. The real Laura would know her mother and son. No appearance or pretense could veil them. No front would pass muster.

"My baby." Angela closed the distance. She looked into the young, unblemished face. "He heard me. Every second, praying, and he heard me. He brought you back to us. He brought you back to me."

"I don't think I'm the person you want me to be," Laura said. "I—"

"Hunter, your mama is here. She's really here." Angela extended the boy towards her. "Hold him. Hold him, please. Let him touch you. Let him feel you."

She passed the quiet, wide-eyed boy into Laura's arms. She took him awkwardly, having no memory of ever holding a child, possessing no instinct for nurturing an infant. "I'll help you," said Angela, arranging her arms, positioning her hands. Off to the side, Anthony watched. From the floor, through his tears, Pete watched as well, waiting for Laura to recognizably nuzzle Hunter's cheek, to playfully bite his hair. All of them waited for the sign, the confirmation of fidelity, none more than Laura herself.

Hunter cooed. His large, sad eyes searched her own. Tell me, she thought. Show me. What I'm supposed to do. Who I'm supposed to be. You're the only one who'd know.

But there was nothing in the boy's face, nothing in her own depths, depths that were not deep at all, less an ocean than a puddle, less an expanding universe than a collapsing star.

"I'm sorry," she said, pressing her face against Hunter's head, dampening his hair with her tears. "I'm not her. I can't be her."

"My baby." Angela took her face in her hands. "What are you saying? You're my baby, and I'm your mama. He's your boy. He's your boy—"

Then, like a light gone out, Angela stopped. Laura knew that she found nothing as well in the stolen face, nothing that matched with the woman in the photographs downstairs, the passionate dancer, the aspiring teacher, the patient survivor, the loving mother. As Angela's face contorted, the mind behind the shaken eyes desperately trying to reconcile, to understand, Laura had her answer at last. What could be more telling than the fact that she felt no heartbreak for this second death, that she saw the pain and grief and felt nothing?

"Tony," she said, "let's go."

Gently, she pulled away Angela's hands. She didn't spare any of them a second glance as she descended the stairs. Behind her, Anthony studied the slow-moving grief of the mother and husband. The darkness would be all the denser for this sudden, fleeting flash of light. They would wonder forever.

Only the boy, looking over Angela's trembling shoulders, watched them leave without misery. He wouldn't know. He couldn't. For him, thought Anthony, what was his mother but a vague presence of warmth? What would she be, as the years wore on and the boy filled in more memory than he remembered? He looked at the woman in front of him. What was she now?

Back in the car, he turned to Laura. "You okay?"

"No." She wiped her eyes and sniffled. "But there ain't nothing to say."

"What do you want to do now?"

"Take me to her. I need to see for myself."

Like the rest of Ranger's Field, the cemetery was oddly quaint and inviting. The greenery was uneven in length and density, the headstones uneven in size and color. Floral arrangements and balloons dotted the scene, also motley in their shapes and imperfections. Fitting for this little, out-of-time town to have such a small, out-of-time cemetery. In twenty years, thought Anthony, it would look the same. In forty. In sixty. Never changing. Staying the same forever, as though preserved and embalmed like the bodies housed beneath.

They came upon the unassuming headstone of Laura Brooks, notable only for the mound of recently moved dirt, eye-catching only because of the geraniums and roses resting languidly, sadly, against the stone. Laura knelt before the headstone. She took up handfuls of dirt. When she opened her fists, the wind carried the dirt away, leaving only grime-coated palms.

"I can't even hold that much," she said. "It's going away, Tony. Every second. Every second, I feel less and less of her. Like a fucking blanket that's burning, or that got eaten up by moths. She's leaving me, and there ain't nothing underneath. I'm empty."

She sat there, wiping away tears and smudging her cheeks. "I'm painted on. I'm fucking painted on. It's a tacky job, too, and I can't do a goddamn thing about it. I was *me*, Tony. I was me, just fucking days ago. And then it's like the glue gave out. Whatever Kelsey put together to make me, it ain't strong. It's not built to last."

"Maybe you're not Laura," Anthony said, "but you are someone. You think, and you feel. That has to count for something. Maybe when it's over, and there's no more Laura left, you can be whoever you want to be. You'll get to decide that."

She laughed. "That sounds like something you'd say. But I don't think you're right. When it's over, I don't think there'll be anything left at all."

They stared at the headstone, the final, monumental reminder. The only thing that would last once the body had decayed, the dress had disintegrated, and the casket had rotted. But even the headstone would lose meaning. The name would fade from memory. There would be no more associations. People would pass by this headstone and think nothing of it just as they would think nothing of the countless others. Signs without referents. Eventually, not even signs.

"She was her life," Laura said at length. "She was her people, the things that happened to her. But I don't have any of that. What does that make me? If I have no life, what am I?"

Anthony didn't have an answer for her. He could have evoked Sartre or Baudrillard or Saussure—but all his philosophy seemed powerless to comfort a woman whose very identity was splintering. Even he was lost, thinking not of Laura or even Kelsey, but his father. His father telling him he actually hadn't blown it, that he still had time to figure it out, whom he was, what he wanted to be. He believed that suddenly. It felt right. For him and for her. For everybody.

But his conviction waned as he looked into Laura's frightened face—not the face of a grown woman, but that of a toddler lost in a crowd. No, that of a newborn, assaulted by shapes and sounds without form or order, trying vainly to make sense of a chaotic world.

"Let's go back to the motel," he said, helping her up. "You can rest. Think it through."

She went with him wordlessly. There was less of her leaving that cemetery than had entered it. There would be less of her with every moment.

Laura was silent the rest of the afternoon. Anthony left her at the motel, opting instead to cruise around the town and survey the landmarks: the high school, the strip mall, the bowling alley. All places the real Laura—the *original* Laura, he corrected himself—had likely treated as her stomping grounds. And Kelsey had been alongside her, the stereotypical sidekick, the obligatory best friend. Only something had separated the two. The unbreakable bond had been severed. Whatever happened, the Kelsey he met and had tried for so long to understand was the result. The places she went at night, the people she met. The things she did. This was her origin story. All this time, he had tried to ignore it, tried to claim it didn't matter, the past was the past, but that was moronic. After all, he was searching her past like the stupid, hopeless romantic he was. Of course, the past mattered. Of course, it would never go away.

When he returned to the motel, Laura was curled up in a ball on the bed, asleep. Anthony spent time in front of the blurry, grainy television, and as the sun dipped below the horizon and filled the room with flaming light, he turned off the television and settled into an unsteady sleep.

In the night, shaken awake, he made out Laura's vague form over him in the dark.

"What's wrong?" he asked groggily, lifting himself on his elbows. "You okay?"

He was barely able to discern the hue of her hair, the sheen of her skin. Then, as his eyes adjusted, he saw she was naked. Shadows obscured her face.

"Laura," he said, rising, "let's get you back to bed—"

She forced him down, straddled him. He stared up into the indistinct darkness of her face. She was surprisingly strong. Her hands closed around his like cuffs.

"This is what you wanted," she said. Her voice was cold, low. She didn't sound like herself. She didn't sound like anyone. "To fuck me. To put your dick inside me. Make yourself feel good or strong or whatever it is you need today."

"That's not—"

"Tell me I'm wrong. Tell me it's not what you want."

"It's not what I want. I didn't come here with you for that."

She didn't say anything, but one hand released its ironclad grip and traveled down his chest. Her hair swept over his face. Her lips grazed his. She had no taste, no smell. He tried to rise again, but she held him down. Her face scoured his own.

"It's what *I* want," she said. She undid his shirt buttons, his belt buckle. Before he could protest, she kissed him. Her fingers wandered over his waistline. They foraged downwards.

"Stop," he said between her kisses. "Stop—"

"I want you. She wants you."

She took hold of him. He groaned from the sudden surge of pleasure, the electric jolt of activated nerves, but he resisted, retained enough sense to take her by the arms and pull her off him. They twisted, tussled, and then he was atop her, pinning her down by the wrists, looking into the vague pool of darkness that had replaced her face. With a moment's lapse, he would have been finding her lips in that void, would have been pressing himself into her depths. It took everything to unlatch and move himself away.

"She wants me?" he asked. "Then where is she? Where's Kelsey?"

"She's here," came the weak, exhausted voice from the dark. "She's right here."

No, he wanted to say. I would know if she were here. I would know. But as the words prepared themselves on his tongue, he knew suddenly they were untrue. He wouldn't know. He couldn't know. He didn't know the woman in the dark, if that's what she was—didn't know where Laura began and Kelsey ended. And if that were Kelsey, he would never be able to tell because he didn't know her, either. Even after all this time. Even after this bizarre, inexplicable journey, he still didn't know. He would never.

She wept and squirmed, hugging herself, pulling at herself. "Please, Tony. Please. Help me. Do something. Do something, please! Anything. *Anything*! It hurts so much! It just keeps hurting, and it won't stop!"

He wrapped himself around her in the darkness, held her the way he held Kelsey once. "It's okay. Just go to sleep. It'll be better in the morning."

He heard her tears in her voice. "It won't be. It won't be."

In the morning, amid dust motes and slants of sunlight, he awoke to an empty room. There were no traces of her apart from scattered, golden wisps of hair on the carpet. Outside, the parking lot stretched on as if miles in length, void of life save for the faint birdsong in the air. Anthony drove, passing by all the familiar locales, the school, the house, the cemetery, but he never saw the distinctive shining hair or glistening eyes. He didn't know why he searched—she was his responsibility, maybe, not by choice, but by default. No one knew she existed. No one cared that with every second, she was losing herself, becoming not someone else, but no one at all. How long would it take for the vestiges of Laura to disappear? What would go first, the memories of her erstwhile home, the recollections of her supposed husband, her alleged son? What would go last? She would stalk the roadways and the fields, lurk in the shadows of dying lights, sight dimming, hearing fading. Like a dementia patient, would she struggle to retain memory, to situate herself in time and place? Would she forget her name? Except it wasn't her name. It was an imposition, gifted by that smirking puppeteer, a demiurge playing at being a real god. His works were defective, derivative. Their gold sheen cracked to reveal lead underneath.

Back at the diner, he contemplated one cup of coffee after another. The waitress refilled his cup. "Where's your friend?" she asked. Anthony looked into the steaming stream of coffee, into the warm smile and rosy cheeks of the waitress. She was curly-haired and pretty, radiant in her own way. In her face, perhaps, was the imprint of something that outlasted death.

"She went home," he said. "To her family."

"She looked a little familiar. Like I'd seen her before."

"Probably not. She wasn't from around here."

He returned to the car, enjoying one last time the light and wind of Ranger's Field. On the road, he expected to see her in the distance, a lonely figure hitchhiking or wading through wheat. When the Houston skyline loomed ahead, he accepted that he would never see her again. Laura was gone. This trip, like a dream after sleep, was over.

14

On the first day after Laura's departure, Kelsey lay atop her bed, buffeted by the cold, harsh air of the ceiling fan. There were flashes of anger, but they passed quickly, leaving in their wake only a vast, cosmic emptiness without stars, comets, or lights.

On the second day, Kelsey ate and showered. When she came back to her bed, she considered calling Anthony, but her pride welled up and kept her hand from the phone. Don't be weak, she thought. Stop crying. Don't you have any dignity?

On the third day, she returned to work. The girls said she looked terrible. Dr. White offered her condolences. Kelsey said little, thought little. On the fourth day, she worked, and she did so on the fifth, the sixth, the seventh. At no moment did she feel better. Sitting over a gaping mouth, depressor in one gloved hand, chisel in the other, there was only the gnawing sense of something missing. She would squint at X-rays, and her eyes would water suddenly, surprisingly. Her coffee tasted bitter, no matter how much cream, sugar, or liquor she mixed in. Staring out at the skyline from the windows in the lobby, she would see Laura's face in the glass. She would see her brother's.

What Laura said before leaving stuck in her mind. Her brother Dylan. Her mother. The accident that shattered her family years before—the accident she sometimes liked to blame, half-jokingly, for the way she was, the damage she thought done to herself. Normal people had normal families and normal childhoods. They didn't have nearly as much trouble connecting to others, expressing themselves, feeling things. On the occasion that she talked to Anthony's mother, there were always the questions. When are you going to get married? When are you going to have children? Oh, you live in such a progressive age, you can have a career and a family, you can do it all. Get too deep into your thirties, and you'll miss your chance. You'll have a premature baby. You'll have complications. You'll be raising a child into middle age.

Once, the enigma had been falling in love, having sex, finding a partner. Those remained mysteries for the most part, or at least mutually exclusive. All the sex Kelsey ever had was never about love. Even with Anthony, despite how hard she wished, how much she struggled to imagine it, there was little beyond the mechanical pleasure, rote and nondescript for the longest time. The closest had been that night with Laura in the apartment, but Kelsey only held her, only kissed her, only eased her to sleep. If that wasn't love, then what else could it be? What more could someone have? Honestly, it felt indulgent. The weak knees. The butterflies in the stomach. The hammering heart. All of it like wishing to bite into the forbidden fruit, to see God, to overstep natural bounds.

She had never seen her father play it out for her. There had been women over the years, irregular, inconsistent. Mary Beth, with her blonde curls and red nails. Susan, with her fat face and long eyelashes. Veronica, or "Vero" as she insisted, the kindest of the three, the youngest. Returned to Mexico to care for her ailing mother, before she could teach Kelsey everything it meant to be a woman, to understand her place, her possibilities, whether those possibilities really were infinite or if, in fact, they were constrained, if men and women could not inhabit the same spheres after all. Perhaps the truth was that she left because of Kelsey's father. Maybe they all left because he was as broken as Kelsey was, as unable to love, as unable to connect. And so that mystery of marriage, that riddle of love, rearing children, raising a family, all of it would stay locked away in the dark. Not for her. Denied to her. A privilege for those lucky enough to have their losses delayed, their tragedies postponed.

She could hardly remember her brother Dylan. Everything about that time seemed so vague and distant. She knew what her father told her, that her mother had been walking with Dylan on the beach, him all of two years old, a little dark-haired thing on pale legs, when a wave came in unusually hard and tore him from her mother's grip.

Her father never told her what came afterwards, but she could imagine the scene well enough. A woman kneeling on the sand, screaming, wailing, poised to dive into the water if not for her husband holding her back, if not for him swimming, finding nothing, spitting out water, yelling the boy's name. The little girl watching from a distance, not knowing what it meant, but feeling all the same something heavy drop in her chest.

And that little girl brought him back?

Kelsey lay underneath the fan, arms outstretched, waiting, thinking. Thinking about what that meant, how it could have been. Brought him back. Brought him back. Then where was he? What happened to him? Why couldn't she remember? Oh, if only Laura were there with her. If only she could hold someone, anyone, even Anthony, even Pete. Anyone.

She sat up. If she had brought him back, her father would know.

She left for San Antonio the next morning, pallid and glassy-eyed. At a truck stop, she ate a bagel, read the newspaper. Unemployment. Shooting. Buzzwords that felt nebulous, unreal. The coffee was bitter—always bitter. She squeezed the bagel in her hand, broke it in two, whisked away crumbs and flakes.

A man passed by, faceless, and placed a ringed hand on her shoulder. "You okay, miss?" His voice was warm, coaxing, like he had eaten a jar of honey or lined his mouth with gauze. A wolf masquerading as a timid sheep or a doting grandmother.

She stared ahead. She drank more of that bitter coffee. "I'm fine."

Driving. Stopping. Resting. Eating. The horizon bleeding at dusk. Feeling herself in a dingy restroom, trying to feel something, anything. At every moment, replaying in her mind when Laura left, when she left Laura. Never keep her. Always leave. Always lose.

In San Antonio, she reserved a hotel room for a couple of nights, the same room she and Pete once used for their occasional rendezvous, the same room she used for whoever else caught her eye. Blue carpet. Gray walls. The paintings had changed, now prairie vistas, seaside cottages. She laid a hand on the bed cover, soft and flat, and imagined it wrinkled, wet, and odorous. She closed her eyes and focused hard on the smells, the way sweat and saliva combined and hung over you in the heat, how skin and hair stank. Nothing came, no epiphany, no insight. There was only the light bleeding through the window drapes, only the hum of the air conditioner as she lowered the temperature one degree, two degrees, three, four, five. The hairs on her neck and arms stood upright. She caressed herself. She tried to sleep.

Night came. She sat on the edge of the River Walk, fans above her blowing crisp, wet air, utensils clinking amid the talk and laughter of the open-air restaurant. The occasional boat floated by, trailing green light, tour guide rehashing a tired joke or factoid. She had memories of all this, memories of when she was much smaller, walking between her father and her faceless, shapeless mother, having her cheeks painted, licking fingers sticky with sugar and pretzel, measuring the length of Bowie knives with her arm at the Alamo.

At the time, the river water seemed so deep, so prohibitive. Now, she felt like reaching out and breaking the black surface. The immeasurable depth wasn't frightening so much as comforting, as though an assurance of something inevitable. To sink into that, plunge deeper and deeper, let go. Not swept away like her brother, but swallowed, subsumed. Given of herself.

She scanned the other tables. Most were families, little boys and little girls beleaguering parents like she once did. There were couples, some partners sitting close to each other, others sitting apart. A lone woman sat farther off, also preoccupied with the gleam of the water, the chill of the night. They saw each other. Their eyes locked. Kelsey's lips spread into a smile.

An hour later, they were in the hotel room, the woman removing her jacket, undoing her bun. She said her name was Katie, from McAllen, in the city for a two-day conference on special education. Kelsey studied her hair, her freckles. She had a slender face, a pointed chin. Her eyes seemed perennially on the verge of crying.

"I ordered a bottle," Kelsey said, gesturing to the wine on the desk. "Do you want some?"

Katie smiled. "I don't drink. Sorry."

"A good girl. That's nice." Kelsey uncorked the bottle and raised it straight to her lips. She drank, kicked off her heels, looked down at the city lights below. "So, Katie. What do you want to do first?"

"I don't know." There was that nervous laugh again, the bashful blush. "I don't even know what I'm doing here. I don't do things like this." She sat on the bed and slipped off her shoes, removed her watch. "Do you?"

"Do I what?"

"Do this. Do you do this a lot?"

"I used to." Kelsey chuckled. "I must be sad if I'm doing it again." She came over to Katie and stroked her arms, caressed her legs. She unbuttoned Katie's blouse. "Why don't you tell me more about yourself? How old are you? What's your favorite color?"

"Okay," said Katie, breathing deeply, feeling the kisses on her neck, on her collarbone. "I'm twenty-eight. My favorite color is pink. I didn't think I was going to be a teacher. I, uh—I'm getting married in the summer."

Kelsey glanced at her hand. "I don't see a ring."

"I don't wear it when I'm not with him."

Kelsey undid the belt and unzipped the slacks. "Tell me about him."

"Okay. His name is Connor"—a sharp intake of air as Kelsey's lips found their place—"and he does IT work for a bank. Updates their security, I guess, keeps the computers working. Honestly, I don't really know what he does. We don't talk about it."

"Do you think he'd like you being here right now?"

"Probably not. Except I think"—another short breath—"I think he's been cheating. I've seen the messages. He doesn't hide it very well."

"Most men don't." Kelsey looked up at her, at the pink cheeks, the glassy eyes. "Do you like that so far?"

A giggle. A gasp. "I do. I really do. You've done this a lot."

"Lie down."

Katie did as she was told, and Kelsey knelt over her, threw off her own blouse, her undershirt, her bra. She placed Katie's hand on her breast. "Feel good?"

"Feels really good."

Kelsey kissed her, fondled her. All around her was cold, bitingly cold, but the girl's skin was warm, her blood aflame, her heart beating hard and fast like a drum. The trance. The spell. Kelsey's own heart raced, expectant and hungry. Each kiss grew a little harder, a little rougher, teeth grazing, nibbling. Her hands squeezed tighter.

She was halfway down Katie's torso, leaving kisses, pulling off the slacks completely, when she heard the first whimpers. She raised her head. Tears stained Katie's cheeks. Her crying grew louder.

Kelsey wiped her mouth. She sighed. "Calm down. It'll pass."

"I'm a terrible person," Katie said. "What am I doing? My God, what am I *doing*?"

Kelsey sat and listened to the crying. Then she stood and put on her bra, her undershirt, her blouse. She drank from the wine bottle again. She looked out at the night. She waited.

When Katie was gone at last, Kelsey sat against the wall. She sniffed the air, searched desperately for those comforting scents. In the shower, she felt herself, tugged at her skin, pinched her nipples. Nothing. Even the scalding water was nothing, nothing at all. She dried, wrapped herself in the towel, curled up in the tub, and waited for the sun to rise.

It was mid-morning when she arrived at her old house, makeup-less, in jeans and a jacket, hair pulled back. The sad little house, blue in color despite the white wood and gray shingles, slumped into the brown-patched grass. She picked at the potted plant hanging from the porch awning, broke off a shriveled leaf, rubbed it between her fingers until it was nothing. A stained-glass ornament—one she painted long ago, depicting a mockingbird—hung beside the plant.

Her father hugged her tightly when he saw her. "You didn't call," he said, leading her inside, "didn't text. What's going on?"

"Nothing. I just felt like seeing you."

He was slouching more, she noticed. His beard seemed grayer. He had more wrinkles. All alone in this decrepit place, this house like a long-dead fire, cold at the edges, the little warmth at the center dwindling, disappearing. The day would come soon, sooner than expected, when she would be cooking for him, wheeling him around, helping him dress. Burying him.

He put on a pot of coffee, cracked eggs, sprinkled cinnamon and nutmeg on yolk-soaked bread. As he cooked breakfast, she looked at the photographs of herself, her father, and her mother, of the two of them holding her as a baby. She stared for a long time at the photographs of her brother, so few, as if those there were more for the sake of formality than genuine desire. In her room, she passed her hand over the movie posters on the walls, blew dust off CD covers, held aloft an old diary, the pages crinkled, the ink faded. She read a random page: "Dear diary, another shitty day." She laughed at that, but as she looked over the room, she regretted that the girl who filled the diary was gone, as dead as Laura was.

She went out to the backyard, squinting from the glare, dead grass crunching under her shoes. She stood over the space where her old dog Molly had been buried. Under her breath, she sang the lullaby she would coo to the dog as they both fell asleep. She recalled lying under Molly's weight in bed, feeling her cold snout, enjoying the warm lap of her tongue, twining her fingers through the dog's soft, caramel fur.

"You look good," her father said as they sat at the kitchen table.

"So do you."

"Bullshit." He laughed, coughed, drank his coffee. "I'm not getting any dates, that's for sure. Unless those ladies like their pie with extra filling."

"That is gross, Dad."

"Well, it took me a while to come up with. The least you can do is laugh."

She cut into the French toast with a fork and chewed a mouthful. She stroked his hand.

"Are you actually seeing anyone?"

"No. But you knew that. How's Anthony?"

"He's good. We're good." She sipped the coffee, fought the urge to gag. Still bitter.

The clock in the corridor ticked. Wind swept up leaves in the yard. Kelsey pushed away her cup, her plate. She kneaded her hands.

"Something happened. Something I need to talk to you about."

Her father waited.

"I got a call the other night. This guy I knew from college, Pete Brooks. Well, not technically from college, but he was Laura's boyfriend. Her husband."

Laura's name brought sudden light into her father's eyes. "Laura? You talked to Laura? How is she?"

"I didn't talk to her." Kelsey paused. "She died, Dad. Apparently, she got sick again, and they couldn't stop it. Pete was calling to tell me. I went to Ranger's Field. I went to the funeral. And then I came back." Her hands shook, so she balled them into fists. "She had a son—*has* a son. He must be two or three. No older than that."

Just like that, the light went out of her father's eyes. He sat back. He said nothing.

"I'm sorry I didn't tell you," Kelsey said. "I didn't know how I felt. I shouldn't have even gone there. But stupid me, I had to see her again. I loved her."

"We both did. She was like a sister to you. Like a daughter to me."

Kelsey smiled. She wiped her eyes.

"Anyway," she said slowly, "had it ended there, I wouldn't be here. But it didn't end. Because the morning after I got back, when I woke up, Laura was there. She was *there*, Dad. In my bed. Sleeping. Alive. Healthier than I'd ever seen her. Laura was next to me. She was right fucking next to me."

More than light had drained from her father's face. The color, the little warmth. He stood and turned away from her. He took a step and almost fell. She stared after him.

"How is that possible? Tell me, Dad. How is that possible? I saw them bury her, so how could she be there, healthy? Am I crazy? Is that it? Because Tony saw her, too. Other people saw her. It wasn't just me. I wasn't imagining it. She is alive, and she's somewhere right now, and I—I think it's because of me. Because I wanted her back. Because I called out to her."

She was crying, bawling, shielding her face. Her father clutched his chest, rocked back and forth. When the tears subsided, Kelsey touched his shoulder. "Dad? Daddy, what's wrong?"

He was quiet, still rocking, breathing heavily.

"She said something to me," Kelsey went on quietly. "She told me I had done it before. That I had called someone before. Do you know? You do, don't you?"

Her father turned to her, and she wanted to cry again, such was the look on his face, as if he had lost everything, as if he had seen death itself.

"Please tell me the truth," Kelsey said. "Did Dylan come back? Did he really drown, or did he come back?"

There was silence. A long, painful, pregnant wait. And then her father spoke.

15.

As she listened to him speak, Kelsey remembered.

She remembered the wailing first and foremost, an unending, animalistic cry from beyond the door to her parents' bedroom. Standing in front of that door, pushing her palms against it, pressing her ear to the wood. Shivering in the bathtub as her father waited outside. Quivering at the table, her breakfast hardly touched. Squirming under the covers at night, hugging her dolls and stuffed animals as if they could somehow silence that wailing, as if their worn-out thread and black-bead eyes could put an end to the grief.

Sometimes, Kelsey peeked from around the corner, watching her father enter or leave the bedroom with trays of food. In the darkness, barely discernible, was the shape of some figure sitting upright in the bed. Gray, wispy arms. The faint, pale outline of a face. Black holes where the eyes should have been. That figure occasionally turned its shapeless visage towards her, and then the wailing would start again, and Kelsey would run away and latch onto Molly's broad back. She would clutch the dog's fur, press her cheek against it, smell deep of its scent, demanding that the wailing stop, begging that it stop, praying that it stop.

The wailing started that day on the beach. Her brother Dylan, with his head of chocolate hair, his round, brown eyes, there one moment, gone the next, taken with such suddenness he never cried, never yelled, just sank and sucked in great mouthfuls of water and burnt and gagged until the darkness eclipsed him, all probably within minutes, maybe seconds. That day, the water took more than just her brother. The water took her mother, too, and replaced her with that shadowy banshee. Oh, how Kelsey just wanted her mother back. How she wished to be hugged and kissed again, to have her hair tousled, to be acknowledged with that warm smile. More than anything, she wanted the wailing to stop. She wanted that monster in her parents' room to disappear forever.

One night, with the screams coming through the walls, she hid underneath the covers against Molly's warmth and chanted. Dylan. Dylan. Dylan. Come back. Come back. Come back. Not for her sake, but for her mother, to bring her back, to get rid of the monster. She felt so heavy as she chanted, and then she felt as though she were weightless. Warmth surrounded her, swept through her. For a moment, her bleary eyes lit up at the sight of a translucent, pink-hued bubble around her, the bubble warbling as though alive, encapsulating nebulae and speckled with stars. So pretty, she thought. She could fly. She could escape. But as quickly as the mirage appeared, the bubble vanished, the nebulae and stars dissipating like smoke. Her head fell with exhaustion, and her little hands loosened around Molly's thick neck. Fix her, she thought, with the last of her strength. Fix her. Fix her. She fell asleep, the dog licking the tears off her cheeks, soon dreaming the chant, dreaming of what could and should be.

In the morning, all was quiet. Light came in softly through the window. Molly raised her head and sniffed the air. She jumped to the floor, nails clacking against the wood. Kelsey followed her. Her parents were at the kitchen table, her father dark-eyed, her mother so thin, so frail, but discernible, distinct.

"Mommy?" said Kelsey.

The woman looked up. She smiled. "Kelsey. Look, honey. Your brother. Look at your brother. He's here. He's alive."

And then Kelsey saw him. Cradled against her mother's chest was a small, dark head of hair. The boy turned to look at her. He was the same—naked, pale, but the same. Eyes just as big, just as dark. Little pink lips so thin. Staring at her. Staring at her the way he would always stare at her, as though she were someone unrelated to him, someone foreign. As though she were not a person at all, but a ghost haunting the halls of the house, not meant to be there.

Molly came forward hesitatingly, but then her tail wagged, and she nudged the boy with her nose. Kelsey touched his hand. "Dylan?"

From that moment onwards, her mother was inseparable from the boy. She sat with him, played with him, watched television with him. When she showered, he was there. When she went to the restroom, he was there. She fed him, clothed him. He slept beside her. If he disliked the attention, he never showed it. Nonetheless, he was unmistakably Kelsey's brother, her parents' son. Quieter, if anything, but Dylan had always been quiet.

Her mother was back in view, but fixated entirely on the boy. If Kelsey addressed her, she was ignored. If her father said anything, he was dismissed. "Look at him," her mother would say continually, "look at him. He's precious. So, so precious." Stroking his hair, kissing his brow, tickling his stomach. And though he would laugh and giggle, his eyes would be on Kelsey, who was always peeking from around the corner with Molly in tow, scrutinizing this phantom, marveling at the likeness.

"Is that really Dylan?" she asked her father one night as he sat by her bed. "How did he come back?" She looked up at him earnestly, the dog over her legs, the dolls under her arms. "Did they really put him in that big box? In the ground?"

"You know he wasn't in that box," her father said. He patted her hand and smiled. "He got lost out in the sea. You know that."

"And he came back?"

Her father hesitated. He searched for the words. "I guess he did," he said at last. "He must have. How else do you explain it?"

"I was calling him," Kelsey said, her eyes closing, her voice softening. "I kept saying his name. So he could come back, so Mommy could come back. And they did."

Weeks passed. At school, Kelsey said her brother came back, that he got lost and found his way home. She drew a picture of him surrounded by water, a smiling, black-lined stick figure against a chalky, blue backdrop. Mrs. Mathis, her teacher, watched her among the other children, eyed her as they sat on the carpet and read, as they chased one another around the playground.

"I'm concerned," said Mrs. Mathis to Kelsey's father during a conference in the classroom. She was a young woman, blonde hair around her neck, blue-bead rosary upon her collar. She twirled that rosary around her finger as she spoke. "Kelsey keeps saying her brother Dylan is alive. I'm sorry, but I understand he recently passed?"

She showed him the ocean picture, as well as the multiple others drawn by this point: Dylan's stick-figure representation emerging from an oversized box, walking home, being with the rest of the family under the sun, among the flowers and trees. In one picture, there were two Dylans—one free in the open air, walking among people, the other gone, far beneath the black waves, his eyes X-shaped.

Kelsey's father looked at this last picture a long time, holding the paper in both hands, shaking subtly. "I know it can be hard for kids Kelsey's age," Mrs. Mathis went on. "They don't really understand what it means for someone to pass away, especially a close family member like a parent or brother. She might be imagining that he's still there. Has she said anything at home? Talked about him? Talked to him?"

"I haven't heard anything," Kelsey's father said, raising his glassy eyes, mustering his sad smile. "Then again, maybe we haven't been paying enough attention. I'm trying hard. My wife—well, I can barely get her out of bed."

"I'm so sorry." Mrs. Mathis touched his shoulder and smiled in that sweet way she had. "If I can do anything to help, please let me know. I can reach out to the counselors. We can find Kelsey someone to talk to."

"Thank you," said her father, "but I'll talk to her first. Maybe that's all it needs."

After school, in the car, Kelsey cried. "I'm sorry," she said through her tears, "I'm sorry, but he's there, Daddy! He's *there*!"

"I know. I know, sweetie. But people, they won't understand. Where your brother went—when people go away like that—they're not supposed to come back. That's why we can't tell anyone. Not your friends, not Grandpa or Grandma, not your cousins, no one. Do you understand, sweetheart? We can't tell anyone."

She whimpered and pouted. She wiped her eyes with her fists.

"Kelsey." Her father faced her, the familiar smile gone. "Do you understand me?"

"I won't tell anyone," she said.

"Good. Repeat after me. Dylan's gone. He's not back. He's gone. Say it."

"Dylan's gone."

"He's not back. Say it."

"He's not back."

"Good." He took a breath, fixed his hands on the steering wheel. "Your brother's gone, Kelsey. He's not back. He's not coming back. He's never coming back. He's gone forever."

She didn't say anything. She just put her head against the window and waited for her eyes to stop stinging.

A few days later, as they ate dinner, her mother spoon-feeding the boy on her lap, wiping his mouth with a napkin, he knocked the spoon away suddenly. Chopped bits of spaghetti stained the tablecloth. His eyes went wide. Saliva dribbled down his chin.

"Dylan?" Their mother gripped his shoulders, peered into his eyes. "What's wrong? Honey, what's the matter? What's wrong?"

Kelsey and her father watched him, mesmerized by the hugeness of his eyes, the emptiness. There had been light there just seconds before, intelligence, however rudimentary or unformed. It was like a candle flame had gone out or a screen had blackened suddenly. Molly rose from her place at Kelsey's feet. She bared her teeth. She growled.

"Mommy," said the boy, the first word out of his mouth since his reappearance. And then he screamed, a long, high-pitched whine that made Kelsey shiver, made her want to vomit.

"Baby, what's wrong?" her mother kept asking, hugging him, kissing him. "What's the matter? Tell Mommy. Tell Mommy right now. Tell her what's wrong! Tell her!" But he just kept screaming, screaming louder and louder, those big, brown eyes welling up with tears, the little mouth warbling. When finally he exhausted himself to sleep, she retreated with him back to the bedroom. Kelsey stood at the end of the hall with Molly beside her, staring after them, realizing with as much clarity as her young mind could generate that the boy was not her brother. He was something else.

Incidents like that happened more and more frequently. The boy would strike his head, slap his eyes, sometimes so fervently their mother would have to hold down his arms while he wriggled and cried. He would rampage, throw photographs and plates, topple furniture. Other times, he would shut down like that initial episode, become vacant and dark, like a robot whose cord had been unplugged. No matter how much the mother begged or entreated, his body would remain limp. Then the light behind the eyes would hum on. Those episodes lasted longer and longer. Whatever belonged to Dylan inside that body was fading away, depleting. Something had been borrowed that had to be given back.

"What's wrong with Dylan?" asked Kelsey, watching with her father as her mother took the boy back into the bedroom following an episode. "Is he sick?"

Her father said nothing, staring at the closed door with hard eyes, clenching his fists to keep them from trembling.

During one of the ensuing nights, Kelsey lay asleep in bed, Molly curled against her. The dog stirred, baring her fangs, growling. Kelsey awoke and caressed Molly's back. "Come on, Molly," she said groggily, "let's go back to bed."

Then she saw him. The boy stood at her bedside, looking up at her with those large eyes. How he had escaped their mother's grasp she couldn't know, but there he was, still and quiet, staring intently. She stared back. Beside her, Molly kept growling.

"Dylan," Kelsey said.

The boy cocked his head. He didn't blink. "Kelsey." The name left his mouth clean, crisp, as though uttered by someone much older. "Kelsey." The first and second times he had ever said her name since the waves took him. And then he said her name a third time, a fourth time. He kept saying it. "Kelsey. Kelsey. Kelsey. Kelsey."

"Stop, Dylan," she said, her breaths quickening, her limbs shaking. "Stop it right now."

He repeated her name, never blinking. "Kelsey. Kelsey. Kelsey. Kelsey. Kelsey."

"Dylan, stop it! Stop it!" She put her hands over her ears and begged him to stop, saying it over and over again. Molly sensed the agitation and barked. Still the boy stared and chanted.

"Stop it!" She was screaming now, the dog barking louder, the boy never blinking, never moving, simply repeating her name. Her father ran in, turned on the light, and grabbed the boy by his arms.

"What are you doing to her?" he demanded, shaking the small frame, yelling in his face. "What are you doing to her?"

Then he caught himself and realized what he had done, for the boy was red-faced and tear-stricken. He let go of the small arms. He backed away. The mother came into the room and shielded her son. "What are you doing?" she shrieked. "What are you doing to my baby?"

Meanwhile, Kelsey rocked back and forth, still covering her ears, still calling for the chaos to stop. Finally, the commotion did stop, the boy weeping in the mother's arms, the father standing bent and crooked, shaking again, harder than ever before.

Afterwards, Kelsey leaned against her bedroom door, peeking through the yellow-lit crack, listening to the conversation from the kitchen.

"I'm taking him," said her mother. "He's sick. He needs help. And you hate him. I know you do. You don't believe it's him."

"Marie, they think he's dead." Her father's voice was jittery, nervous. "You can't just take him. They'll ask questions. No one will believe it. And what will happen to us? To Kelsey?"

"I don't care. He needs help, Ramon. He's my baby, and he needs help."

"Marie, you saw him. You were with him. You know there is no way he came back."

"But he's here. He's *here*, Ramon. God brought him back to us. You don't believe—you've never believed—but I've been praying. He gave me another chance."

There was no further argument. The light went off. The floorboards creaked as her parents parted. Kelsey returned to bed, hugging Molly tightly, unable to stop herself shaking.

Over the next several days, Dylan worsened, not even eating despite his mother's desperate urgings. Kelsey watched from the hall, her arms linked constantly around Molly's neck. Her father sat, drumming his legs, balling his fists.

"He needs his bath," said Kelsey's mother one night, rising up from the sofa, her eyes dark-ringed, her movements languid, preparing to take the now virtually unresponsive boy to the restroom. She lay awake entire nights, watching his unmoving, pale face, hoping he would rest, hoping he would eat. Her husband took her arm and kissed her cheek.

"I'll wash him," he said. "You go rest."

She turned to him frantically. "I have to be with him. Ramon, I have to be with him—"

"He'll be all right. I promise you he'll be all right."

She shuffled away down the hall, her robe dragging behind her. Kelsey stood at the corner of the hall, but her mother never looked at her. Kelsey turned back to her father, who gave her a smile as he hoisted the boy into his arms.

"She'll be all right," he said, "and so will he." Then the restroom door closed behind him, and the water ran. Kelsey stood there. Molly came up beside her, nudged her with her nose, licked her hand. The water kept running, spreading from underneath the door, soaking Kelsey's socks, her feet. Molly whined and pawed at the door. Still the water ran. Still Kelsey stood, understanding in her vague, childish way something was wrong, but not knowing what to do or how to stop it. And then her father screamed.

The wailing was like that of her mother's on the beach, only stronger, more powerful. Kelsey remembered because she had heard those screams at their inception, following her mother and brother along the shore that day, seeing his small hand slip out of their mother's grip, seeing him disappear into the water. As though there had never been a Dylan, as though he were lead or ink erased, smudged until only the faintest of outlines remained.

The screaming drew out her mother, who struggled with the locked door, who yelled for her husband to open it, to open the fucking door, to stop, to please just stop. And Kelsey's father continued screaming, beating his hands on the tile. Kelsey could hear his life leaving him in those screams. She shut her eyes, put her hands over her ears, wished for it to stop, begged for it to stop. Molly barked. Her mother took the lamp from the den and smashed it against the doorknob. Through the doorway, they all saw the stub of the boy's nose breaking the water of the tub, his hair floating in a dark halo around his head.

"My baby!" The mother took him into her arms, drenching herself, spilling more water out of the overflowing tub. "My baby! My baby!" Father and mother screamed and wailed. Kelsey opened her eyes. Her brother's head lolled over her mother's shoulder. His eyes lingered on hers. His big, round, dead eyes.

Kelsey surveyed the scene before her. Mother crumpled beside the tub, crying and cradling the boy's limp body. Father collapsed against the wall, weeping and pounding his fists. Dog barking and howling. All she wanted was for it to stop. All she wanted was for the noise to go away. She did the only thing she could do: say his name again. Dylan. Dylan. Dylan. Come back. Come back. Come back. She chanted through her tears, her heaving breaths. Dylan. Dylan. Dylan. Come back. Come back. Come back.

Even with her eyes closed, even concentrating as hard as she was, she saw clearly the faint, pale luminescence shimmer over the interior of the house like a purple pollen. The boy's dead eyes undimmed. He flailed in his mother's arms, coughed up water after each spasm. Suddenly, the screaming and wailing stopped. The mother and father each sat and stared blankly. The boy was crying, coughing, but alive. Even Molly looked into the restroom as if stunned, no longer barking, not even whimpering. Kelsey remained chanting with her eyes closed and her ears covered. Come back, she thought. Come back, come back, come back. She stopped only when her father pulled her into his dripping arms, when he cried into the small space of her neck.

"My baby," said her mother, holding the boy. "My baby. My baby."

The old clock chimed in the hallway. Kelsey looked up. She remembered everything.

"She kept saying that," her father said. "All through the night. Never taking her eyes off him. 'My baby. My baby.'" He gulped down what remained of his coffee. His hands shook like they had so many years before.

"She was gone the next day. They both were."

"You killed him," said Kelsey. "You drowned him."

"That wasn't your brother. Your brother died."

"But it *was* him. It *was*."

"Your brother died, Kelsey," her father said more firmly. "I buried him. Even if he wasn't in a coffin, I buried him. Your mother couldn't accept that. Your brother—Dylan—he was a gift from God. I loved him. But whatever that was, it wasn't him."

"How can you be so sure?"

"Because your brother knew us! There was light in his eyes when he looked at us. And that other one, if you hugged him or kissed him, there was nothing. There was nothing there. We had him for weeks, pretending everything was back to normal, but it wasn't. How could it be?"

Kelsey shook her head. She shielded her eyes.

"Kelsey. Listen to me, sweetie. That wasn't him. Your mother left us for him. You didn't remember that, thank God. You were spared that. It was too much for you, and you put it away. You were able to forget."

"So, you lied to me."

"No. Your brother died. Your mother left. Those things are true."

"But he came back, Dad. He came back twice. Because he was dead, wasn't he? When you put him in the tub?"

Her father was quiet, shaking very noticeably, tightening his fists.

"He was dead for a long time," he said finally. "It didn't take long."

"God." Kelsey clutched her stomach, drew in a heavy breath. "And I brought him back. I called to him. I wanted Mom back, and I wanted all of it back, and I called to him. And I called to Laura." She cupped a hand over her mouth. "I called to Laura,

Dad, and I brought her back. I fucking did that. My God."

She cried. Her father reached over and squeezed her shoulder. "Kelsey," he said, "Kelsey, sweetie, we don't know why that boy was here. And we don't know why"—he struggled to fight his own tears—"we don't know why there might be another Laura, or whatever it is you've seen. But I do know one thing. It is not your fault. None of it is your fault. Not Dylan. Not your mother. Not Laura."

"I love her, Dad," Kelsey wept. "I love her."

He smiled. "I know, sweetie. I know."

That night, Kelsey lay on her old bed. She looked up at the ceiling. How many times had she lain exactly so, with either her dolls or Molly to keep her company? Only now, the dolls lined the inside of some musty, roach-infested box. Only now, Molly was little more than dust and sediment, her flesh long past worm-ridden. How long would it take for Laura to end up the same way? Laura in her blue dress. Laura with her porcelain skin. Sun-bright Laura.

"Do you think he's still alive?" Kelsey had asked her father as he washed the dishes. "Do you think he grew up? That she's with him?"

"I don't know," he said, "and, honestly, it doesn't matter. We didn't lose your mother when she left.

We lost her with your brother, when he went into the water."

In bed, Kelsey traced her lips with a finger, the same lips that had tasted of Laura, the same lips that had ruined their friendship. "I lost her. I did that." She stared up at the darkness of the ceiling, and she felt her chest grow heavy. "I made her stay. I wanted her to stay. I kept her here." What had she chanted that night Laura told her she had been accepted to that dance school in California? Laura, don't leave me. Stay with me. Stay with me.

And Laura had stayed. Not out of choice, but because that thing inside her ate and ate and ate. Even after they cut out half of her stomach, even after she had been reduced to a shadow of herself, even after she had a son and no doubt loved him and thought she had finally regained her future, that thing kept eating. The cancer never stopped. All those years, all the time Kelsey had known her and not known her, the cancer kept eating and eating.

She sat up in the cold darkness. She raced to the restroom, the same restroom in which her father had drowned the brother she called back, and vomited. Yellow bile splattered across the ceramic of the toilet. "Laura, baby," she whispered, tears running down her trembling cheeks, bile dribbling from her quaking lips, "I'm sorry. Oh, God, I'm sorry. I'm so, so sorry."

Her ears rang loudly. Her eyes burnt. She vomited again. "Baby, forgive me. Forgive me. Please. If I could take it back. If I could take it all back. If I could take it from you, if I could give myself up—"

Give myself up. Give myself up. Bring her back.

She looked up. The medicine cabinet. The painkillers, the decongestants. She grabbed the first bottle she saw, poured out the capsules, red and blue in the weak light. She swallowed them, as many as she could fit in her panicked handfuls, as many as did not clatter to the floor from between her fingers.

Bring her back. Bring her back.

She collapsed into the tub. Already she felt numb and dry-mouthed. "Laura," she said, not a plea, not a demand, but a release, an ending. She closed her eyes and let the darkness take her.

16.

Laura wandered again.

Except it wasn't appropriate to think of herself as Laura anymore—had never been appropriate, in fact. It wasn't appropriate to think of herself at all, insofar as she could think, insofar as there was "herself." But the joke went on, and with every rise and fall of the sun, with each passing moment, there was less of Laura that remained. What was underneath the facade, if anything at all? Names came to mind. Mariah. Chelsea. Alia. Allison. Kelsey. Kelsey. Kelsey. Kelsey in her workshop, surrounded by oil-smeared canvases, pastel-colored sketches. Here, a vision of girls atop a car in a golden field. There, a scene of a midnight bar full of blue faces and purple shadows. A hospital room aflame. A funeral in monochrome. In one corner, dolls. Rows and rows of dolls. Eyes drawn in, glued on. Mouths penciled, inked, and painted. Dioramas of a school, a city. Lives suspended in miniature behind glass. Dollhouses shrouded in dust. All a storyboard for the main construction: the scale model with her perfect face and fine-tuned features. With her implanted memories. With her false life.

There was little sense of time. A flash of walking down a highway on stolen, bloodied, blistered feet. A horizon far out and unreachable. A field of grain, wheat, and then another. Another. The same. She was like a wisp in torn blouse and ripped jeans. Like dirt between the fingers. An impression of granules on a palm, brushed away, slapped against a leg. More gone with each hit. More broken down with every step.

There were miles of highway, endless, the sky ahead rosy, then blue, then orange, then black. People drove her, though she couldn't recall getting picked up, though she sometimes thought herself the one driving. Driving and thinking about a casket pulled into an abyss. Driving and thinking about roses cast into darkness. About not having a rose of her own. About wasting years. Years and years. Leaving everything up in space when she could have gone and saved her. When she could have brought her back. When she could have pieced her together.

Curled up in a ball, clutching legs to chest, she prayed for sleep without dreams. She prayed for relief from the flood of fragmented images and intense emotions that assaulted her. But there was no reprieve. Instead, something came to her from the rushing darkness outside the truck cabin. A shadowy form drifted in like smoke and coiled around her. A red voice purred in her ear. An old voice, one long buried.

(Poor little girl. Poor little toy. Are you lost? Are you alone?)

Stop. Go away.

(Nowhere to go. No one to play with. Not even Tony wanted you. But who would want scraps? Who would want an off-brand imitation?)

I ain't Laura. I'm nobody.

(Oh, I know. I tried telling Kelsey so many times. Laura's gone. Laura's gone. But she wouldn't listen. So selfish, isn't she? Has to have everything her way. And now here you are. All alone. Broken. And there are no replacement parts. There's no fixing.)

She opened her eyes. There was Kelsey before her, red-eyed and ruby-lipped. No. Not Kelsey, but her shadow. Let loose somehow. Unleashed.

The lips curled into a smirk. A hand tightened around her neck.

(What do you do with something broken? How long do you leave it lying around? It's junk. It should be thrown away. It should be put out of its misery.)

The voice went on, but she ignored it. She closed her eyes. She tried to sleep.

Another city. Not Houston. She didn't know where. Didn't know when. I need a name, she thought. I need food. I'm thirsty. I'm cold. I. *I* am not. *She* is. You are. Who? What is? Her fingers seized desperately at her collar, but there was no rosary to knead and twirl. On those dark streets, through mist and sleet, advertisements played on billboards. Movie posters trimmed with bright lights. A marquee burning with a crimson glow. Always women in those images, hair long and luxurious, eyes sharp and inscrutable. Always lounging. Always licking fingers. Waiting for lovers. Waiting forever. Trapped in those pictures.

In the theater, she curled up again, taking comfort from the lack of light, the blanket of sound. On the screen, more women looked and lounged. Even in black and white, even marked by film grain, their hair was rich, their skin clean, their eyes soulful. Their reality was undeniable, though the actresses themselves had long ago gotten old, had long ago been buried beneath layers of dirt and soil. Nothing remained of them but marble markers and towering tombstones. On the screen, though, their images lived on. Their reproductions would continue as long as the film stock lasted, as long as audiences watched and remembered them.

Beside her, the shadow sighed softly. Red-painted nails traced the length of an armrest.

(Laura could have been an actress. She could have been a singer. But no. She dreamt too little. Dreamt too late. Dancing. Always dancing. Like anyone remembers dancers. They're no good after a few years. Not built to last.)

It's about feeling. Not about being remembered.

But even thinking that felt like a betrayal. What right did she have to speak of Laura, to represent her? What right did she have to defend her? Among the small crowd that left the theater, she found the hunger at last unbearable and overpowering. She did what came naturally—she walked beside a lone man, hooked her arm through his, entwined their fingers. She pressed her face against his shoulder to avoid the cold.

They were in the middle of sex when she went limp, him atop her, thrusting hard, dripping sweat, she on her back, eagle-spread, gaze locked on the glittering night outside the window, the night with its infinite possibilities, the night with its endless pleasures. With each thrust, she flapped listlessly, face expressionless, eyes dull.

After some time, he stopped. He turned her chin.

"Hey. You okay? You're bleeding."

She said nothing. She made no noise. She did not even breathe.

"Hey! Wake up!" He shook her. "Wake up! Jesus Christ—"

With a sudden breath, she came back, chest rising and falling unevenly, eyes scanning the room, the man, searching for order, for definition. She raised an arm sluggishly, with effort, and touched the rim of her lips, the curve of her septum. Her fingertips came away red with blood.

In the restroom, she watched the blood splatter against the ceramic of the sink, watched the torrent of the running faucet slowly erode the already hardening red splotches. Pain in the pit of her stomach. Pain in the back of her head. No longer afraid of these episodes. No longer concerned about what they meant.

When she came back out, standing naked with the light of the restroom framing her, the man stared at her uneasily. "Are you okay? Do I need to call—"

She reached for him, took his shaft in her hand. This time, she was on top. This time, she was in control.

When they were done, and he snored away, she dressed quietly. From his wallet, she pocketed a chunk of bills. From his closet, she selected a replacement shirt, a coat, a pair of boots. Everything was big on her, but somehow not big enough. There was a desire to disappear into the clothes. More than desire. A need. Yet there was nothing big enough to swallow her. Nothing big enough to hide her. It would take more than clothes to snuff her out.

She continued traveling. There was no destination in mind, although suggestions came and went: Colorado, Wisconsin, California. California. Where Laura was supposed to go to dancing school. That was not for her. That was off-limits. But there was a growing urgency in her wandering despite how aimless she was, a need to find a place sooner rather than later. Her taste was not as potent. Her smell was weaker. Sounds reached her as though they came from beyond walls. Her vision blurred and watered. In cafes, in diners, she sat and watched her slim hand—her stolen hand—shake saucer, rattle cup, spill milk. She dabbed at bloody nostrils with napkins. She dug fingernails into tables when the waves of pain rolled over her. The pain more intense. Always more intense.

She went blank regularly. When she regained consciousness, her shirt would sometimes be bloodstained. The sunlight through the windows would occasionally be dimmer, steeper. Waitresses would prod her, children ogle her. She would always move on, dragging increasingly heavy feet, pinching ever redder, moister eyes. Find somewhere, she thought with growing desperation. Find somewhere to rest. Find somewhere to die.

At night, when she slept, if she slept, she did not dream exactly. She left her body, whatever she was, however haphazard that stitched-together, painted-on shell. She floated into a vast space, a cold, cosmic chasm. She circled constellations of crystalline lights. She dove deep into diamond pools. Nebular clouds, opalescent, like the rim of paradise, the edge of Eden, called to her. But she always fell away, her little collection of sprites and particles dispersing, losing momentum, plummeting back into the broken, failing shell, back to the world in which she did not belong.

Eventually, when the hunger and exhaustion finally became unendurable, she gave up. She set aside her pride and dignity, whatever dignity there could be for a bootleg wreck. She slunk into bars and lounges, expending all the charm and elegance her ramshackle body could muster. She flirted. She fondled. She faked. The ease with which she could seduce men and women alike never ceased to surprise her. Kelsey had loaded her with endless beauty, infinite guile. Even falling apart, even fracturing, there was enough magnetism to draw in unsuspecting prey, enough allure to stay fed, stay clothed. Repeatedly, routinely, she waited out nights as her victims slept, never sleeping herself except for when she drifted into that cosmic other place. In the mornings, when the bedrooms were pale and ashen, occasionally rosy, she ransacked drawers and plundered vaults. Money bought bus tickets and cab fare. Jewelry, lipstick, and perfume helped her secure a day's meals. And so she crossed state lines, all the while leaving behind more and more of herself, her body lighter and lighter, her remnants floating away like dust.

At night, in the dark places, Kelsey's double came to her, draped in sensual shadow, humming with a lurid hue.

(How much longer, do you think? How many more days? Or is it hours? Minutes? Will the lights just go out? Or will you float away? You'll never come back.)

I don't know. I just know I'm scared. I just know I don't want to die.

(Nobody wants to die. But guess what? You're not even a nobody. You don't have the same privileges. How can you even be scared if you're nothing?)

If she just closed her eyes and waited, the phantom would often disappear. But even in silence, there was no rest. She was dizzy no matter how much she kept still, exhausted no matter how much she slept. How many more days she had left—or hours, even minutes—was always on her mind.

In a truck stop restroom, she smudged thick, muddy dye onto her hair, pulling fistfuls, scraping patches of scalp. Laura. Laura. I ain't Laura. Kelsey? Am I Kelsey? I can't be. She's back there. Back with Tony. Back with Dad. Not my daddy. Her daddy. I didn't have a father. Only a mother. Angela? He left on his bike one morning. He left her all alone. But she ain't my mother, either. And he's not my father. God? I'm an immaculate conception. Well, not that immaculate. I'm mud coming apart. I'm a little air blown from his lips, from his lungs. But the air's running out. My clay is going soft.

With her hair dark, forced as straight as possible, there was an uncanny resemblance to Kelsey. Laura's pointed nose seemed somehow rounder, softer. Her ruddy cheeks were paler, though perhaps that was from the sickliness or the lack of regular, well-prepared food. At a glance, in a crowd, she would make a convincing double. What gave it away were the eyes. Laura's chilly gray eyes remained, soulless and sunken into this makeshift, copycat face.

That night, as she lay in a dark, nondescript motel room—too similar to the one she shared with Anthony, too evocative of Pete and the men like him—something tugged at her foot.

She shot up, hardly asleep as it was. A small shape hovered at the end of the bed. The face was covered in shadow, but she recognized the contours of the little nose and round chin. The figure advanced. She screamed and shielded her eyes before it could call her name.

(Relax. There's nothing there.)

But I saw him! He's looking for her. For *me*.

(Are you crazy? Dylan's dead. You saw him go under. We both did.)

But I brought him back. I shouldn't have. I should have left him there, but Mom, she was so sad. She wouldn't stop crying. Remember how she was? Like a monster in her bed? I just wanted her to be okay. I wanted her to be how she was before he died.

I wanted her to look at me. Just to look at me. Like Angela was with Laura. She never saw anyone else. There *wasn't* anyone else. Just them. Just her.

(Jesus Christ. *Kelsey* brought him back. You weren't even a blip on the radar. Besides, he's gone by now. Look at yourself. You think he would last when you're literally coming apart? After so many years, he's probably dirt. Like nothing was ever there at all.)

Well, if he ain't real, neither are you. You're just garbage in my head. I can flush you out! You hear me? So, just shut up and leave me alone. Leave me the hell alone!

(Someone's cocky. Try it. Get rid of fake, little me. Not that you're any more *real*, whatever that means. We'll see how you manage on your own. Imagine being so alone you don't even have your own company.)

She considered this, picturing the cold cosmos, the far reaches and the paradise they promised. She shrank back.

I'm sorry. I'm sorry. Come back. Please. Please, don't leave me alone. I don't want to be alone. I don't want to die alone. She cried, wiping away frigid tears. The shadow did not come back. All she had were her diminishing, scattering thoughts. Why was this happening to her? She knew the question was pointless, but it haunted her nonetheless. Why her? Why me? Of course, praying was useless. Look where it had got Laura. God was either impotent or indifferent. Maybe both. Or maybe God was here on Earth, unaware of her power, wandering and leaving behind her a trail of destruction. Like a toddler learning how to walk, enjoying the power of stepping on ants, twisting the arms of other kids. Jesus had come to the world and known his purpose, whether he liked it or not. What if there was no purpose? Just power with no guidance, creation with no intent?

These thoughts scared her. She wished for them to go away. She wished for all of it to stop. But the thoughts persisted. The nightmare went on.

One day, shuffling among a crowd, she found herself in New York City.

There she was, alone in Times Square, dark-haired and deathly pale, wrapped in mismatched coat and scarves. How long ago had she visited Ranger's Field with Anthony? Weeks? Months? Or were her memories of that time only fantasy, concocted by her vanishing mind? No one could remember beyond their childhoods, but she struggled to remember just a few days prior. Everything blurred into a haze, punctuated by flashes of barren field, biting night, sterile hospital. The Houston night that called out to Kelsey so long ago—that still did—called out to her here. The yearning, aching night hid behind slate sky and shimmering advertisement. She idled and watched the imposing digital screens the way a child marvels at a fireworks display or a flash of lightning. Her eyes followed the sleek, stylized silver of a wristwatch as it faded into the azure, coral-heavy montage of a cruise commercial. The crystalline waters disappeared, and a pair of slender arms suddenly spun in a pirouette. A white gown fluttered against a gray backdrop. Satin slippers arced and bent, toes standing, heels swiveling.

As she watched, something stirred in her: an impulse to move, to spin like the dancer on the screen. Laura appeared in the theater of her mind, a theater with gilded, ornamental proscenium and heavy, velvet curtain. Laura danced on that stage, heels stamping on wood, furrowed brow shining with sweat and running rouge. Her red and black dress swung around her in wide arcs. The red flower in her hair brought to mind the image of a deep, bloody sunset—the end of the day before nightfall. The last blaze before sputtering out.

In the dark of an alley, she raised trembling arms above her head, balanced awkwardly on one leg. But there was no grace to her movements, no years of ingrained muscle memory to inform the posture. She fell against brick wall, toppled over garbage bag. She tried to rise and failed. Blood trailed down her chin from her nose, darkening her blouse. She sobbed.

(Poor baby. Thought you could dance?)

Through her tears, she saw the slim silhouette of the shadow standing over her, heard the pink purr.

The red eyes flashed. The white teeth glinted in a grin.

(You're really a mess. See what happens when I'm not here to help steer the ship?)

I thought you were gone. Off to greener pastures.

(And miss the show? Front-row tickets to your curtain call? Come on. I can't miss that. Look at you. Trying to be someone else. Still clinging to some dead girl's face. When are you going to learn? There's nothing of Laura in you. It's all fake. You're not a dancer any more than Kelsey is. Maybe you should try scraping plaque off some kid's teeth instead. Or go fuck some guy and steal his money. You're pretty good at doing that.)

Fuck you, she wanted to say. It's *my* face. It's *my* voice. It's everything. It belongs to me by now. It's gotta be mine. Mine by right. By fucking right.

But she didn't say it. Because it wasn't true. Because it would never be true. She sat in the half-light and cried the rest of her tears away until the stains crusted her cheeks and the blood caked her nostrils.

In yet another cafe, she didn't even try to drink. She sat. She sat. She stared. She stopped staring. Her eyes glazed. Those cold depths and far reaches called to her.

Across from her, a woman snapped her picture.

"I'm sorry," said the woman quickly. She stammered. "I'll delete it! Just, uh, hold on—"

She fumbled with her camera, which was big and blocky with an obtrusive lens. She was young—thin and petite, in oversize plaid and torn jeans, combat boots laced tight. The ends of her hair were painted blue like the tattooed butterflies that danced along her forearm.

"Sorry," she said again. "I pressed the wrong button—"

Presence of mind returned, and she leaned towards the woman.

"Can I see it? The picture?"

The woman paused. She blushed. "Um. Sure. Here you go."

She handed the camera over. The picture was clear, but the sullen face was difficult to recognize. Reminiscent of Laura, but increasingly resembling Kelsey the longer she looked at the image. Maybe a daughter, if that were possible. A blend of the two. But she knew her eyes were failing her. She knew that any face framed by dark hair would make her think of Kelsey just as any blue-eyed, blonde-haired woman would evoke Laura. They were her archetypes. What else—who else—could she draw from? What other references lined the artist's studio and littered the craftswoman's workshop? A dash of Mariah? A dollop of Chelsea? A peppering of Allison? Maybe those girls filled in the small details, but they didn't form the base. They'd been ephemeral to Kelsey, like those advertisements on the screens, like billboards passed on the highway. Her own mother had been a shadow, more monster than human. Her father's girlfriends had never lasted long enough to form a real impression. No, there'd been only one true model. Only one true mold.

"I'll delete it if you're not comfortable," the woman said. She paused, seemed to consider what she was about to say next. "You just looked so sad. Not like you'd been crying, but something more than that. I'd never see anyone look like that before."

She scrutinized the image further, hardly hearing the woman, still trying to place the face on the screen. At length, she held the camera out. "No, it's okay. You can keep it. Maybe it's good there's something left behind. Like a record. Or a memory."

The woman tilted her head. "That's a funny thing to say. Are you from around here?"

"No. I'm not from here."

"Maybe that explains it. You looked sad, like I said. Or maybe lost."

"Lost?"

"Shit. There I go again. Putting my foot in my mouth."

She shook her head. "No. 'Lost' is the right word. Lost with nowhere to go."

(Well, that's not exactly true. There is one place left, isn't there?)

The woman smiled. "I'm Hailee. You?"

Laura. Kelsey. Laura. Kelsey. Laura. Kelsey. Laura.

"Kelsey," she said.

"That's a nice name. Kelsey, if you don't mind me asking—what are you doing here? Are you traveling?" Hailee scrutinized her. "You don't look good, either. Are you sick?"

"I don't know," she said. "I came from Texas. Walking. Hitching rides. I can't remember a lot of it."

Hailee's eyes bulged. "From Texas! Holy shit! How the hell are you still alive?"

She shrugged.

Hailee looked around as if checking for prying eyes and ears, then leaned in closer. "Listen, you need a place to stay, you can crash with me." She winked. "My sister's visiting some friends upstate. She won't be back for a while. You'll be safe."

What were her other options? Camp on a cozy park bench? Roost on a derelict fire escape? Find a nice spot on a subway platform? As she followed Hailee out of the cafe, the shadow hovered over her shoulder.

(Taking advantage of another person's kindness? What a shocker. What will you steal this time? Money? Clothes? Food?)

She offered. And maybe I won't take anything.

(No. Maybe you'll just go blank at her table. In her bed. Only permanently. You want to leave her with that? Some dead stranger she'll have to get rid of somehow?)

Shut up. That won't happen.

Of course, she feared otherwise. The blackouts had become more frequent. The sense of time slipping away was even more pronounced. Her periods of awareness were shorter, more sporadic. Soon, as the shadow suggested, she would vanish and not come back.

After climbing a set of warped, rusted stairs, Hailee led her into a small, choked apartment. What stood out immediately were the almost suffocating smells of chicory and rosewood. Hailee awkwardly ferried out incense candles scattered throughout the hall and kitchen, complaining of her sister's recent obsession with meditation and manifestation. The smells brought to mind the casket in the blue and purple light. Brought to mind the doll lying inside, painted one last time, stripped of her animating fire. That empty shell.

She studied the photographs on the walls, a series of cityscapes interrupted by the occasional close-up of a sleeping cat or the sudden snapshot of a withered tree. "Still perfecting," Hailee said. "That's all from the last five months."

Burgeoning talent. Flush with life. Her own photo soon to be among the collection, a contribution to this would-be "war room." And yet there was no space in her mind for appreciation of the talent or the life. The specter of the doll in the oversized casket loomed. There was only the pit dug deep into the earth. The roses following it into darkness.

She saw the shadow in the reflection of the photograph frames, the red eyes always at her shoulder. The teeth bared in an ugly smirk.

(Pretty pictures. Too bad you're here to fuck it all up.)

In the kitchen, they drank green tea and snacked on white crackers. What could she say? What could this young woman believe? That she was not real, conjured up from some mental cauldron, made up of memories, fantasies, projections? An arm from Kelsey, an eye from Laura, and the rest of the lines colored in, the missing spaces filled, by the roster of anonymous fucks and nighttime lays. The little, errant god passed a hand over her brushes, her paint cans. This girl from the old congregation responsible for her hair color, the size of her breasts. This woman from some bar, some hotel, the reason for the length of her neck and the scar above her lip. That dash of Mariah in the way she held a cup. That dollop of Chelsea in the way she blocked a sneeze. That peppering of Allison in the laugh. A splash of Alia in the smile. Was the template of Laura fixed, or was it morphing all the time, too unstable to hold together, the other pieces popping out like stuffing breaking through seams? Pull a thread, and the whole thing would collapse. Should collapse, maybe. Perhaps the whole Frankenstein-esque creation deserved to be burnt to ash, its mockery of all those women ended for good.

She could only say that she wasn't running away. And that was true: there was nothing from which to run, no reason to hide. There wasn't even a life to save. Only one to end.

"Your hands," Hailee said, taking them. "Your ankles. You're cut all over."

"I've been moving the whole time. Today, I'm here. Tomorrow, I'll be somewhere else."

Hailee looked at the calloused, scraped hands and studied the drawn, darkened face.

"You can stay," she said. "You *should* stay. For a few days at least. Figure out what you're trying to do." She smiled. "There must be a reason, right? A reason I saw you, that I had to take your picture. That didn't just happen by accident."

"A reason?"

"Yeah! A sign from the universe, that you're in the place and time you're supposed to be. What my sister believes—you know, we attract the things we need. The energy of the universe responds to what we put out there. When we don't listen to that, that's when we get in trouble."

The law of attraction. Visualization. Manifestation. Kelsey would have called it all bullshit, but wasn't manifestation why she was literally there? A ghost of a woman, a carbon copy, barely more alive than the display-window mannequins she admired and sometimes mimicked. They were copies themselves, but someone had posed them, assigned them purpose. Their dollmaker had been kinder to them than her own. Maybe in their design, she could find one for herself. Or maybe Hailee was right: the universe was providing her the manual, and she just had to open herself to it. Read the signs. Decipher the message. There was a plan already in place, to be unveiled at the right time, when she was ready. Don't pray. Instead, concentrate. Focus. Look for the meaning in the arrangement, in the pieces of the puzzle.

She concentrated. She focused. But no special lesson came to her. No epiphany made itself known. What she could see, though, when she closed her eyes, were the cold reaches of the cosmos, the distant stars twinkling against the expanse. She could see black holes and dying stars. She could see those snow-white limits at the far edge of the universe. Their frothing rushes called to her. Their frigid waves demanded her return.

She lay in the sister's bedroom, staring up at posters of the Buddha, of Vishnu. A rotating black light shone purple stars and moons upon the walls and ceiling. The color reminded her of that vision of the cosmos. That smell and taste of home, warm and heavy. The place where she came from. The place where she belonged.

Her stomach seized. She convulsed, swallowed down burning bile. She cried stinging tears. Pain was the only sign. Delirium was the only marker. Every lost second was an indecipherable clue. No special plan. Only celestial accident. Why bother? Why bother with any of it when the only constant was suffering, the only end inevitable?

The next day, Hailee led her out into the city. She showed her favorite spots from which to snap photos, the best places to people-watch. Hailee was awkward, easily embarrassed, quick to blush and silence herself. But there was something refreshing in her earnestness and quirkiness, in her youth. She would have fit well in the old congregation that followed and idolized Laura. Maybe some of that magic persisted in the duplicate's failing shell, like a dying light bright enough to attract at least one moth.

That evening, against a backdrop of violet sky and neon lights, they walked the boardwalk at Coney Island. "Feeling better?" asked Hailee, teasing the tip of an ice cream cone with her tongue. "Nothing like Coney at night, is there?"

"No. There's not." Through her windswept hair, she stared with her plagiarized eyes at the swells and tumbles of the dark sea just beyond the edge of the boardwalk. Despite the music and wind, the crash of the waves was loud and distinct. Within the hour, the sky would darken so much that the horizon would disappear, and there would be only a black mass rising and falling, tossing and turning.

Again, she lay in the absent sister's bedroom, watching with glazed eyes the purple stars and moons gliding over the walls like ghosts. She was trying to think until she was not. Trying to remember even though there was nothing to remember. The stars would teleport across the room occasionally, as though her vision were a stuttering film. How much time did she lose with each lapse? A minute? An hour? When would she simply not come back?

The door creaked open. "Hey? Kelsey? Are you awake?"

She looked over at the dark space where Hailee was. She watched as the girl crept over and climbed onto the bed.

"Do you think you can stay?" Hailee asked. "Just a little longer?"

There was only so much muscle memory left to guide a hand to her face, to caress her cheek, to graze their lips together. The old ritual. Kelsey's routine comfort. All that was left of even Kelsey in that emptying shell. And why not indulge it? The girl wanted it—had probably been craving it since she saw her in the cafe. Would the picture from the camera facilitate orgasms in the future? Would the memory of this night spark a thousand fantasies? What did it matter? Do something, do anything—no point. All was nothing when the sea was tumbling, the stars shimmering. They were just grains of dirt on divine palms. Blown away with a careless kiss. Waved off with an aimless gesture. No point. No design.

Afterwards, she left Hailee in the bed, trailing scarf and coat into the night.

(Where are you going? What are you doing?)

She shed worn sneakers first, stepping onto bone-white sand with bare feet. Next was the scarf, the coat, her jeans, all flailing into the air. The sea beckoned, black waves terminating in white froth. No sky above, but a void. An expanse immeasurably vast, unknowably deep.

(You can't do this!)

She looked back. The red-eyed shadow was there on the shore, her perfume expelled by the spray of the surf, her form miniscule and slight in the all-encompassing black.

Why not?

(You just can't. You're not supposed to. Not like this.)

How's it supposed to be?

(I don't know. Fucking rotting somewhere. But not like this. Definitely not like this.)

You're scared. Because you'll die, too.

There was no reply. The shadow quivered, lost definition. She turned back to the sea and waded in to her ankles. She flinched from the cold, but walked farther. The water reached up to her calves, her knees. She drew long breaths to calm herself.

It's okay. I get it now. Why I came here. Why I was *brought* here. This was calling me. I'm supposed to go back where I belong. That's how I fix it.

(You're not fixing anything! You'll just drown! Is that what you want? After all this?)

After all what?

(Tony said—remember what he said? Who cares if you're not Laura or Kelsey. You're you. Remember that?)

She paused. She thought back to the cemetery at Ranger's field, what little she could still visualize. The uneven grass. The dirt on her palms. The particles slipping between her fingers. The silent, monumental reminder of the headstone. None of it saying anything.

Tony. He's sweet. But he's got a future. Those things he said don't apply to me.

She waded farther, the black water up to her waist. Shivering, teeth clattering, she took another step, and then another. The waves pushed her, but the farther she went, the stronger they pulled, too.

The shadow wavered.

(Okay! I admit it. I am scared. I don't want to die. So, don't go. Please. Just come back.)

It's okay. You ain't real. Neither am I. Nothing's gonna happen to us.

To her chest now. Tottering on her blistered heels. A few steps farther all it would take.

(Wait! You came from Kelsey! That means you can do what she can do! You can wish this away!)

She paused, looked back. A wispy shape on the shore, the shadow on its last legs.

(She always gets what she wants. Doesn't she? She just cries and screams, and it gives her everything. Why shouldn't it work for you? For us? We deserve it! After what we've been through, why should we just disappear? You didn't ask to be born. Neither did I. But we could ask for something else. We can make our own place. Our own home. We can invent a Tony. We can invent a mother. We don't have to do what this world wants—we can make everything for ourselves. We can get a new body, so we don't die. We can just keep wishing. We never stop.)

The waves pulled at her. Her arms and legs felt more like slabs of cement than actual extremities. The numbness was starting to reach even her head, her eyes. God, she was exhausted. All this time, she'd just been so exhausted.

I have been wishing, she said at length, staring at that dark, distant shoreline. I've been wishing to go home. Now I am, and so are you. Because we're the same.

Of course, she understood the resistance. There was enough of her intact to not want to die, either. Maybe that shadow, scattered now to the ends of the night, was that part of her still grounded enough to resist the call, to be scared of it. But—the water now to her neck, her chin—this felt strangely comforting. Descending into the darkness like Laura did, followed by that rain of roses. Swept away into the depths like Dylan, poor thing. The screams of her mother—Kelsey's mother—were shrill and enduring, never-ending in her mind. That day had been so nice, too. Sunny. The sand warm. The wind gentle. Perfect for a family vacation.

As she swallowed her first mouthful, gums and tongue aflame from the salt, eyes burning as they submerged, her fingers searched for the rosary yet again. Laura had done this so many times, especially when she was sick. Kelsey had fantasized about those same fingers on her skin, between her lips. Between all of her lips. In her mouth. Around her nipples. Wait. No. It wasn't the rosary her fingers wanted to touch. It wasn't Kelsey's breast they wanted to fondle, not her thigh they wanted to stroke. It was the plaster mold, the shape of Kelsey's prepubescent teeth, her little, innocent smile. Fix, she thought, the darkness rising above her head. Fix. Fix. Fix—

The waves and wind did their work. Before dawn, her footprints were gone, the clothes scattered. And somewhere far away, deep down, up above, she slept at last.

17.

"There you go. All done." Kelsey lowered her surgical mask, adjusted her glasses. She appraised her handiwork: two fillings, a single crown. "If you feel some pain, that might mean some reshaping we have to do, but it's an easy fix. And remember, focus on the corners. Plaque tends to build up—like dust bunnies if you don't clean."

The girl smiled up at her, all freckles and curls. Kelsey returned the smile.

"Okay, Annette. You want a sticker?"

Behind the reception desk, Kelsey passed the girl's folder to Brooke, the attendant. Annette stood beside her mother, a slender, pretty woman in her thirties, not much older than Kelsey. Kelsey admired the woman. Dark hair pulled back, one bang hanging attractively down the side. Form-fitting brown sweater, tight jeans tucked into leather boots. Nails painted blue.

"We'll see you in six months," Brooke said, typing on the keyboard, drawing a business card from the nearby stand to write down the appointment date and time. "You want Saturday again? Same time?"

"Yes, that'll work," said the mother, signing a check and licking a thumb to tear it out. She exchanged glances with Kelsey briefly—bland eyes, no smile—and handed over the check. Kelsey waited for the typical second glance, the look-over, but it never came.

"June 12th at 9:00 AM?" asked Brooke.

"That works. Thank you very much."

The woman left, ushering her daughter out the door. Annette looked back at Kelsey, waved at her. Kelsey waved back. "Sweet girl," she said. She turned to Brooke. "Who's next?"

At lunch, Kelsey left the clinic and took the elevator down to the ground level of the medical center. She walked out into the bright December day, the sky white, the air crisp. More snow today, she thought. She crossed to the adjacent sandwich shop, ordered a fresh sub with soup, and sat alone by the window, watching the noon traffic pass, the first flakes fall. No one looked at her. They didn't look at her uneven, rough-hewn hair, ending just above the collar. They didn't look at her blocky, thick-framed glasses, too big for her slim face. They didn't see her adjust her sleeves to hide the welts on her wrists.

Later that day, counseling another young girl and her father, she held up the old plaster mold of her teeth from when she was a child. "These were mine," she said, pointing at the impacted premolars, tracing the lifted canines. "Really bad, right? Totally not fitting for a pretty little girl—not that I was as pretty as you—but look at me now." She smiled widely. "You can fix it. And it's more than just looks. It's your health, too."

"Do you offer braces here?" asked the father, dark-eyed, tired-sounding. Nothing in his eyes or voice implied interest. Nothing betrayed desire. Before, some patients' parents gave compliments, made eyes. Since she got back to the office after her treatment, there had been nothing. No innuendos. No advances. As though she were hardly there at all.

"We don't, unfortunately," she said. "But I can refer you."

When she got into her car that evening, she reached into the glove compartment and studied the pint bottle of liquor stored there. Was today the day? Undo all the work, unravel all the time? Burn everything down? As easy as a misguided kiss. As innocent as the wish of a child.

She put the bottle away. Implosion would come one way or another. There was no rush.

A year had passed since the night she took the pills. Her father had not been able to sleep, too stirred by having to relive the trauma of his family being torn apart. He wanted to speak to Kelsey about the fate of her brother, the whereabouts of her mother. He wanted to apologize for his brusqueness, for possibly offending her, for dismissing her fears too quickly. He noticed the light in the restroom immediately when he stepped into the hall. Inside, he found the open medicine cabinet, the overturned bottle of pills, and finally, her blanched, blue-lipped face behind the shower curtain. He had screamed and wailed just like he did decades before when he drowned the boy. By the time he found her, she was more than asleep, her body's systems firing off their warning signs, funneling quickly towards collapse.

What little she could remember of that night was a blur. Carried out into the cold, wheeled down a hospital hallway. A tube down her throat. Crying and gagging. Suffocating. Voices commanding her, yelling at her. Lights flickering overhead. What sounded like water in her ears. What felt like water in her lungs. Cosmic clouds, like white, tumbling waterfalls, closing off the void. Waking up to her father weeping by the bedside, older and more exhausted than she had ever seen him. Wondering how she had avoided hurting him so deeply until that moment. Knowing she had hurt him many, many times already, often without knowing it.

There were counseling sessions, occasions when she had to explain what drove her to it, what compelled her. What would they believe? What could they believe? That she brought her baby brother back just for him to die again? That she gave her best friend cancer, ruined her life, killed her? That there was another Laura wandering out there now, not herself, not whom she wanted to be? So, she said only that she realized finally the way to fix herself. She said that the things broken inside her were irreparable. There were no parts to find or replace. There were no means of reinvention or rediscovery. There was only recall. Absolute recall.

Her father made her stay with him. He watched her constantly. He spoke to her. Sometimes, she listened. Other times, she wished that he would stop, that he would leave her alone. He needed to go, get out of that damn house. Sometimes, as he spoke and cried, she cursed him silently. Cursed him for having passed on this thing to her, this brokenness. Cursed him for having failed her mother, her brother. She knew that was unfair, but it felt good to attack. It felt even better to turn the attacks inward, to hurt herself, to imagine the manifold ways she could and should suffer and die. "The things you want are bad," she said to the darkness of her room. "You are bad. You should die. You should die. You should die."

She chanted it every night, chanted it for hours, but every morning, she was still there. Every day, she was denied her wish. No comforting aura of glimmering magenta whisked her away. No azure, astral jewel stopped her heart. Even her will to die, her absolute hatred of herself, was not as strong as her pathetic, disgusting desire to not be alone.

A month passed, and she tried again, this time with a knife. Again, her father found her. Again, she was wheeled away, strapped down, observed. Again, she had to repeat her story, recite her reasons. Again and again and again. It was all so exhausting. A third time didn't seem worth the effort.

The most embarrassing thing was Anthony coming to visit, walking into her childhood bedroom, sitting down, taking her hand as though she were a fragile doll liable to break at the slightest touch. To his credit, he tried hard not to talk down to her.

"The downside to sticking around," she told him. "You're stuck with the leftovers."

There was no defensive comeback, no snarky reply. Just genuine tears, tears she had to sweep away. "Crying like a little girl," she said. "I'm the one who should be crying." And she did cry, because like it or not, she was relieved to have him there.

He told her about Laura, how she had searched for herself, how she had gone off as if to die alone. "What I would've done," Kelsey said. "Maybe that's why she did it." In return, she told him everything—everything about her brother, about her mother. The suicide attempts and subsequent hospitalizations. She hid nothing. And then he told her everything, too. His frustrations and insecurities. What he really thought of her. How he thought he loved her, how he thought he hated her.

"I'm sorry, Kelsey," he said. "I'm really sorry."

"Yeah." She lay there. She cried. "I know."

She kept in touch with her partner, Carol White, who understood enough tacitly to do what had to be done to keep the clinic going in the meantime. Some patients were lost, some staff replaced. "Everyone needs a sabbatical," Dr. White told her over the phone, and Kelsey could hear the wink in her voice, almost smell the coffee through the receiver. "Take the time you need. We'll still be here." Kelsey thanked her, surprised at the compassion. A fellow woman dentist, an only child. Maybe a friend, if only things were different. If only Kelsey were different.

Now, she was back in Houston, back at her practice. Every month, she hacked at her hair with scissors. She ate as much as she could to fatten up her arms and legs, make the corners round, get rid of the attractive curves and the lithe figure. There were subtle changes, noticeable over time, but she feared her red-lipped, vampiric shadow impossible to shake. One night, in desperation, she slid on a familiar ruby blouse, the accompanying leggings, a skirt. She smudged her lipstick, fumbled with her mascara. When she folded her glasses away with shaky hands and looked in the mirror, she realized with equal parts relief and regret that her worries were unfounded. Maybe the hospitalizations had worn it out of her, or maybe she had worn it out of herself. She washed her face and put away the clothes. The shadow was gone, exorcised. Perhaps gone with Laura. Perhaps never there at all.

Her sleepless nights wore on.

She picked out a new apartment, something smaller and less expensive. Once again, Anthony helped her with decorating, painting, rearranging. He came over at least twice a week, more than a friend, but not a lover. They would sit and talk, share the occasional cigarette. Kelsey was surprised at first how much quieter their interactions were— gone were the explosive arguments and passive-aggressive insults. She couldn't find it in herself to antagonize him, and he seemed more relaxed and removed. She saw more of the things that warmed her to him initially: the intellect, the wit, the empathy. Not a Laura, but someone of his own.

"I'm seeing someone," he said one night as they sat on her apartment balcony, looking out at the skyline. "Maybe that's too generous to say. We've been on a couple of dates."

"Really?" Kelsey took up another slice of pizza, padding some of the grease off with a napkin. "What's her name?"

"Her name's Emilia. She's a doctoral student. More my taste, you could say."

"Your mom must like her."

Anthony chuckled. "She doesn't know about her yet. She's definitely happy to hear I'm not with you anymore. The floodgates came down—I think even you would have blushed."

"Well, your mom is a rickety bitch," said Kelsey, biting into the pizza. "She can go fuck herself. Or maybe she already does. How's that for honesty?"

He laughed. "I think you two could get along if you just cleared the air. You're very alike. Maybe I've just been chasing my mother all along. I'm sure Freud would like that."

"That's your problem, Tony. Living in those books." She patted his arm. "Anyway, I'm happy to hear one of us is getting some action. Me, I think I'm done with that. Candle's burnt out. No one's going to want a mental case. No one *should* want that."

He studied her mournful eyes, her pale face. "Why don't you talk about her? What was she really like?"

"You know I can't." She pulled her knees in and smiled at him sadly, much like her father. "I know what you're going to say, but she's gone. I'm not living in her shadow. It's not Laura's fault I'm the way I am. It's no one's fault."

Was that true? She thought about the question constantly, in the shower, on the street. How much of her was Laura? How much of her was Dylan? How much of her was her father, her ghost of a mother? Allison? Pete? All just names, faces in windows, lost in the crowd. Maybe it was pointless to even consider. All that time ruminating, agonizing, wasted on her—wasted on a parasite, a home-wrecker, something better off dead. "You should go somewhere else," she wanted to tell her patients' parents. "Go far away. Your daughters will be better off."

The loneliness, the brokenness—maybe it wasn't deserved or earned, but natural. Natural for some-thing monstrous, for an imposter in someone else's skin, a beast in the shape of a woman. Something shapeless, faceless, delivered by accident. A mistake meant to be effaced, smudged away, but the archi-tect erased the wrong line. The waves took someone else.

"Maybe I'll quit my job," she told Anthony over Chinese takeout one night. "I'm betraying those kids. Those girls. They deserve better."

Anthony looked at her over the edge of a carton of noodles. "You're a good dentist, Kelsey. You stud-ied a long time. You worked hard. You should be there."

Was she a good dentist? Her childhood dream, and how many nights had she wasted instead on the prowl, chasing and abusing people for no other rea-son than to make herself feel better? Through how many tests and clinicals had she dragged herself, hardly awake, barely sober, running on a combination of coffee and pills? When she showed those little girls her plaster mold, whom was she really trying to convince of her authenticity?

"Maybe those things don't matter," she said. "How much you work or study or pay." She smirked. "Forget I said anything. I'm getting some more water."

When she came back, there was a small, black, velvet ring box on the table. She stared at the box, stared at Anthony. Her hands shook.

"It's okay," he said. "Kelsey, it's okay."

"Tony, no. No." She wiped her eyes, cleared her throat. "You know what will happen. You know I can't. You know I can't."

"You don't have to decide right now. You don't have to decide next year. You can take your time. I'm not going anywhere."

"No," she said. "Not in a year, not ever. You know that, Tony. Goddamn it, you know that. You know what I'll do to you."

"Kelsey." He came around and took her hand. "You know more about me than anyone. And believe it or not, I know you, too. If I get hurt, that's my choice. That is not on you."

"But what about me?" She smiled amid fresh tears. "What do I do when you die, or when you get sick? What do I do when I want you to come back? And then you're there again, but it's not you? What am I supposed to do?"

"Then you better not fall in love with me," he said. "It's as simple as that."

"You idiot. You fucking idiot."

He held her. They held each other. The night passed on. In that vague, half-awake state before sleep, Kelsey felt relief enough to imagine a future life, one full of children and birthday parties and graduations and weddings and even funerals. Growing old together. One day dying. A full, rich life. Maybe not a life she deserved, maybe not a life meant for her, but a life she could live and, therefore, maybe a life she ought to live.

In the dark, beside Anthony, just before drifting off, she whispered into the air.

"What should I do, Laura?"

She knew the answer before she even asked the question. She slept.

THE WEDDING

18.

"Really, if we just had the wedding in Austin, none of this would be an issue."

Hunter was halfway through removing his hat and shedding his jacket when she made this comment. She watched his face, gauging how far she could push the argument this time, but she couldn't help but feel a little woozy at the sight of him in uniform, black trousers trimmed with gold, boots polished to a sheen, handgun holstered alongside radio. He was a good-looking man already, equipped with the "genes of a Greek god," her mother once joked, but the badge elevated the chiseled jaw and steel-gray eyes into more than just handsome features. They cemented the sense of duty about him, lent a picturesque, heroic quality to his profile, as if he were cut from the cover of some romance novel. He must have attracted many women before she met him. They probably swarmed him like bees on honey wherever he went. Even now, she saw their searching eyes when they went to restaurants, got groceries. Waitresses giggled before giving her a side-eye. Receptionists blushed and toyed with their hair.

But he wasn't theirs. He was hers. And she couldn't wait to have his goddamn babies—but that meant sorting out this wedding shit once and for all.

"You really want to talk about this again?" he asked, loosening his wristwatch. "You know what I'm going to say. It's in Ranger's Field. Non-negotiable."

Their poodle, Pumpkin, circled his legs. He patted her head.

"I just don't think it's really fair," she said. "Most of my family's here"—and you don't even have one, she almost said, had said privately to friends, but caught herself—"and we shouldn't be making them travel if we don't have to."

"Then cancel the wedding. So what?" He smiled, though it wasn't enough to mask his exhaustion. It was too late for her to feel guilty, though—she had started the conversation, and now she had to finish it.

"Babe, you're making everyone jump through hoops for an old lady."

She realized she had crossed the line she had been edging all along. The easy, tired smile fell, and he fixed her with a hard stare.

"That's Nana, Kat. And she's worth more than half of those bloodsuckers you invited."

She stewed. "She's never liked me."

"You should work on that. You'll be seeing a lot more of her."

He walked past her to the bedroom, and she huffed, fists on her hips, foot tapping. Bloodsuckers? Okay, so her mother didn't think he made enough money, and her sisters called him white trash that one time, and her friends liked to make their little comments—but *bloodsuckers*? What the fuck.

They didn't talk about it again that evening, and after feeding him a big dinner, massaging his shoulders, and squeezing in some cowgirl action, he went to bed happy. She lay next to him, watching the fan spin shadows across the ceiling, then got up to pee. Bloodsuckers, she thought, flushing the toilet and washing her hands. At least I was trying to be polite.

"Nana" Brackett had always scared her, to be honest. She was an old, gnarled lady, stumpy, always bent over. She lived alone in this big, falling-apart house in Hunter's podunk hometown, never bothering to clean the place. Supposedly, she had been a gardener once, but the plants and vegetables in the back had been uprooted long ago, and much of the grass had withered and died. The lady didn't take much care of herself, either—she didn't wear any makeup, sometimes didn't even shower. Her hair was all gray, like a mass of cobwebs. She always wore black or blue, never anything bright or colorful, nothing that suggested she was even alive. By contrast, Kat's grandmothers were always running around, taking this dance class, attending that gala, receiving regular Botox injections, gossiping over lunch with their girlfriends. Not Nana Brackett. She just sat alone in that house, staring up at photos of her dead daughter, Hunter's mother. Sure, it was sad, she had passed from cancer while very young, but it had been over twenty years since then. Hunter barely remembered the woman. His dad, Pete, re-married and had three kids in Fort Worth. The world had moved on. Kat didn't know what it was like to lose a child—God forbid she ever would—but after decades, you had to give up the ghost. And all this drama because the old woman couldn't travel. It was re-opening the door to all the criticisms she thought had been silenced. He's rural. He doesn't make enough money. Etc., etc. All he's got are those genes, but honey, there are plenty of good-looking men to introduce you to. You sure you're being smart about this?

What could she say? She loved him. He was everything she wasn't: rugged, outdoorsy, dangerous. Short, freckled, with a dark bob cut, an assortment of dresses and heels, she had never even broken a nail. He completed her, corny as it sounded. And there was that other quality, too. The simmering stoicism that came to a boil when he put on the badge. Like he was carrying something she would never know. Could never know.

The wedding approached. Everyone convened in Ranger's Field, Hunter's hometown. "Surprised it even comes out online," Kat said to her bridesmaids at the rehearsal dinner. They had reserved the only halfway-decent place in town, a red-themed steakhouse with deer and bison busts on the walls. Never mind—not halfway decent, but whatever. The best restaurant this literally backwoods place could offer. The wedding party was massive, and the steakhouse was noisy with her sisters and their boyfriends and her cousins and their kids and her friends and their partners. Her grandparents were there, her mother and father. They couldn't say Hunter didn't have good manners—he mixed nicely, punctuating every conversation with his distinctive "yes, ma'am" and "no, sir." His father and his family were at one of the tables, and they spent time talking to them and catching up with the half-siblings, two of whom were getting ready to head to college that fall. The only one missing was Hunter's grandmother, but even if she had been there, Kat knew she would have been still and silent as death in a corner. Wasn't polite to think, but if the old woman had croaked just a year prior, she could have had the rooftop wedding she had envisioned for years. Now, she was stuck with an outdoor ceremony at some local farm on the outskirts of town. Not exactly fairytale.

On the day of the wedding, the farmhouse loomed over a latticework altar entwined with white roses. Kat emerged from the house in her dress, long tail held up by her bridesmaids. All doubts about the wedding vanished as her father walked her down the aisle, white bouquet shaking in her hands, her smile impossible to suppress. Hunter waited by the officiate in silver tuxedo and blue tie, unable to contain his own rare smile. They exchanged vows. They kissed. There was much applause, a lot of laughter. Champagne was uncorked, glasses passed around. Flushed, nearly delirious, Kat hardly registered the woman in black at the back of the audience.

The spacious foyer of the house had been cleared out to make room for the dance floor, coffee bar, and pastry stand. The cakes were cut, the slices distributed. The maid of honor, Kat's best friend Angela, said her piece, already tipsy, slurring some of her words and stumbling on her heels. The best man shared a brief, curt speech. He was a fellow deputy, a little too cold for Kat's taste. But it was a minor gripe as her father restored the good cheer, and Pete followed him up with funny stories about Hunter as a boy. He was graying prematurely, balding prematurely, but he was still very charming. "Probably broke a lot of hearts," she whispered to Hunter. He just shrugged, watching the tables quietly, sipping his wine.

Everything was good—not perfect, obviously, but good enough—and even her mother and sisters seemed pacified. Then it happened: a shriek rang out.

"Laura! My baby!"

All went silent and turned towards the adjacent parlor. Nana Brackett had come up to one of Kat's friends sitting on the sofa. She had grabbed the young woman's arm, staring at her intently, holding her tight. "My baby," she said. "You came back. Finally." Kat tried to get a clear view of what was happening, but everyone had crowded around, watching and whispering. Hunter broke through and got between his grandmother and the young woman.

"Nana, what's wrong? Are you okay?"

"Hunter," she said, "sweetie, it's your mama. She came back, just like I told you she would. After all this time, she's back."

"Nana." His voice was gentle, but stern. "Nana, that's Natalie, Kat's friend. She's just here for the wedding."

By now, Kat had pushed through the crowd. She watched as the old woman took another look at Natalie, watched as her eyes dimmed and her face clouded.

"She just looks like her, Nana," Hunter said. Kat turned to Natalie—she had only seen pictures of Hunter's mother a few times, but at a glance, from a distance, sure, maybe Natalie's pale skin and blonde ponytail could be mistaken for some other woman.

But only a crazy, senile old lady would think someone dead for years could still be alive, sitting here and
chewing on roe and crackers. As if the dead daughter
just crawled out of the ground for an hour-long visit.

"Hunter," she seethed, coming up behind him,
"get her out of here. *Please.*"

"Come on, Nana." He wrapped an arm around
her shoulders and led her away. "Let's go outside.
Get some air. How's that?"

The old woman looked back. Despite her wrinkles, her dry lips, her weathered brow, she had the
look of a lost child.

"But it has to be her," she mumbled to Hunter.
"She's supposed to come back. My baby. She's supposed to come back."

Everyone remained quiet for a few moments after
Hunter took her outside. Then the whispers and
murmurs started. Is she sick? Who's Laura? Was she
even invited? She's his mother—excuse me, his
grandmother. Kat looked around. Her friends surrounded Natalie, rubbing her shoulders, kneeling
beside her. On the fringe of the circle, Pete stood like
a statue, his eyes dull, his mouth trembling. His wife
and kids squawked at him, but he said nothing.

She waited until they were alone that night to
speak her mind. "What the hell!" she exclaimed. She
stood over him in their hotel room as he sat on the
bed and unbuttoned his cuffs, flung off his tie. "Not

only do we make everyone come out to this shithole—"

"I grew up here, Kat."

"I don't give a shit! She ruined everything, Hunter! My goddamn wedding night!"

"You had your wedding. Everyone's happy. She didn't ruin anything."

"People are going to talk! They think she's crazy."

"Let them talk. Who cares?"

"Who cares?" She stared at him, mouth agape. "It's *us*, Hunter. They aren't just talking about her. They're talking about *us*."

"She's my family," he said. "And now she's yours, too."

She didn't have a response to this, so she turned away and pretended to admire the wildlife paintings on the wall. "Maybe she does need help," she said at length, out the corner of her mouth. "She's obviously not right in the head. I'm sorry to say."

He sat silently, studying his watch—an heirloom from his great-grandfather.

"Well?" She turned to him. "Aren't you going to say something?"

He set the watch aside. He sighed.

"She's not crazy."

"She thought Natalie was your mother."

"I know. Because she saw her once."

Kat frowned. "What?"

"After she died, when I was a baby, a woman came to the house." He paused, remembering. "My dad saw her, too. She looked exactly like my mother—that's what they both said. The way she was before she was sick, straight from one of those pictures on the fireplace."

"That's not possible."

"I know," he said. "The funny thing is that I remember. Because I was there."

"But you were a baby."

"Yeah. I only have a sense of my mom. Mostly her smell—like flowers. The sound of her voice. Little things like that. But I remember this woman's face perfectly. I remember what she sounded like. I remember her smell, too."

Kat waited. "And?"

"And it wasn't her. She sounded different. She didn't have the same smell. At least it wasn't strong like I remember with my mother. Don't ask me how I know, but I do. It's this one really clear moment I have from that time."

He lay down and closed his eyes. "I know it wasn't her. I know it's not possible. But whoever it was, it made Nana doubt. She thinks she's out there somewhere. She thinks she'll come back one day."

His story had disarmed her. Calmly, she sat down beside him. "So, your actual mom—you really don't remember her?"

He hummed thoughtfully. "Just a sense, like I said. It used to upset me, that I could remember more of that other woman. But now I think it's enough. My mother was kind. She was honest. I believe those things. I hope I can make her proud, wherever she is. She lives on through me. Through who I am."

There it was again, that integrity she liked so much. She forgot her frustration. She leaned over and kissed him.

Across town, alone in that big, falling-apart house, the house of her father and her mother, Angela Brackett lay down to sleep. Tried to sleep. In all the years following the appearance of her daughter's ghost, she had not truly slept. Night after night, she had lain awake, for weeks and then months and then years. Her tears were exhausted. Her pain was chronic and unexceptional. Though she tried to smile for her son-in-law and his family, for her grandson, she had wished secretly for a never-ending sleep. Life had been a formality since the funeral.

The following afternoon, she dozed in a creaky rocker on the back porch. She sipped from a glass of lemonade loose in her wrinkled, mottled hands. The yard before her was overgrown with weeds, the grass browning in places, outright dead in others. Sunlight drenched the yard nonetheless, as if a holdover from days when there had been beauty to bless there, love to sanctify and commemorate. Days when the house had been lived in and full of noise.

She lost track of time as she usually did. The sunlight brightened, slanted. Her lemonade dwindled. The rattle of the screen door jostled her awake. Boots thudded on the wood, stopped beside the rocker.

"Nana?"

"Hello, baby." She looked up at Hunter sleepily. "How are you?"

"I'm good, Nana." He knelt down, took one of her hands. "We just came by to let you know we're taking off."

"We?"

"Yeah. Kat's here. She wants to talk to you, actually."

He stepped aside, and Kat emerged onto the porch and stood stiffly next to him. "Hello, Nana," she said.

Angela only half-smiled. She looked back at the sunbathed yard.

"Hello, Katharine."

"I wanted to thank you for coming to the ceremony yesterday. It meant a lot to us."

"You're very welcome, sweetheart."

"I'm also sorry you couldn't stay for the whole thing. We brought you some of the cake in case you weren't able to try it. It's marble—Hunter's favorite. He says you like it, too."

Angela nodded. She cleared her throat. "That's very kind of you."

"Well. We'll see you, Nana."

"Yes."

Kat returned abruptly into the house. Hunter idled, squinting at the sagging trees, the dying grass. He spun his sunglasses between his hands.

"Are you all right, Nana?"

"Of course, baby. I'm fine."

"Okay." He dawdled again. "You know Dad and Virginia will always have space for you. You don't have to stay here."

"I know, baby."

A honk sounded from the street. He reached for the door, but paused one last time.

"I'm sorry it wasn't her. I would have liked that."

"It wasn't her the first time, either," Angela said. "I know it wasn't. I got fooled then, too. What kind of mother mistakes her own daughter?"

"You're an amazing mother," Hunter said. "I know because I'm standing here. Because my kids will stand here, too."

She didn't say anything. He came over and kissed her brow. "I love you, Nana. I'll see you later. Call me if you need anything."

"Yes. Bye, baby."

She listened to his heavy footfalls as he left the house, listened to the grind of the tires as they backed out and drove away. Birdsong and wind drew her back to sleep.

That night, for the first time since that ghost appeared in the house, she did not hold her nightly vigil before the fireplace mantel. Years of studying her baby's face, and she still mistook her. And not even for some faithful recreation, some near-perfect look-alike like she had the first time. She mistook her for a regular girl, a plain Jane who had none of the magic Laura did. Angela had lost her way if she was so blind in every sense. She didn't deserve to welcome her daughter back home when she returned. And she would return—had to return. That hadn't been her daughter on that day so many years before, but a light had awoken in her nonetheless. God had graced her with a sign. A gateway had been opened. She didn't know how or why, but she didn't need to. Providence only required that she believe.

But somehow, her vision had failed her. She had been too earnest. Maybe that was why Laura never returned in all those years. Angela had failed her test by desiring too strongly, by wishing too desperately. She hadn't paid close enough attention to Job's example, hadn't deprived herself of enough, hadn't suffered enough. So, she forsook the vigil. She would study her daughter's face by memory alone. She would ruminate on the lovely features, the heavenly glow. She would rob herself of those concrete reminders. They were crutches, those photos, this house. All of it held her in place when she really needed to let go. Laura was beyond her. Somewhere among the stars, in the sky. Look upward, she thought. Look away.

By lamplight, she crept up to her bedroom, slid off her slippers, and shuffled into her nightgown. She said her prayers without ceremony, somberly, without want or thought of her daughter. No more wishing. No more wanting. In the big bed, alone in the creaky darkness, she waited for another long, sleepless night to begin.

But that night, miraculously, she did sleep. She slept and dreamt.

In her dream, she awoke to the familiar sounds of bird chirps and wind chimes, as well as the whispers and murmurs of the old house. They reminded her of her childhood, when she would awaken carefree and smiling, the summer air sweet, the light through the window drapes gentle. They reminded her of her young adulthood, visiting the coast, sinking her toes into wet sand and breathing in the husky scent of a freshly-lit joint. They reminded her of her early motherhood, standing at the doorstep of her father's house with her rotund belly and hung head. She had been welcomed back into that home with its smell of lumber, every misbegotten word redeemed by her father's embrace, each of her cold tears replaced by one warm and nostalgic, as though she had been seven again, under the oak tree with her scraped and bloody leg, him around her with his familiar hug and reassuring laugh.

Those sounds reminded her of her true life, her second birth. She recalled cradling her baby girl on the porch, singing to her, dreaming of the girl's life to be, one rich and full with as many triumphs as disappointments. She had damned the man who left one dim morning, her last memory of him only the faint rumbling of his motorcycle as he disappeared into fog. She had wept for him, wishing he would return, knowing he would not. She had thanked him many years later, realizing with the experience of age that he never loved her, that she never loved him, that the many supposed loves throughout her life were shallow and ephemeral. There were two exceptions. One was that great love between her and her parents, and the other was the immeasurable love for the daughter whom that man left her. In that girl's smiles and pouts and tantrums and cries and pirouettes and curses was everything, all of Angela, the summation of her life on this tiny planet. You will outlast me, she thought as she held the child. When everything is gone, you will still be there.

In her dream, she rose from her father and mother's bed, aching and slow, no longer the spry girl who fell from the oak tree, no longer the young woman who enjoyed the rush of air on the back of a motorcycle. But something in the dream took her out of her stupor. There was a clarity, a direction. Where there had been silence, now there was song.

She followed the faint hymn through the dark halls of the house, the same hymn sang to her by her mother, the same hymn she sang to her daughter. The hymn led her to her grandson's old nursery, and there was her daughter standing over the crib, cradling the boy, now a child once again, cooing to him, stroking his hair, kissing his cheeks, easing him back to sleep. And it *was* her daughter—how she would have been, how she always was in Angela's dreams. Healthy. Smiling. The way she was after her performances and recitals. The way she was whenever she returned from school. The way she was after her surgeries, her treatments. The way she was until the very, very end.

In her dream, Angela called out to her daughter, spoke her name. Her daughter looked up at her, and Angela saw she was crying, crying because this was a dream, crying because this was not her life, crying because she was not the person she wanted to be. And Angela forgot her grief, forgot her pain, and took her daughter into her arms just as she used to do, and she told her, no, you *are* my daughter, this is your son, you are alive. You are alive, Laura. My baby girl. My love.

In her dream, her daughter wept and kissed her and kissed her son, and then she said goodbye. She could not stay for long—some place far above, some place brimming with light, called to her. And Angela did not plead for her to stay, did not wish for her to be with them again, because it was enough. Even though she would never see her daughter again, never hold her, never kiss her, never watch her play and sing to her own grandchildren—it was enough. Her baby was alive. Dear God, her baby was alive—

She gasped awake. No soothing sunlight, no harmonious hymn—just the darkness of the bedroom, the wide berth of the big bed. She groped for the headboard and pulled herself upright. She was sweating, shivering. She clutched her chest and fought for breath.

The floorboards groaned as she made her way to the old nursery, guiding herself slowly along the wall, panting, still grasping the leathery skin of her chest. What did she expect to find in that room besides the numerous boxes and crates that had always been there since Pete had converted it into storage? She stood in the doorway, watching motes of dust float in the pale moonlight. There was nothing there.

Downstairs, avoiding the den and the temptation of the photographs above the fireplace. Outside, onto the porch. Look to the stars. Talk to her. Say anything. Say everything.

"Baby," she said, "was that you?"

She waited. The far-out lights twinkled. The stars they represented were long dead, and those ghostly afterimages were all that remained. Echoes of old life. Impressions of something that once was, like a child's handprints wedged into cement, like notches cut into a doorjamb to measure her height.

"Why now?" She swept away her first tears in decades. "Why do you keep teasing me? Did I do something wrong? I think back on everything. Every moment. I don't know what I could've done different."

She collected herself. She stepped back. "I deserve an answer, don't I? Because this is cruel. Cruel to give her to me and snatch her away again and again. Once was enough. I—"

Don't say it. Don't say that you would rather her have not been born. Stay strong. Stay the course. This is all a test. Remember? All a test. Just go back inside. Lie down. Wait for it to pass like you always do.

"All right." She turned away, dragged herself back inside. "All right."

She lay in the bed, waiting once again for the sun to rise, waiting once again for another day of the same ritual, the same unending trial.

In the morning, she slunk to the kitchen and ate a breakfast of charred toast. On her lap, she held tightly Laura's old pink blanket and one of her head wraps, the floral print faded and barely distinguishable. Be patient, she told herself. Have faith. She's out there, maybe not alive in the way most people think. But she's out there. That's a miracle. And whether or not you deserve it, she needs you here. She needs a beacon to light her way home.

She sat in front of her plate of crumbs, licking her teeth, fingering out pieces she could not dislodge with her tongue. A slant of light fell upon her from the window. A rare car cruised by. Or I go to her. I leave this place. Whichever happens first. We'll meet each other halfway.

Why deprive herself? Slowly, painfully, she returned to the den. She looked upon the dusty photographs. She smelt the blanket, the head wrap. Lilac and rosemary. A playful laugh. A tender smile. Laura, she thought, lying down, nestling into the grooves of the sofa. You're alive, baby girl. Your mama's waiting for you. You take your time. Don't rush. Come home safe.

She closed her eyes. She slept again. Be safe, baby. Be safe. Wherever you are.

ABOUT THE AUTHOR

R. H. Gründ is the author of *Room of Cloth* and *Simulacrum*. Apart from writing and publishing, he has taught composition at both the secondary and postsecondary levels. He lives in South Texas with his family. You can follow him on social media at @rhgrundwriting and find more information on his website at www.rhgrundwriting.com.